THE

BLACK RIVER
CHRONICLES

LEVEL ONE

THE

BLACK RIVER CHRONICLES

LEVEL ONE

by David Tallerman
and Michael Wills

DIGITAL FICTION

PUBLISHING CORP

To my co-author, with thanks.
– David

To the members of my first dungeon party of so very many years ago: Craig, Brad, Alex, Peter, Terry, Evan, Scott, and our esteemed master of disasters, Stephen. Thank you for the adventures and the lasting friendships.
– Michael

FOREWORD

Welcome to The Black River Chronicles. Yes, it's a book. Yet another book, in a world that already has so many. So why this one?

We will always need heroes, and will always want to read stories about them. And heroes aren't the biggest, strongest, fastest, and best; being heroic is making the right moral choices, and pushing ahead when you're afraid and don't know what to do, and facing your own doubts and weaknesses. Being biggest, strongest, fastest, and best helps, but no one starts out that way.

So, how *do* heroes start out?

Well, fantasy stories are as old as humanity, magic being the "what if" awe and wonder factor we've talked about by firesides for centuries, that will solve our problems or spank evildoers or right terrible wrongs or bring us all joy and fun and freedom from drudgery. (Don't buy that? Well, there's a reason it's called "fantasy.") Fairytales became knightly romances became our modern written fantasy genre, and in that genre, classic works have introduced or popularized specific words (*The Lord of the Rings* giving us "ranger" in its fantasy sense, for example). In like manner, fantasy "classes," rogues and wizards and so on, have come to us from roleplaying games.

Which, along with such perennially tricky questions as to how to handle fantastic languages so a modern reader can understand what's being said, or how it is that dragons and trolls and humans in a given fantasy world can all understand each other, hands us another quandary: How do people who wander a world with weapons, making a living "adventuring" (often doing things modern real-world governments might label "banditry" or worse), come to wear such class labels, with specific abilities or powers to match? If adventurers come from diverse backgrounds, how is it that they fit so often and so neatly into these categories some of us call "classes"?

Is there an academy somewhere, turning out rogues and rangers to meet the world's needs?

Well, as a matter of fact, there *is*.

The Black River Academy of Swordcraft and Spellcraft.

And this is its story. Or rather, the beginning of its story. Not when it was founded or what went right or wrong back then, but rather *our* first look at it.

This is one wannabe ranger's tale of his experiences at a place that trains adventurers before they set out into the world to have adventures. Like a driving school sending real-world folks out into the world behind the wheel of hurtling largely-metal things that all weigh more than a ton, training adventurers to a certain standard before unleashing them on the wider world, out all on their own, is a Good Idea. As in, *not* doing so is decidedly a Bad Idea, and dangerous for all concerned. And in this case, "all concerned" really means "all creatures living in the same world."

But then again, doing so—when magic and sharp weapons and roguery are involved—can be decidedly dangerous, too.

Especially when novices don't know what they're doing.

And when you add deception to the mix, everything becomes more dangerous.

Especially when everything's wrapped up together in one place: The Black River Academy. A powder-keg of ambitious students being sent on actual adventuring missions, with sometimes cantankerous tutors doing the sending.

Putting magic, danger, deception, and adventure together

means not necessarily all that much fun for anyone directly involved, but *lots* of fun for us, the readers.

And believe me, this book is a lot of fun. Surprisingly realistic fun. Enjoyable, immersive fun. "I want more" fun. And there's a promise that this fun *will* be followed by more. At the same time, all on its own, this book tells a great tale that comes to a satisfying ending.

Magic, danger, deception, adventure...and friends. As unlikely as it seems at the beginning of the story, there's friendship ahead. Good friends.

And you can never have too many good friends.

Ed Greenwood
Writing from The Archmage's Chair

I

Durren had spent the entire morning being mediocre at archery.

Archery was a hard thing to be really mediocre at. It was probably easy enough to be downright bad. Three or four students certainly fell into that category: their shots peppered the outer rings of the targets, the ground before them and the straw bales beyond. One boy, lanky and amber-skinned and surely from beyond the Middlesea somewhere, had somehow managed to fire over his shoulder, nearly taking his own eye out in the process.

Durren felt sorry for them, for not every type of body was suited to the bow, and likely a couple of them would never be much better than they were now.

The truly excellent pupils he watched with more interest. They were a boy and a girl, with nothing apparently in common except that their poise and aim were practically flawless. Practically, but not quite: the girl had a tendency to loose an instant too early, while the boy drew to the left and downward. They were exceptional, but Durren felt satisfied that in a straight match he could have beaten them both.

Instead, he'd spent the morning being mediocre, to the best

of his ability. Mostly he placed his shots in the middle ring, sometimes straying towards the outer when that grew too boring—or when he became worried that his consistency would draw the attention of today's tutor, a tall and sharp-eyed woman named Tallowbyne. By the time noon drew near, the urge to try for a perfect bull's-eye was making the backs of Durren's hands itch. He felt as though that black-dyed circle was mocking him.

Just as he had convinced himself that one extraordinary shot would be mistaken for an accident—he might even make a joke of it, pretend to have astonished himself—there came a fearful clanging from the Old Tower. A dozen different bells hung there, used on their own to signal the hours and sometimes in combination for special messages. Durren had never before heard them all ringing together.

"Wait where you are," Tallowbyne instructed, when two dozen sets of enquiring eyes turned her way.

So Durren slung his bow over one shoulder and waited, gaze roving the courtyard, at once curious and nervous to see what could justify such an unusual measure.

The main courtyard of the Black River Academy for Swordcraft and Spellcraft, an enormous space confined by the rambling outer walls on two sides and by the academy buildings on the remaining two, was divided unequally between the four classes. The region here in the crook of the walls belonged to the rangers, the walls extending outward to allow them distance to really test their archery skills. The fighters, to the left, had a large, collapsible arena and a row of training dummies made from wood and straw. The wizards' area was similar, with targets set on poles, some of them disconcertingly person-shaped. The principal difference was that their section was often on fire; Durren suspected it was no coincidence that the well lay in that quadrant. Lastly, the farthest corner belonged in theory to the rogues. In practice, it was usually empty—or else the rogues were even better at sneaking than anyone dared guess.

In the three months Durren had spent at the academy, he'd never seen the four regions used at the same time—perhaps to avoid the risk of a stray fireball incinerating some poor fighter, or a misfired arrow picking out a wizard standing too near the edge of their allotted area. Yet, now, students were filing in from three directions, one group arriving from the main entrance and the others from side doors at the end of either wing. There were the fighters, showing off to each other and everyone else, a mass of bulging muscles and vacant expressions. There were the wizards in their loose-fitting robes, clumsily carrying staves almost as tall as themselves. There were the rogues, looking sheepish to be out in the open like this, trying always to edge away from each other. If Durren had had to guess, he'd have said that every first level student at Black River was out there, all together in one place for the first time.

The very centre of the courtyard was given over to a stepped platform. Durren had wondered on his first day what it was there for, and had since given the question no more thought. Now he understood—for ascending the steps on the far side was a familiar figure. Head Tutor Adocine Borgnin had spoken to Durren just once, when he'd first arrived at the academy, and Durren had found him grave and intimidating. Now, upon the stage, Borgnin cut an imposing figure.

He was dressed simply but well, in a cape of darkest grey, boots that reached almost to the knee, and a tunic of black felt, the slashed sleeves of which revealed a crimson lining beneath.

His hair and beard were both trimmed short, the latter in a spike beneath his chin. Durren would have struggled to judge the Head Tutor's age, and only from rumour did he know that Borgnin was the second youngest Head Tutor the academy had ever had.

Borgnin cleared his throat, a sound like the cracking of a whip. "New students of Black River," he said, "you have been here for three months now, and as such it's time that you began the next stage in your education. All of you have proved a certain aptitude in your chosen classes.

"However, to be a good ranger, wizard, fighter or rogue is not merely to be capable alone. Often in life you will be called upon to work with others whose abilities differ from but complement your own. Fail to do so and you'll be of no use to anyone, not even yourselves. Therefore, today you will join a party, and henceforward you will undertake expeditions with that party…beginning the moment you leave this courtyard."

At that, the gathered students, who had stayed politely quiet until then, let out a collective murmur. Durren, however, remained silent. He felt that if he opened his mouth even slightly he might choke. A coldness had begun in his heart and chilled him all the way down to his fingertips. How could no one have told him about this? But then the tutors never told you anything, and the higher level students barely acknowledged those less capable than themselves.

"Moreover," continued Borgnin, "you will be staying in the parties decided today until you all have levelled up. The crucial word in that sentence is *all*. From here onwards, the four of you will level up together, or else you never will. A single failure will hold back their entire party."

This time, the murmur was more of a collective gasp. The

unfairness of what Borgnin had said was appalling. Half of those in Durren's own class were only days away from being awarded their second level, and Durren had no doubt that the same would be true for the other classes. And unlike level one, level two actually *meant* something; it was an acknowledgement that you understood at least the basics of your trade.

For many, that promise would have been the only thing making these tough first weeks bearable: all that had kept them going from early morning exercises through to late night study, sustained them during endless, tiresome lectures, let them endure the ceaseless criticism of tutors. Now here they were, being told that any one of their fellow students could halt their progress for good. Worse, everyone knew that if you failed to level up in your first six months then automatic expulsion would await. Expulsion, through no fault of your own! Durren could read the thought in so many of the gathered faces, written in a mixture of shock and horror.

Borgnin cleared his throat once more. "Your parties," he said, "have already been determined, based on your performance until now and what circumstances your tutors feel will best allow your skills to flourish. These assignments are not open to debate. You may not trade party members, and you will be expected to behave towards your new companions with respect. You will have no leaders; all decisions are to be made by mutual consent. That is all. The allocations will now begin."

With that, Borgnin spun on his heel, and was striding off towards the academy buildings while the import of his last words was still sinking in.

Another, older tutor took his place, a woman Durren didn't recognise, though her stark black clothing and obvious discomfort at being in public implied that she was part of the rogues' class. She had a scroll in her hands, and without preamble she began to read. "Party one to consist of, from the wizards, Nirma Faxis, from the fighters, Dunt Brevin, from the rogues, Elias di Torkender, from the rangers, Lyra Escafleur. Come forward and join your party mentor."

Durren noticed then that a stocky man was waiting at the base of the platform, and that nearby a queue of other men and women had formed, some of whom he dimly recognised as yet more faculty members: professors, assistants, instructors, librarians and even a couple he'd seen working in the kitchens. Clearly, whatever being a party mentor involved, it was a task requiring every available hand.

Durren watched as the chosen four hurried over from their separate quadrants. Lyra Escafleur was the girl who'd been excelling at archery all morning, and she marched off with quiet confidence to join her new companions, all of whom looked just as capable. Then the stocky man led them away in the direction of the buildings, and the tutor moved to the next entry on her list.

Thus the morning progressed. The rogue tutor read a set of names, the selected four gathered to meet with their mentor, and then together they trooped off towards the academy. The process was a slow one and seemed to go on forever.

What most bothered Durren, however, was that there appeared to be a clear logic to the order in which his classmates were being summoned. The best students had gone first, and then the better ones, and now the remainder consisted of the deeply average and the basically hopeless. Did his tutors really have such a low opinion of his abilities? Could his attempts to not draw attention have misfired this badly?

The names had long since begun to blur together, so that

Durren was barely listening by the time his was finally called. Flustered, he found himself repeating in his mind what the tutor had said, even as he hurried forward: "Party eighteen to consist of, from the wizards, Areinelimus Ironheart Thundertree, from the fighters, Hule Tremick, from the rogues, Tia Locke, from the rangers, Durren Flintrand. Come forward and join your party mentor."

Durren tried to gain a discreet first view of these three that he was doomed to be spending so much time with. He saw the wizard girl first, the one with the extravagantly long name—and nearly had to stifle a laugh, for he couldn't have imagined anyone less well-suited to it. Areinelimus Thundertree was a dwarf, one of the few Durren had seen, and, though he was only of moderate height, her head wouldn't have reached to his chest. The overall impression wasn't improved by the glasses she wore, the lenses of which were so thick that he wondered how she could see through them at all. She was round of face and body, and her robe was at least a size too large, its shapelessness suggesting that Thundertree had tried to adjust the garment herself, with no knowledge of sewing or even of what clothes were meant to look like.

Nearing the stage, Durren turned his attention to the other two members of their prospective party. Approaching from his left was the fighter, Hule Tremick. Hule looked entirely typical of his class. He was at least a head taller than Durren, and suitably broad. His pinched eyes and flattened nose suggested a lifetime of failing to dodge punches, while his belligerent expression implied a fondness for throwing them without good reason. His only distinguishing feature was that his close-cropped hair was so pale as to be almost white.

As for their fourth member, Durren only saw her at the last

moment. Her face was sharp-featured, her eyes the pale grey of an overcast sky. There was something almost feline about them, just as the slight point to her ears made Durren think of a cat's. Her skin was of a darker grey that merged imperceptibly with her cloak—for she was dressed entirely in black, a particularly dense shade that made following her movements difficult. Of the three of them, she was the only one who looked like she might be more than capable in her trade of choice. She was also the first dun-elf Durren had seen and, for all he knew, perhaps the only one north of the Middlesea. Certainly, her kind were not a common sight these days.

Feeling those pallid eyes of hers flick his way, Durren glanced aside quickly, realising too late that he'd been staring. He found himself looking instead at a squat, sagging man not much taller than the dwarf girl, who frowned back as though he'd been waiting for hours rather than minutes. As the four of them formed a line, he introduced himself with, "I'm your mentor, Colwyn Dremm. Hurry up now!"

With that, Dremm was away, marching towards one of the smaller doorways that let off the courtyard. Durren found himself hurrying to keep up, this time taking care to keep his gaze fixed on nothing. It was beginning to sink in that he'd be spending a great deal of time with these people, and that it might not be the best idea to make too early a bad impression.

Beyond the door, Dremm led the way through a series of unfamiliar passages, in a wing of the vast building Durren had never had cause to explore. The embossing on the walls, a simple design of an inverted sword against a red background, implied that this section belonged to the fighters.

Durren felt as though they must have walked half the length of the courtyard outside by the time Dremm halted to open another door. The room on the far side appeared to be some sort of huge storage cupboard. Three walls were lined with shelves, the one to the left crammed with rucksacks and the others busy with such a range of objects that Durren could hardly begin to take them all in.

"Take a pack appropriate to your class," Dremm said. "Don't worry, they're all the same. And you may select one item each. Choose wisely, because you won't be allowed to change your mind until you've levelled up."

Now that Durren looked, he realised that the rucksacks were divided into four categories, each section marked with a class crest. Those intended for the rangers were more easily identified, however, by the laden quivers sewn into their left side.

Durren hoisted one down as instructed, and then turned his attention to the remaining shelves. They were covered from top to bottom in bric-a-brac, with objects of every size and shape competing for space. There were already a great many gaps in evidence, where previous party members had seized what Durren assumed to have been the choicest items. Still, more than enough remained to make the possibility of choosing seem all but impossible.

Durren's gaze fell on a wooden pole, nearly double his own height. Chopped into three, it would have kept the wizard girl in staves for life. What its actual function was supposed to be, though, Durren had no idea, and its sheer uselessness appealed to him. How were you even meant to carry it?

Reluctantly he forced himself to consider other possibilities: a set of glass jars containing some murky substance, a white cloth sash, a miniature kettle, a stone the size and shape of Durren's flattened palm that glowed with its own dim light. None of them appealed. Then, turning his attention to the highest shelf, he saw something that immediately called out to him: a coil of thick and sturdy-looking rope.

"I'll take this," he decided, stretching to his full height to lift it down. Only as he did so did he discover that the angle had hidden the coil's true dimensions from view; the rope was so long that it would probably have stretched from the courtyard to the tip of the Old Tower, and appropriately heavy. Durren almost considered changing his mind, but the rules likely prohibited indecisiveness, and even if they didn't, he'd have been too embarrassed.

The rogue girl—Tia, that was her name—had made her choice almost immediately. Now, Durren realised that she was glaring at him, though whether because he'd taken so long or because she disapproved of his selection he had no way to guess.

"You never know when a good length of rope will come in useful," he pointed out defensively.

Her answer was to give the slightest of shrugs—as if to suggest that nothing he did, no matter how stupid, could possibly concern her—and to turn her back on him.

Durren had been the last to pick, he realised, for their mentor was watching him as well. Seeing that his decision was made, Dremm stalked off again, back into the passage, and Durren was left trying to stuff the rope into his too-small pack without at the same time tripping over his own feet.

Dremm led them up one staircase and then another, and Durren noticed that the embossed designs upon the stonework had changed. Now they represented a staff with an orb atop and stylised lightning bolts spitting out across a yellow backdrop; evidently they'd passed into the region of the academy reserved for the wizards. A minute later and they'd arrived at their next destination, this time a door of ancient black wood with runes picked out in gold upon its panel. Dremm knocked and from within a voice called back, "Come in."

The chamber was large and hexagonal, with narrow slit windows spaced around the outer three sides. The centre was given over to a sunken area, the same shape as the room, but floored with tiles of red and black rather than with flagstones. On the far side, an elderly man sat upon a high-backed chair, a staff propped against the arm beside him. From his lengthy and unkempt beard and air of mystified distraction, Durren assumed him to be one of the professors in wizardry.

"This," Dremm said, "is Hieronymus, and he'll be managing your transportation, along with certain other matters of a magical nature. Best to treat him with the utmost respect, lest you find yourselves stranded somewhere unpleasant."

The man named Hieronymus nodded sagely. Then he reached into a sack beside him—a sack that Durren realised, with alarm, was wriggling ever so slightly of its own accord. "You will be accompanied by an observer," the old wizard said, "which will project your endeavours back to a scrying pool here at the academy. In this manner, your mentor can make sure you aren't getting yourselves into too much trouble."

Does that also mean they'll come to our rescue when trouble finds us through no fault of our own? Durren wondered.

Then his gaze fell on the object in Hieronymus's palm, and Durren barely resisted the impulse to take a hurried step backward—though the thing couldn't possibly have done him any harm. The observer was not much bigger than a curled mouse and, perhaps more to the point, it had no limbs. It had no anything, in fact, except a single eye, almost as big as its body and currently watching the four of them with patient interest.

While Hule and Tia were watching the observer as warily as Durren was, the dwarf girl, Areinelimus, seemed entranced by the little creature. "We should call it Pootle," she said. But she clearly hadn't meant to speak out loud; realising that the rest of them were looking at her, she blushed and stared hard at her feet. So quietly that Durren could barely catch the words, she explained, "Pootle was the name of a rock-slug I had when I was little."

Durren had no idea what a rock-slug was or why anyone would want to have one. But if he had to be followed around by a floating eyeball, then it might as well be a floating eyeball with a ridiculous name; he had a feeling he'd have bigger concerns soon enough.

As though to illustrate that point, Dremm spoke up again. "Your mission is in a rat-kind village some miles to the east. A merchant caravan has reported that a chest of valuable goods was stolen, and they would like their property recovered. As you know, rat-kind are a cowardly folk, but that's not to say they aren't capable of aggression, so consider yourselves in hostile territory. You'll recognise the chest by the heron crest branded upon its lid.

"Once you've recovered it and are out of danger, speak the words 'homily', 'paradigm' and 'lucent' to your observer, in that order. The transport spell will reverse, returning you here. Take note that the incantation will only work if the four of you are all together, within arm's reach, and if your observer deems you to be in no imminent danger. The radius of the return spell is somewhat imprecise and we can't have you bringing along any stray passengers. Do you understand all that? Yes? Excellent."

Durren wasn't at all certain he'd understood, but Dremm had allowed only the briefest pause for him to say so. In any case, he wasn't prepared to be the only one to admit ignorance. At least he felt that his memory was up to the task of remembering the words Dremm had given them. *Homily, paradigm, lucent,* Durren echoed in his thoughts.

"Then, if there are no questions, it seems we're ready to begin. Step down into the pit," Hieronymus asserted, in a tone that made the lowered area before them sound like the depths of the underworld.

Areinelimus went first, perhaps because of all of them she was the least intimidated at the prospect of magic being worked upon her. Tia followed, keeping her distance, and Durren and the fighter, Hule, stepped down almost at the same time.

Durren could hear, now, that Hieronymus was chanting beneath his breath. Durren couldn't make out any of the words, or be sure they were words at all, but the sound made him feel strange, deep in the pit of his stomach. There were lights, he realised, popping at the edges of his vision like tiny fireworks. Where the lights appeared, the room beyond seemed smeared, as though it was a still-wet painting that someone had rubbed with their finger. Then the room was melting away, as insubstantial as a dream in the moment before waking.

I have a question, Durren thought suddenly. *I've got plenty of questions. Like, are you really sending me into certain danger with these people I've only just met? Like, what happens if things go wrong? Or, given that none of us have the faintest idea of what we're doing,* when *things go wrong?*

But by then it was too late. By then, Dremm, Hieronymus, and the entire room were gone—and Durren was falling through the skin of the world.

2

It came as a shock to realise that he was still on his feet. For an instant Durren had been convinced he was plummeting, through a bottomless tunnel of streaming purple and gold, the walls of which might have been close enough to touch or as far away as the stars in the sky.

Yet here he was, upright, with apparently all of his limbs still in their right places, and around him a scene quite different to the one he'd been seeing only moments before.

Durren had half expected that they'd materialise right in the centre of the village, surrounded on every side by angry, knife-wielding rat-kind. He had already slipped his bow from his shoulder and his free hand was twitching towards the quiver on his back. Wherever they were, though, it certainly wasn't a village, of rat-kind or of anything else. He was confident, in fact, that they'd arrived in a forest. The one thing causing him to doubt was that his head was still spinning, in a way that made his vision blur and his stomach altogether too eager to spill its contents.

Durren took a deep breath, and slowly the spinning steadied. Of the others, only Hule looked worse for wear. Tia was already casting those pale eyes of hers over the surrounding trees, as though at any moment one of them might reveal itself to be an enemy, while the wizard, Areinelimus, gazed about with all the trepidation of a child trying to pick out the perfect picnic spot.

"Where are we?" Durren asked, since he felt as though someone should say something. But he also spoke softly, because, like Tia, he was half ready to believe that there might be rat-kind hiding behind every tree.

Tia pointed to a gap in the dense foliage high above. "There's smoke," she said.

Durren followed her finger. Sure enough, upon the patch of blue sky were traced wavering lines of grey-white. He didn't understand the significance at first, but then it came to him. Smoke meant fires and fires meant people—or, in this case, rat people. At least they wouldn't be wasting half the day wandering lost in this forest before their quest even began.

The dwarf girl, meanwhile, was still glancing around the clearing with obvious fascination. Perhaps feeling Durren's eyes on her, she turned towards him. With a timid smile, she held out her hand, as though they'd just stumbled into each other at a formal banquet. "I'm Areinelimus," she said. "After my grandfather. But no one ever calls me that. All of my friends call me Arein."

Something, perhaps only the eager way in which she'd said it, told Durren that in truth no one had ever called her Arein. He hoped she was a better wizard than she was a liar, and the thought made him feel unexpectedly sorry for her. "Good to meet you, Arein," Durren said, shaking her outstretched hand. "I'm Durren Flintrand."

"Oh!" Her eyes widened. "Like the Luntharbour Flintrands? The merchant family?"

"I'm a distant cousin," Durren said hurriedly.

But Arein continued undeterred. "I heard they even lend money to princes and kings, and that they own half of Luntharbour, and…"

"I wouldn't know about any of that," Durren told her.

"Oh." She looked crestfallen. Then, abruptly, her former good cheer was back. "Well, anyway, it's nice to meet you, Durren Flintrand."

"I am Hule Tremick," the fighter announced suddenly, in a manner that suggested he wasn't entirely happy that others were being paid attention when he wasn't. He was careful to pronounce every syllable of every word, as though speaking was something he had to put considerable thought into.

"Hello, Hule," Arein said, and Durren nodded in acknowledgement.

That left only Tia. Durren thought at first that she'd vanished, but then he noticed her standing a little way off, beside one of the thicker trees, her cloaked silhouette merging almost perfectly with its trunk. He sensed she'd been following their conversation, though nothing about her posture gave the impression of interest.

"Your name was Tia, wasn't it?" Durren called.

She spared him the briefest of glances. "Yes." Then she was staring again into the wilderness. "And you should probably keep your voice down. There are rat-kind nearby."

She was right, he'd almost forgotten. Abruptly the thick foliage all around felt less safe. It would have taken only a little imagination to populate the darkest patches with glaring rodent eyes.

Durren had never met any rat-kind, and he knew of them only by their reputation, which wasn't good. They were considered to be at best scavengers, at worst thieves and bandits. He certainly wasn't surprised to hear that they'd have robbed a merchant caravan, though he guessed it had been a small and poorly protected merchant caravan—because rat-kind were also known for their cowardice in the face of any real threat. Which begged the question, did four first level students from the Black River Academy for Swordcraft and Spellcraft qualify as a real threat? The answer, Durren suspected, was probably not.

"We should come up with a plan," he decided.

To his surprise he realised that Arein and Hule were looking at him expectantly.

However, it was Tia who spoke. "That's easy," she said. "Wherever there are most guards, that's where the chest will be."

She seemed particularly sure of herself for a level one student, Durren thought. Perhaps she'd been getting in some extracurricular practise. That was a notorious problem with training rogues, many of whom would inevitably end up as thieves of one sort or another, be it as agents for one of the great houses or simply as common crooks. Anyone being taught the necessary skills to survive in that kind of life was apt to realise how those selfsame skills could be turned to their own benefit, enough to alleviate the hardships of a student life. But was Tia the sort to do that? She seemed, somehow, too serious to turn her hand to petty crime.

"So," Durren said, "we need to get an idea of the layout. That means finding somewhere high up. Is anyone any good at climbing trees?"

"Hule says we storm in and take the treasure," Hule stated, far too loudly.

Had the fighter really just referred to himself by his own first name? "There are only four of us," Durren pointed out. "And we don't know how many of them. Anyway, I'm not sure we're meant to harm them. I mean," he finished lamely, "we don't know the full circumstances." It hadn't occurred to him until then that he might have to loose an arrow at a living target before the day was out.

"Pah! Rats!" was Hule's only response, as though the value of rat-kind lives could be summed up with those two words.

"I don't want to hurt anyone," Arein put in. Her voice was small, and she looked devastated at the thought. "There must be a better way."

"That's what I'm saying," Durren agreed. "We get a good view of the place and, like Tia said, look for the spot that's most heavily guarded. Then, once we know where they've got the chest stashed, maybe Tia could sneak in while the rest of us cause some kind of a diversion. I don't know, something like–"

"But where *is* Tia?" Arein asked.

Durren looked round. She'd been standing next to that tree—or had it been that one? His eyes searched the edges of the clearing. Maybe she'd gone a little way into the forest? Maybe she'd taken it upon herself to follow his suggestion and clamber into the treetops? Or...

"Oh no," Durren murmured. He'd been replaying the last minute's conversation in his mind, and had recalled the last time Tia had contributed. "Come on," he said out loud, "we have to go."

"You don't think...?" Arein asked. Durren had already begun striding in the direction of those slender columns of smoke, and she had to hurry to catch up. "I mean, you don't think Tia would have...?"

"I don't know," Durren said. But he thought he did, and that she would have. *Wherever there are most guards*, she'd said, *that's where the chest will be*—and now she was nowhere to be seen.

Glancing back, Durren noticed that the eyeball creature— *Pootle, I suppose that's what we're calling it*—was following, though at a sufficient distance to keep all three of them in view. *But not Tia*, he thought. *What happens when one of us gets into trouble on their own?*

As though to answer the unspoken question, Pootle abruptly shot off in the direction of the village. Its speed was extraordinary; one instant it was there behind them, the next a vanishing blur. Seconds later and it was back, trailing them as sedately as before.

Well, at least one of them knew where Tia had run off to. If the thing had had a mouth, or had moved slowly enough to follow, then the knowledge might even have been useful.

Through gaps in the trees, Durren could see the village now, a cluster of squat buildings walled in mud or clay—and stretching far enough into the distance that the word 'town' might have been more appropriate. There was a steep bank descending on the nearest side, perhaps intended for drainage. So far its incline and the dense woodland had concealed their approach, though Durren could see plenty of rat-kind scurrying about in the gaps between huts.

The forest's edge seemed an ideal spot to regroup, and to think through just how they were meant to go about finding one person amid so large and hostile a place—especially given that that one person was Tia, who'd spent the last three months training to be as hard to find as possible. Durren wondered if there was any way to work a too-long length of rope into their plans, decided there probably wasn't. At any rate, the worst thing they could possibly do would be to rush in unprepared…

Which was precisely what Hule was doing at that moment. He was, in fact, already halfway up the bank. For a moment Durren seriously debated leaving him to his fate—until Arein broke from cover too and dashed after the errant fighter. Probably her intention had been to try and drag Hule back, but he had a good lead on her by then, and her legs were barely half the length of his.

Still a part of Durren argued for staying where he was, or perhaps dashing in the opposite direction. It was only a small part, though; Hule could go hang, but the prospect of the dwarf girl being gnawed by ferocious rat-kind was more than Durren's conscience could withstand. In a moment he'd slid from the security of the trees and was running at full tilt to catch up.

By then, Hule was across the mud-spattered boundary of the village, and Arein was only a little way behind. A dozen rat-kind had already frozen in the midst of whatever they'd been up to and were staring with beady eyes. Durren found it hard to read expressions from such inhuman faces, but he felt comfortable in saying that not one of them looked pleased at the sight of these three intruders.

Durren held up his hands in what he hoped was a placating gesture. "This is all a big misunderstanding," he suggested, though he had no idea if rat-kind even spoke Central. "We were looking for our friend, you see, but she obviously isn't here. So we'll be on our way, and you can all go back to…to whatever it was you were doing."

Not one single rat-kind went back to what they'd been doing—or gave any impression of having understood a word he'd said. Durren considered trying again, perhaps louder and more slowly; but he couldn't persuade himself that doing so would accomplish more than his first attempt had. Instead he found himself staring back at them, entranced by their strangeness.

Durren didn't know if rat-kind were people who looked like rats or rats that looked like people. The question had never seemed important until now. At any rate, he certainly hadn't expected them to be quite so rodent-like. They were small, smaller even than Arein, and though they walked on their broad hind legs, they did so in a way that suggested they could as happily drop to scamper on all fours. Their hands—should that be forepaws?—were more developed than a rat's, yet at the same time not quite like human hands, with the four fingers slender and gnarled.

Like rats, they came in a variety of shades: most were brown or grey, but a few were a snowy white, and an even rarer minority had splashes of one colour upon another. Their protruding jaws were shorter than a rat's would have been, though long enough to be called snouts. Most startling were their perfectly black and irisless eyes, the sight of which sent a shudder down Durren's spine. By comparison, the fact that they had long pink tails whisking the air behind them seemed almost ordinary.

Durren had understood in theory that this was a village, but only now did he begin to appreciate just what that meant. He'd expected the place to be populated entirely by armed rat-kind ready for a fight, but of course it wasn't like that at all: there were children hurtling about, women with pink and wrinkled babies bundled in their arms, chickens scratching in the dirt, even the clang of a blacksmith's hammer resounding from somewhere nearby. This was these people's home, and here he and his newfound companions were, intruding without any hint of welcome.

For all that, however, there was certainly no lack of sharp objects appearing in rat-kind paws. They were an industrious folk, or else skilled at stealing implements suited to their size. Much of the ironware was obviously intended for more domestic purposes—one grizzled rat-kind was threatening them with a hoe—but there were actual blades to be seen too, mostly knives and stubby short swords.

Hule had had his own sword in hand since the moment he'd crossed the perimeter. Now he raised the weapon above his head and bellowed, "Tremble, vermin! Return what you've stolen or taste my steel!"

If Durren could have crawled into a hole at that moment, he would have—not because he was afraid, though he was, but because he'd never been so embarrassed in his life. Dying was one thing, but dying in such idiotic fashion, with this loud-mouthed cretin by his side? That was something else altogether.

He realised that, almost without his noticing, his fingers had plucked an arrow from the quiver on his back. Now they were fitting the shaft to his bowstring. This situation was about to turn very bad, for them or for the rat-kind, but most likely both—and when it did so, it would happen quickly. They weren't going to be rescuing Tia, that was for sure, and their best hope now would be to get away intact. Only, Durren suspected that they'd already passed the point where the rat-kind would just let them walk away. What they needed was a distraction—something suitably dramatic.

He looked round for Arein, realised she was behind him, trying to stay out of sight in his shadow. "Do some magic," he muttered from the corner of his mouth.

"What?" She couldn't have sounded more shocked if he'd

asked her to divert the gathered rat-kind by juggling live toads while balanced on one leg.

"Magic. You do magic, don't you? You're a wizard, aren't you?" Durren realised he was no longer whispering, and tried to get a hold of himself. "They've probably never seen magic before. Can't you do something to frighten them? Just a fireball would do. A lightning bolt. Can't you do that?"

Arein looked positively terrified now, like a rabbit that found itself staring into the maw of a wolf. Clearly there was no use expecting help from her; Durren just hoped she'd manage to run without too much encouragement, if the opportunity should come.

But was it likely to? He was beginning to doubt. The armed rat-kind were circling around them, cutting off their retreat. The women, with their scrawny, blush-skinned infants, were retreating indoors. And even if the rat-kind weren't looking for a fight, Hule evidently was: his face was scrunched in fierce concentration, his eyes darted feverishly.

One rat-kind, a large specimen with a wickedly curved knife in hand, squeaked something at the others and took a step closer. Like all of them, he'd been keeping his distance from Hule and Hule's sword. Now, however, he looked as if he might be readying for an attack.

One or two of them would have no chance against the fighter; even if Hule was hopelessly unskilled, his greater reach gave him the advantage. But half a dozen rushing at once might just take him down before he could inflict any serious harm. Sure enough, as Durren glanced sideways, he saw that the circle of surrounding rodents was beginning to close.

Durren made his decision. He wasn't willing to kill these people, not unless there was no possible choice, but nor was he going to stand here doing nothing. He brought his bow up, took aim—even as, beside him, Hule tensed like a cat about to pounce.

The rat-kind who'd spoken took another half-step forward, bringing him almost within range of Hule's outstretched sword, and Durren knew that this was his last and only chance. For just an instant he wanted to miss: this would be far too good a shot, the kind that would have tipped his tutors off immediately. Then his brain caught up with the circumstances, the fact that all their lives depended on him—and he loosed.

The rat-kind jolted backwards as though yanked by invisible cords. He crashed into the wall of the house behind him and stayed there, despite his best efforts to tear himself free. The fletching of Durren's arrow was just visible quivering beside his tufted ear, where the shaft had pierced the baggy hood of his garment.

The other rat-kind took a collective step back. Durren had moved so fast that half of them were yet to realise why their companion had been whisked through the air. That left him ample time to draw and nock a second arrow. He aimed at one, shifted to another, hoping actions would speak more loudly than words had done: *Your friend is alive because I chose to miss, and maybe next time I'll choose differently.*

Then a screech rose from far to their right, shrill and piercing. The sound was totally inhuman, and Durren realised he must be hearing some kind of rat-kind cry. As he glanced in that direction, he caught the briefest glimpse of a black-clad form vanishing between the trees. They were gripping something in both hands, clutching it tight to their body.

The figure was Tia, of course. And she was stealing back the stolen treasure chest. While the three of them had been achieving nothing except to place their own lives in danger, she had single-handedly completed their quest.

Well, she had if she could survive the next few minutes, anyway.

Some of the surrounding rat-kind broke off to give chase, but most didn't. There was already a group pursuing Tia, tumbling down the bank even as Durren watched, and they weren't lacking for numbers. Tia might have accidentally provided a brief diversion, but that wasn't going to save the three of them.

Durren realised he could hear a low mumbling coming from behind him. When he glanced back, Arein's gaze was distant, and she was gesticulating at the empty air with her free hand. Just as Durren was beginning to wonder if the fear hadn't curdled her brains, he remembered what he'd asked of her barely a minute before. He hadn't had much experience with the casting of magic, but he was willing to believe it might look a lot like this.

Sure enough, there came a gasp from the assembled rat-kind—and at the same time another sound, a sort of muted whoosh. Durren glanced about, unsure at first of where the noise had come from. Then he raised his eyes and saw the thin tendril of smoke crawling from a nearby rooftop. Even as he watched, smoke became fire: only a few sputtering sparks at first, but then, without warning, the entire dome of matted straw was alight.

Another whoosh came from the left. Another roof began to belch smoke, and then licking flames. A third, deeper into the village, followed suit.

Durren looked back at Arein. The impression of distance had cleared from her eyes, her hand was still, and she was staring at the now-blazing rooftops in horror.

She wasn't the only one. Already panic was starting among the rat-kind. Suddenly, three stray humanoids were the least of their concerns. Now the question was more of choosing between their stolen treasure and their burning village. A crooked well was visible further down the mud-paved street, and the majority of nearby rat-kind were eyeing it in such a way as to suggest that stopping their homes from burning to the ground appealed more than a fight they might not win.

There wouldn't be a better opportunity. "Run!" Durren yelled. To set an example he spun around, grabbed hold of Arein's overflowing sleeve, and dragged her after him.

He was half sure that Hule would stay for the fight he'd seemed so eager to provoke, but then the fighter was pounding past them. Together the three of them tumbled down the slope towards the gloom of the forest. But Durren didn't need to look behind him to know that at least some of the rat-kind weren't willing to give up so easily.

Nor was that the worst of their worries. For Durren had just remembered a crucial detail from what Hieronymus had told them, one he'd barely given any thought to at the time. Hadn't the old wizard said that the transport incantation would only work if the four of them were together and within touching distance?

So it wasn't enough for them to survive. It wasn't even enough to escape. Unless they could catch Tia before the rat-kind did, none of them were going anywhere.

3

They had two things in their favour. First, the rat-kind appeared to have no ranged weapons; a couple of bows, even a slingshot, and Durren, Hule or Arein would surely have been dead by now. And second, the rat-kind were far more concerned with catching up with Tia than they were with capturing the three of them. Durren could hear the larger pack far off to their left, communicating in long, chittering sentences and ear-grating squeaks.

Then again, since Durren was trying to reach Tia too, there was a limit to just how much that helped them.

So Durren used those back-and-forth calls for guidance and plunged into the forest, heading for where he believed the main horde to be. For the moment at least, he appeared to have become the party leader: Hule seemed content to sprint along beside him and when Durren looked over his shoulder he saw Arein close upon their heels.

He had thought Arein would be the death of them, but she was a surprisingly good runner. She'd hitched up her robe with the hand not clutching her staff and was managing to keep up a steady pace without any sign of flagging. Obviously there were at least some advantages to a dwarfish constitution. She didn't have much of a lead on the half dozen rat-kind that had chosen to pursue them, but at least she was managing to keep it.

Durren's lungs were already beginning to ache. He could feel himself slowing. His vision was blurred, the speed of the chase whipping tears from his eyes, and he was afraid that he'd put a foot wrong and go tumbling. For the forest was growing denser as they penetrated deeper, the trees clustering more closely, roots jutting beneath a blanket of mould. Whenever he dared glance back, Durren could see that the rat-kind were negotiating such hazards easily, sometimes skipping to all fours to manage a particularly hazardous stretch. Yet they were starting to flag, too—just enough to keep them from closing the last distance.

Only Hule seemed immune to fatigue. He had taken the lead now and was running with easy strides, his breathing steady and measured. Yet nothing suggested that he knew where he was going. If anything, he gave the impression that he was sprinting for the sheer pleasure of doing so. Only by chance was he following the course that Durren had chosen for them, the one that led towards the greater accumulation of rat-kind squealing and so, presumably, towards Tia.

But how long could they keep this up for? And what could they hope to achieve? Even if the four of them should manage to get away, there were more than enough rat-kind on their trail to comb these woods until they were found again. Hadn't Hieronymus also said something about being out of danger? Perhaps the transport incantation wouldn't even work so long as their pursuers were nearby.

Then, finally, Durren saw Tia—though he could easily have missed her. Somehow that cloak of hers found shadows even when there were none to be found; though she was dashing at full tilt, she still managed to pick out brief patches of concealment.

However, she'd come to a spot where her options for cover were limited indeed. Where she was, the underbrush thinned, the trees formed an inconsistent line, and the ground appeared to reach a definite end. As Durren drew nearer, he realised that beyond Tia the land fell away; he guessed there must be a slope or even cliffs. The drop could only be a short one, for the tops of trees jutted into view, but it was enough to severely reduce her options. Having reached that edge, Tia could only continue beside it or swing back into the forest and risk severely narrowing her lead.

At any rate, only her sheer stamina and agility were keeping her ahead of her pursuers. Tia was an excellent runner, better even than Hule. She moved with light-footed, long-limbed grace. Even now, when surely she must be past the point of exhaustion, she seemed to glide across the ground. The rat-kind would never have stood a chance of catching her, were it not for the treasure chest she carried.

It was more of a casket, really, but its weight was hindering her—though not by much. Whatever its contents, it certainly wasn't laden with gold. More likely gemstones, Durren thought, and for a moment he found that the part of him that was his father's son had taken over, busily estimating the coffer's potential worth. A great deal was the obvious answer; no wonder the rat-kind were serious about recovering their pilfered treasure.

It took nearly all the strength Durren had left to catch up with Tia. Even then, she barely paid him any notice. Her expression was one of total focus. She looked as though she intended to keep running for exactly as long as she needed to, whether that should be another minute, or an hour, or the entire rest of the day.

For all Durren knew, maybe she was even up to the task—but he had his doubts. Whatever she might believe, she couldn't maintain this pace forever, and even if she should somehow outrun the rat-kind, that wouldn't be the end of their problems. No, there was only one solution, and he knew she wasn't going to like it.

"You're going to have to…" Durren huffed, "have to…" He felt as though his lungs were ready to burst. His heart was a solid knot of pain. Yet, from somewhere he managed to dredge the last words: "Drop it!"

The look she turned on him was murderous. She couldn't have appeared more disgusted if he'd asked her to fall back and sacrifice herself so that the rest of them could escape.

"It's our only chance!" he managed.

Tia's only response was to pick up her pace.

The cramp in Durren's side was threatening to double him in two now. But if he gave up, then at the least he'd probably never see the academy again, and he might well end up on the point of a rat-kind sword. Tia wasn't going to be persuaded, though, that much was clear. He felt that she was running, now, as much to get away from him as from their pursuers.

They were almost out of options. In fact, Durren could see only one—and however little he liked it, he knew Tia was going to approve even less.

Durren dredged up some final reserve of vigour. He was half sure that his burning muscles would simply refuse him, but nevertheless he matched her pace—and was certain he saw a hint of surprise in Tia's face as he drew alongside her once more.

That was nothing to her expression when he lashed out at the casket.

She realised what he meant to do—only a fraction of an instant too late. Even as she tried to tighten her grip, he had knocked the chest from her hands. She flailed, nearly caught it, fingers scrabbling at the polished edge. But by then Durren had managed to grasp her sleeve, and she faltered, almost slipped. The casket twisted free, struck a rock with a crunch, and even as Tia was slowing to recover it, went rattling over the edge of the cliff.

Durren suspected she would still have tried to go after it, but he hadn't let go his hold on her sleeve, and he pulled hard. Behind them, the rat-kind were skidding to a halt. They could have caught up easily, but instead they were scampering to the edge and gazing downward. As Durren watched, one or two even began to attempt the descent, while the others squeaked and chirruped encouragement.

Tia tore free. For a moment Durren thought that she was going to try and fight the rat-kind—there must have been well over a dozen, for the second group had now caught up too. Instead, she hurried to the edge of the forest. There she struck out in a direction she seemed to have chosen solely because it led away from the rat-kind and their increasingly vocal efforts to recover their prize.

Dizzy with relief, but more so with fatigue, Durren stumbled after. Thanks to him, they'd escaped with their lives. Thanks to him, too, they'd be returning to the academy empty-handed. He couldn't help suspecting that it was the second of those things the others were more likely to remember.

Tia finally came to a halt a minute later, in a small clearing not unlike the one where they'd first materialised. They'd left the cliff edge, the casket and the rat-kind some way behind, but still she hadn't said a word to Durren, and he hadn't tried to speak to her in return. He wasn't even certain he could have for the ache in his chest.

Seconds later, Hule caught them up, with Arein loping along behind him. The moment she stopped, she collapsed into the dirt, legs splayed in undignified fashion, leaning back on her arms and gasping great lungfuls of air. Hule, meanwhile, was glancing around the clearing, as though hunting for something that had been deliberately hidden from him.

"I see no treasure," he declared.

Durren had no desire to answer, but he suspected that failing to do so would only provoke more tactless questions from the thick-headed fighter. "We had to throw it away," he said, and tried to ignore the scoffing sound Tia made at the word *we*. "That was the only way to divert the rats long enough for us to escape."

Hule scowled. "We should have fought them to a standstill," he insisted. "I'll go back and take their treasure from them. Which of you cowards will stand with me?"

"You're staying here," Tia told him. "The three of you have done enough damage."

Hule began to square up to her and then, catching the look in her eye, huffed dismissively instead.

"All any of you had to do," Tia said, each word colder than the last, "was to not get in my way. Those rats would never have known I was there if you hadn't alerted the whole damned place."

"What are you talking about?" Durren snapped, abruptly almost choking with anger. "We're supposed to be a party! You can't just sneak off on your own and do the entire quest without us, while we stand around being useless."

He realised only then what he'd said, and how the other two were looking at him. Arein, in particular, appeared mortified. That expression, not to mention the way her chin was beginning to wobble, made Durren want to take the words back—but he couldn't, because they were the truth.

Durren turned back to Tia. Striving for a more reasonable tone, he said, "You went off without a word, so of course we came looking for you. What else were we going to do? If you'd just let us in on what you were planning, maybe we could have come up with a proper diversion. As it was, you put all our lives in danger."

"Everyone knows rat-kind don't kill people," Tia said dismissively, as though that should be enough to settle the matter. "At worst they'd have imprisoned you until the academy ransomed you back."

"Oh, well. I mean, if that's the *worst*. I'm sure they'd promote us all to level two after that. I mean, the three of us having to be ransomed from a bunch of talking rats? They'd probably have given us honorary tutorships."

"So perhaps," Tia said icily, "you'd have done better to just let the only competent member of the party get on with things. Now, I'm going back to scout around and see if there's anything to be salvaged from this mess. I can't stop any of you from following me, but I'd advise against it."

Then she had turned away and was already stalking back into the forest. Despite the implied threat, Durren would still have gone after her, perhaps have tried to dissuade her—had he not been too stunned to move. Surely she wouldn't really do this again? Surely his words couldn't have fallen so entirely on deaf ears? By the time he'd comprehended that she was serious, that she wasn't coming back, Tia had already vanished.

"At least one among you has some spine," Hule observed approvingly. He seemed quite unconcerned that Tia had abandoned them once more.

"Oh, shut up, Hule," Durren said. "She had a point, you know; what were you thinking, rushing in like that? It's a miracle you didn't get us all killed."

"It wasn't all Hule's fault," a small voice piped up.

Durren rounded on Arein. "No, that's true. Why couldn't you have just done that spell of yours straight away and saved us all a lot of trouble?"

"Hule is no coward," Hule affirmed, as though that somehow concluded the discussion. Arein, though, only snuffled and looked away.

Durren had fully expected Hule to throw a punch his way. In fact, he'd almost been hoping for it. For one of the rare times in his life, he genuinely felt like settling an argument with his fists. However, Hule seemed already to have lost all interest in the matter. He merely snorted through his nostrils, sat with his back against the nearest tree and closed his eyes. It appeared that if he had no choice except to wait, his preferred option was to spend the time not fighting but napping.

Durren realised guiltily that Hule's didn't seem like the worst of ideas. His every muscle throbbed, his lungs felt as though they'd been scraped raw with a sharpening stone, and even thinking straight required more effort than he was willing to devote.

However, as he was glancing around for a suitable spot to make himself comfortable, one well away from the dormant fighter, Durren noticed a sound he should have registered before: Arein was snuffling, very softly. Abruptly, all of Durren's remaining anger evaporated. Of the three of them, he'd already decided that she was the least unbearable, and he felt bad for having lost his temper with her.

Durren walked over to the dwarf girl, knelt beside her. "At least you managed a spell in the end," he tried, realising only as he spoke that it was the exact opposite of the comforting remark he'd intended.

Arein turned a tear-streaked face his way. Beneath those absurdly thick glasses of hers, her eyes were rimmed with red. She had to gulp deeply before she could steady her trembling lower lip enough to say, "And look what I did! Those poor people. For all we know, I burned their whole village down."

Though Durren wasn't convinced he'd mind if a few rat-kind homes had been razed to the ground, he understood that that wasn't the answer she needed to hear. "I doubt it," he said. "They'll have put those little fires out in no time. And, look." He licked a finger, held the digit up before him. "Barely a breeze. Fires only carry on windy days."

Arein looked reassured, but only slightly. "Still," she said, "I shouldn't have done it."

"Honestly, it's not that big a deal. A couple of rat-kind houses will need new roofs, and maybe they'll think a little harder the next time they consider stealing some poor merchant's treasure."

Arein took off her glasses, rubbed at them with the edge of one sleeve. "It's not just that. Don't you know how magic works?" There was surprising dread in her voice, as though she were discussing some virulent disease.

"I think so. I mean, there's all this magic floating around, and if you know how then you can control it, and some things

are magical and some aren't. Nobody much uses magic in—"
Durren had nearly said Luntharbour, remembering only at the
last instant that he'd already claimed not to have lived there. "In
the town where I'm from," he managed. "My father always said
that there's nothing useful magic can accomplish that coin
won't do twice as well."

Arein slipped her glasses back on, and suddenly she looked
very serious. "You don't know how magic works at all," she
said. She didn't sound critical, Durren thought, more envious,
as though he was lucky not to have such knowledge scrabbling
about inside his mind.

"Fine," he said, "then explain it to me. We're stuck with
each other, so I suppose it's time I learned."

Arein considered him steadily. "We are, aren't we? Stuck
with each other, I mean. The four of us. We have to make this
work, somehow. Except that only you and Tia are any good."

That surprised him. "I don't know about Tia, but I doubt
I'm much better at this sort of thing than you are."

"I saw how you shot that arrow. It was incredible."

"That? That was just luck," Durren said quickly. "I was
trying to frighten him, I never thought I'd hit anything. I'm just
glad I didn't slice his ear off, or they'd have probably never
stopped chasing us."

Arein smiled. She had a hesitant smile, but one that lit her
pale, round face, turning it moon-like. "Well then, at least you're
lucky. I'm not even that."

Sensing that she might start crying again if he couldn't
divert the conversation onto safer ground, Durren said, "So
what's so terrible about magic? I mean, making things happen
just by waving your hands and saying a few words, that seems
pretty amazing to me."

At that, Arein actually shuddered. "You must have heard of the unbalance?"

"Of course. My grandmother used to swear by it sometimes. If she stubbed her toe she'd say 'Curse the unbalance!' Or if something good happened then it would be 'Thank the unbalance' instead. She was superstitious like that."

"It's not superstition," Arein said. Her voice was dreamy now, as though she were reciting some ancient lesson she'd long ago learned by heart. "It's not superstition at all. The unbalance is very real. I know; I've seen it."

For the first time, Durren found himself really attentive to what the dwarf girl was saying. He was struggling to keep up with her switching moods, and her seriousness kept taking him off guard; it was easy to forget that she had access to power the likes of which he could only dream. "You've *seen* it?" he repeated.

"The unbalance is the source of all magic in the world. Every wizard can see it. If they choose to, anyway; if they want to be good."

Durren was surprised to hear her say something so vain sounding. Then he realised she didn't mean good in that sense, she meant as opposed to bad. "Why would only good wizards see it?" he asked.

Arein scrunched her brow, as though she'd realised she'd already lost the thread of her explanation. "The unbalance is just a…a *phenomenon*. It's real, but it's also an idea." She chewed distractedly at her lip. "It's hard to explain. But you can imagine it as like a chasm in the ground, except that it runs through absolutely everything. And it's always in motion. Think of the earth constantly shifting, the two sides of that chasm scratching and grating against each other, and then imagine the stones and dirt raining down. Except that with the unbalance it's not any of that, but the raw stuff of reality being scraped loose, falling into our world. That's what magic is: tiny fragments of broken reality."

Durren found that he could just about stretch his mind around that notion, even if it didn't altogether make sense to him. "So magic is bad then?"

"It's not that it's bad or good. It just is. The unbalance is there, and probably existed even before there were people; no one made it. Only, a long time ago, wizards began to realise that the more they used magic, the more magic there was. Using it actually made the unbalance worse—made reality a tiny bit less real. But when you have a hundred wizards in the world, or a thousand, or ten thousand, then suddenly all of those little bits start to add up."

"That's awful," Durren said. He was genuinely horrified. He'd always felt a little distrustful of wizards, but that had more to do with coming from stolid, materialistic city folk than any suspicion that they might be doing something dangerous. "But then, why would anybody think of using magic? And how is it allowed? Surely someone would have rounded up all the wizards centuries ago and..." As his mind ran through the possibilities of what that hypothetical someone might have done, he finished weakly, "asked them to stop."

"It's just the opposite," Arein insisted. "If it wasn't for wizards, things might be much worse than they are by now."

Durren nearly pointed out how that contradicted everything she'd just told him. But he was beginning to learn that she'd get to her point eventually, if he only left her to it.

Sure enough, Arein continued, "The thing is, because wizards are aware of magic, because we can sense the unbalance, we're also capable of healing it. Doing so takes a lot of concentration, but over time the greatest wizards developed rituals that made the process easier, found items to help them focus, that sort of thing.

"So the rule is, whatever magic you use, you have to repair the unbalance by at least a corresponding amount. Any good wizard will try to do more than that, though, to compensate for those who refuse to be accountable for their magic—and those who can't."

"What do you mean, can't?"

"I mean, there are objects and beings that are just basically magical. They don't have any say in the matter, but it would never occur to them to take responsibility either. To them it doesn't matter if the unbalance gets worse and the world grows more magical. Maybe even some of the smarter ones might think that was a good idea. Dragons, for example—dragons are absolutely full of magic. And shape-shifters...have you heard of shape-shifters? They're horrible things, and once upon a time there were lots of them around, but maybe they're all gone now.

"Anyway, the point is, there are all sorts of creatures that are magical just because their ancient ancestors happened to live in a certain place at a certain time. Sometimes all it means is that they look a little strange, like the rat-kind, but some of them have magic in their blood, they can draw on it and..."

Arein stopped mid-sentence, distracted by the tramp of heavy footfalls. When Durren looked over his shoulder, he saw Hule marching towards them—and behind him, Tia waiting near the edge of the clearing. That she was back and wasn't carrying the casket, together with her baleful expression, answered any questions Durren might have had as to the success of her reconnaissance.

If there'd been any doubt, however, it was settled when Hule announced, "The rogue wench has come back empty-handed. Now Hule wants to go home."

Durren assumed that Tia hadn't heard herself being described as 'the rogue wench', since Hule was still breathing. Rather than give the fighter any more opportunities to aggravate her, Durren clambered to his feet. "Thank you for explaining magic to me," he whispered to Arein, and she offered him a timid smile in return. Then to Tia he called, "Are you ready to leave?"

Durren took her silence for a yes. Hule had apparently come to the same conclusion, for he stomped over, to stand beside her impatiently.

As Durren hurried to join them, with Arein just behind, he noticed that their observer was descending from the treetops. Perhaps the creature was somehow responding to what had been said, or perhaps it had only recognised that the four of them were finally all together. At any rate, once they'd formed a circle, Pootle dropped neatly into their midst.

"So how does this work?" Durren asked. "Are we all supposed to say the words at the same time? Do you think we should hold hands?" Seeing the look Tia was giving him, he decided he'd do better to stop asking questions.

"Homily, paradigm, lucent," she hissed, pouring all of her aggravation into those three words.

For an instant it seemed nothing was going to happen. Then suddenly Pootle was glowing bright as a star, the white of its eye somehow expanding, until that was all Durren could see—and the forest clearing was nothing but a vanishing memory.

4

I dislike hyperbole," Colwyn Dremm pronounced. "I tell you this so you'll know that I'm not speaking lightly when I refer to your quest as an unmitigated disaster."

Dremm had arrived mere moments after their materialisation in the transport chamber, having presumably been alerted by Pootle. No one had said anything in the meantime, not even old Hieronymus, who seemed indifferent to their presence and uninterested in the details of their quest. The observer had flitted back to him, had nestled in his lap and closed its one disproportionately large eye. However, on Dremm's entrance it had looked up again, as though it was another member of the party, whose performance was about to be judged.

Dremm's face had been thunderous as he'd entered. But, watching him, Durren sensed a degree of theatrically to his ill temper. Certainly he seemed to be enjoying himself now, as he settled down to what was evidently not going to be a brief critique of their failings.

"It's hard to imagine," Dremm said, "how you could have done much more badly than you did, unless perhaps you'd brought a few stray rat-kind back with you and let them loose in the academy."

He glanced about, inspecting the shadowed corners of the room as if he really expected to find beady rodent eyes glaring back at him. "Should you be given credit for recovering the object of your quest, at least briefly? I think not. In fact, that temporary success has only made matters worse. Even if the treasure isn't scattered far and wide at the bottom of a cliff, it's safe to say that the rat-kind will not be so lackadaisical in guarding it from now on. Thanks to your efforts, the prize this academy was hired to recover is most likely lost for good."

Dremm rubbed at his chin. "Since in all my experience I've never heard of such a miserable performance, I confess I'm at a loss to know what to do. Unfortunately, the academy turned its back upon flogging some decades ago, and any other punishment seems trivial. Though it will embarrass me nearly as much as it will you, I see no recourse but to ask for Head Tutor Borgnin's judgement."

Durren felt as though someone had just trickled ice water down the nape of his neck. He had to grit his teeth not to shudder. Just this morning, everything had been fine. He'd been no more than another unexceptional student of the academy. Now here they were and his name was about to be put before the Head Tutor. The entire situation felt dreamy and unreal; he couldn't quite recall the sequence of steps that had brought him to this point, where his worst fear had come true through no apparent fault of his own.

"Hieronymus," Dremm called over his shoulder as he turned back towards the entrance, "might I ask that you keep an eye on them? I think we can all agree that they've had enough adventures for one day."

Hieronymus chuckled, tapped Pootle on its leathery head.

"Oh, I can do that," he agreed.

Then Dremm was gone, the door slamming behind him.

They were all still standing in the lowered area at the centre of the chamber, where they'd materialised. Durren would have preferred to wait somewhere else; his stomach remained in knots at the memory of that disconcerting interval between places. But the only chair was the one Hieronymus occupied, and the step down to the pit was just deep enough to serve as a seat, so Durren made himself comfortable there instead. One by one—first Arein, then Hule and finally Tia—the others followed his example.

The five of them sat in silence. To Durren's ears, it seemed to have a weight all of its own. Part of him wished that someone would say something; the rest was grateful that no one did. For what, really, was there to be said? Only that they were doomed, and that they'd brought this fate on themselves.

Still, the silence weighed heavy. Even a cleared throat would have gone some way to mitigating it. Durren wondered if he should be trying to reassure the others—or Arein at least. Maybe if he were to blame everything on Tia and Hule, then Borgnin would go easy on her. Then again, more likely he'd only think that Durren was trying to save his own skin. For Borgnin, of course, had no way of knowing that it was already too late for that.

Dremm seemed to be gone for an impossibly long time. Outside the slit windows, the day dimmed towards evening. Somewhere a bird sang, and Durren wondered what it thought there was to sound so happy about. At one point, Hieronymus appeared to have fallen asleep, but a minute later he stirred with a sputter and a mumbling of nonsense words.

Then, without warning, the door opened and Dremm was

back. He looked particularly pleased with himself—at least until he saw the four of them sitting. Together they jerked to their feet, and Dremm approached as far as the edge of the pit, the perfect position from which to look down on them all at once.

"You'll be glad to know," he said, "that the Head Tutor was profoundly interested to hear the story of your exploits."

If a hole had opened in the floor at that moment, Durren had no doubt that he would have hurled himself into the depths. It was the way Dremm had pronounced those words, *profoundly interested.*

"Struck by inspiration on the way to his office," Dremm continued, "I suggested to Head Tutor Borgnin that the four of you should be reduced in level. The Head Tutor explained to me that the Black River Academy has never had a level nought, because there have never in the past been students so execrable as to warrant one. Though he was tempted to invent such a rank just for the four of you, he concluded that doing so would not ultimately justify the embarrassment of becoming a laughingstock amongst our fellow educational establishments."

Dremm smiled heartily, as though this was all a joke and he couldn't understand why only he found it amusing. "Unfortunately, this leaves us with limited options."

Expulsion, Durren thought, *it's going to be expulsion.* He knew so in every fibre of his being. They would send him away, and what would happen then? His imagination nearly failed at the enormity of the question, the awfulness of every possible answer. He supposed that they wouldn't escort him every step of the way back to Luntharbour. And there were other academies, weren't there? But, so far as he knew, none with quite such lax entrance procedures.

What did that leave? What alternatives were there for a

would-be ranger with three months of training and a good eye with a bow? Perhaps one or two, if he wasn't overly concerned with being honest; but Durren wasn't convinced that a life of banditry would suit him. Maybe there was a town out there somewhere that would take him on as an apprentice guard, if he was willing to spend the next few years working for crusts and a straw mattress.

Or—he could go home.

He could go home, and he'd never be able to leave again. He could go home and surrender to that life he'd thought he'd escaped. And had he really believed, or had a portion of him always known? He'd tried to tell himself he had choices, that circumstances could be changed, given enough bravery and determination and a certain amount of foolhardiness. Hadn't he always suspected the truth? That at sixteen years of age he had no choices at all, and no say in his own destiny; that perhaps it wasn't even a question of age and he would never have either.

"Fortunately," Dremm said, breaking in upon Durren's thoughts, "for you if not for the good name of this academy, the Head Tutor is a merciful man, and circumstances have conspired to give you another chance. A member of the faculty has for the first time expressed interest in mentoring a party, and has even gone so far as to say that he'd prefer a challenge— a group suited to quests out of the common.

"Of course, our Head Tutor did not fail to see how fortuitous the timing of this was, and has volunteered your services. It seems to me that this is the ideal solution for all of us: for you because you might yet live down this disaster, and for me because, when you inevitably fail to do so, it will be no business of mine."

Durren wondered if Dremm expected some response; a

show of grateful enthusiasm perhaps? He sensed he should be feeling something along those lines, but the emotion hadn't quite arrived yet. Maybe it was just that the news sounded too good to be true, or maybe that Dremm seemed so suspiciously pleased.

There was no time to worry further, however. For Dremm was already turning back towards the door, with a goodbye wave to Hieronymus, and this time he obviously expected them to follow.

Dremm led the way through passage after passage. Every one was unfamiliar to Durren, and some gave the impression of having been used only rarely. They were lit by occasional torches or by convoluted wells that let glimmers of evening light probe from above. Dremm escorted them up one flight of stairs, down another, and after a while Durren began to wonder if this wasn't simply a cruel and unusual punishment of his devising. Perhaps, having dragged them through these endless-seeming corridors, Dremm would admit at the last that they were to be expelled after all.

However, Dremm did finally come to a halt, before a towering portal the likes of which Durren had rarely seen. The door must have been twice his own height, was proportionately broad, and the iron-bound planks from which it was constructed seemed like relics from another age, so warped and blackened was the wood.

"This will be your last chance," Dremm declared, "and, as far as I'm concerned, it's one too many. I doubt our paths will cross again, which is a great relief. Still, I wish you luck in your future endeavours." He smiled, and there was nothing at all pleasant in that smile. "If only because something tells me you're going to need it. Give my regards to Storesmaster

Cullglass."

Then, to Durren's surprise, Dremm turned and hurried away in the direction from which they'd come, leaving the four of them alone.

Durren and Hule exchanged glances. When Hule's blank expression yielded no answers, Durren looked to Tia instead. For a moment he thought she seemed as uncertain as he felt. Then she caught herself and, stepping up to the door, rapped hard upon the decrepit timbers.

There came no response. Seconds ticked by. Durren couldn't hear any sound of footsteps from the far side, but then the door looked sturdy enough to muffle all except the loudest of noises. Surely there should be a bell somewhere, he thought, and he glanced around for a pull cord. But no, there was nothing.

"I've heard of Cullglass," Arein whispered, from below Durren's left shoulder. "I heard he's a bit...well, you know..."

Durren didn't know, and in that very instant the heavy portal began to swing open, with a groan of ill-treated hinges. The light in the room beyond was low and treacly compared to the corridor, so that at first all he could see of Cullglass was a silhouette, tall and angular.

"Come in, do come in," the shape said. Cullglass's voice was high but rasping, reminding Durren a little of a crow cawing. The storesmaster didn't wait for them, but turned instead and trotted back into the shadows. Seeing no choice, Durren followed, and the others moved with him.

Cullglass took four long paces and then stopped beside a laden table. Durren could see something of his face now. His features were long, particularly his nose and tapering chin, and his forehead was broad, though pinched towards the hairline.

Dark, crinkling eyes glistened from behind narrow glasses, which seemed to perch on the bridge of his nose of their own accord. His beard, the same lank grey as his unruly hair, drooped in a braided cord to the centre of his chest.

As Durren had been considering Cullglass, so Cullglass had been inspecting the four of them. "Now then," he stated, "my name is Lyruke Cullglass, and I am keeper of the academy's stores, movable goods and retired armaments."

At this, he waved with a slender-fingered hand at the room about them, as though trying to encapsulate its contents in the one gesture. Then, with an outstretched finger of the same hand, he pointed at each of them in turn. "And you are Areinelimus, yes? Areinelimus the wizard. Tia Locke, our representative from the rogues. Hule, the fighter. And Durren, the ranger. Do I have it right?"

They each mumbled in the affirmative as his finger passed across them.

"I confess," Cullglass said, "you're not at all what I'd been led to expect. The way Dremm spoke, I'd imagined you to be all fingers and thumbs, knock-kneed and drooling. Between the five of us, I wonder if this initial setback was more a failing of mentorship than of your own abilities? Even the proudest vessel will go astray if its captain is asleep at the helm."

"No, it was all us," Tia said stonily, in a tone that implied that the word *us* applied to everyone but her.

"Oh? Well, then." Cullglass made a clucking sound with his tongue. "Let us put any failure down to beginner's ill luck then. I'm sure even the greatest of heroes had their early hiccups; why, even Severn Urnsalver himself. There are always things the legends choose to omit, my young friends."

If it was reassuring that Cullglass seemed both willing and

eager to brush over their disastrous morning, still Durren wasn't certain what to make of the storesmaster. He was beginning to see what Arein had been trying to warn them of out in the passage: Lyruke Cullglass was definitely an odd sort, even by the standards of a place that housed its due share of eccentrics.

But Durren had had time to look around now, and it was fair to say that Cullglass was far from being the strangest thing in the room.

The space was profoundly gloomy. There were small windows high up towards the ceiling; however, they were closed with shutters of the same dark wood as the door. The only light came from splayfooted braziers of black wrought iron, and those were set towards the centre of the vast chamber, presumably so as to minimize any risk of a stray spark setting light to something precious.

For, as Durren was starting to see now that his eyes were adjusting, the room contained no end of precious things. Or so he assumed, at any rate. Certainly not everything here would have met his father's definition of that word. There were no piles of gold and jewels, no obvious finery. But everywhere were objects so inexplicable and outlandish that Durren had no name for half of them, and surely that must make them valuable also.

There were weapons, of course, of every shape, size, and function. And there were spiked and bladed things he took to be weapons, though he had no idea how they'd be wielded. There were wizard's staves, some crude, some impossibly ornate and elegant. There were hats, gauntlets, scarves and sarongs, boots and garters and snowshoes. A colossal clockwork timepiece mounted upon one wall ticked resoundingly. There were multitudinous glass jars, from some of which glassy-eyed creatures stared back distortedly through the jelly within; others contained only lumps and twirls of gooey red that Durren knew with unpleasant certainty had once been parts of living things. There were bundles of dried herbs, flowers and roots, hung from high shelves. There were a great many books, though only a fraction of those accumulated in the main library. And then there were the objects that Durren could interpret only as shapes, not able even to guess what their functions might be.

The room was a treasure trove. It was a wonder. Any rich merchant or provincial lord would have drooled with envy. Yet the place was also decidedly peculiar, and the more Durren looked the less comfortable he felt.

No wonder Cullglass was a little odd.

The storesmaster had been watching them all this while, perhaps enjoying the expressions of mounting awe upon their faces. Now, however, he cleared his throat and said, "So we've met! An excellent start. And you know that I already have great faith in our future together. As far as I'm concerned, the slate has been wiped clean, and there will be no further mention of today's misadventures. Now I'm sure you're all eager to rest after so taxing an experience."

Cullglass led them back to the door, again drew it open, with the aid of a black metal ring large as his head. Once the four of them had shuffled past into the corridor, he said, "I shall send word for you in a few days' time, as soon I've been advised by the powers-that-be of your next quest. In the meantime, I shall expect the very best things from you all."

And before any of them could think to respond, the door had slammed shut in their faces.

The rest of the week felt particularly uneventful after that day.

Mornings and afternoons were the usual round of exercises and lectures. The former involved mostly sword fighting and archery, with a little knife work and wrestling thrown in. The latter were upon a daunting array of subjects, some of which seemed to only have the barest relation with how Durren had imagined his future career. He appreciated that a ranger needed to be able to fight, that was a given. And though he hadn't fully considered the importance of terrain, of hunting, of weather, he'd come to accept that woodcraft was nearly as valuable as being able to defend himself. But an hour spent on the ideal lining for cloaks stretched his patience almost to its limit, and an even lengthier talk upon the topic of edible grubs nearly broke him. At times he wondered if this wasn't the academy's way of whittling their numbers down to more manageable levels. Certainly it was difficult to imagine anyone actually taking in everything they were taught.

Durren's monthly appraisal with the head of the ranger class, Eldra Atrepis, happened to fall at the end of that week. He wasn't at all surprised when the meeting didn't go well. Not one of his statistics had been judged as improving, not even his strength. He knew he should just be glad that none of them had been reduced after the rat-kind debacle, but still he found the failure dispiriting. At least Atrepis hadn't said too much upon that subject; she had seemed as eager to get to the end of their conversation as Durren was himself.

Still, Durren left Atrepis's office full of needling doubts. He was finding it increasingly hard to tell when he was pretending to be an average student and when he actually *was* being average—or even less than that.

Of course, if he should ever stop pretending he couldn't

shoot straight, his dexterity score would likely double. Yet that was impossible. Suddenly revealing himself as one of the best archers in Black River would be a recipe for disaster. What if he should find himself entered into an inter-academy competition? Or even one of the professional challenges the institution every so often sent its ablest students to? The very thought made him shudder.

All right then, so not dexterity—but with only a little effort he knew he could raise his charisma or intelligence, and where would be the harm in that? More to the point, could the result really be worse than being branded a perpetual underachiever?

So it was that, on the one hand Durren found himself dreading being summoned back to Cullglass's storeroom; on the other, he felt almost eager at times. At least another quest promised a break from all the tedium, tension and self-doubt.

In the event, it was on the tenth day since their disastrous first excursion that the message came. Durren had been beginning to wonder if Cullglass hadn't simply forgotten about them when the summons finally arrived, delivered by a shuffling lad whom Durren took for a minor employee of the academy, probably a stableboy or some such. His brief, mumbled instruction was to go to Cullglass's stores when the Old Tower's bells rang noon.

Whether because Cullglass had sent him at the last minute or because the boy had dawdled, that didn't leave Durren much time. Fortunately, he was in a free practise session just then, so at least he didn't have to make excuses for his hurried departure. He'd taken care to memorise the way back to the stores after his last visit, and managed to retrace the route with only a couple of wrong turns. Still, Durren arrived to find the other three already waiting.

He'd seen nothing of Arein and Tia since their first quest, and had recognised Hule only once, fighting in graceless but energetic fashion in the fighters' temporary arena. Arein gave Durren a small smile that he returned, while the other two barely acknowledged him, Tia especially making an effort to look anywhere else.

This time, Hule knocked, hammering upon the door as though it had done him some personal insult, and the answer came more quickly. Cullglass appeared pleased to see them. Within the stores, the shutters were partly open, softening the murk with bars of dust-laden light. It was possible now to see into the darker recesses of the shelves, and to discern objects that the shadows had hidden before—though Durren wasn't altogether convinced that was a good thing.

Cullglass led the way to an area near the centre of the room that seemed to serve as his office, though the space was hardly less cluttered than anywhere else. Upon the three surrounding tables, amid the accumulated bric-a-brac, were a dozen huge ledgers, two of them laid open and webbed with cramped handwriting.

Cullglass propped himself upon a stool, which only served to make him look like a ragged rook perched on a branch. "Here you are, my young adventurers! It seems an age since last we were together. Have you missed each others' company? Have you craved a chance to prove your worth? Then you'll be glad to know that our Head Tutor has selected for you just such an opportunity. Because the quest I have for you is one that very few—and certainly no students of Black River—have ever dared attempt."

Cullglass considered the four of them appraisingly, as though they were gladiators about to duel and he was wondering where best to lay his bets. "After all," he said, "how would they have? It's no small thing even to see a unicorn, never mind to confront one."

5

"N ot all things are what they seem to be." Cullglass's squinting eyes roved their faces, seeking perhaps for some acknowledgement of the truth in what he'd said. "Take, for example, unicorns. The epitome of grace and beauty, yes? A symbol of peace and quietude, of reclusiveness and modesty." He sighed, as though in disappointment at his own words. "Would that the truth should be so straightforward."

Durren found himself wondering where precisely this could be leading. For his part, he'd never had any opinion on the subject of unicorns, except to know in theory that they existed; Luntharbour had as little time for magical beasts as it did for wizards. Curious as to what the others were making of Cullglass's speech, Durren tried to glance surreptitiously from face to face. To judge from Hule's features, the fighter was thinking nothing at all, and Tia hid her reaction as perfectly as she always did. Arein, however, was certainly showing a response: her eyes were wide and Durren could have sworn she was trembling.

"In the end," continued Cullglass, "a unicorn is a beast like any other. Most are good. A few are not. They have their territories, and they resent seeing them trespassed upon. Being beasts beyond the natural, they are capable of more than mere animal cunning. One might even say that they understand how to be cruel."

Arein was looking more uncomfortable than ever. "No," she murmured, "that's not right."

She seemed not even to have realised she'd spoken until Cullglass's gaze fell on her.

"I mean…" she stammered. She took a great gulp. "What I mean is, unicorns are *good* creatures."

Cullglass's expression was solicitous. "As I said—yes, most are good, without a doubt. A few, though, a very few, are not. Every barrel must have its bad apple."

"No, I see that," Arein agreed. "Only…" But she didn't seem to know how to finish her sentence.

"These are ugly truths, my dear, but ones we must face today. Areinelimus, I must ask you to trust in this matter to the wisdom of your elders, which in this instance means myself. Because what I'm trying to tell you may well prove to be the difference between life and death for you and your young companions. Do you understand?"

Arein squeaked something that might have been *yes*, and stared hard at her own feet.

Cullglass took a deep breath, as though the diversion had disrupted his carefully ordered thoughts. "What, in the end," he asked, "is a unicorn but a horse with a spike upon its brow? An intelligent beast with its weapon always drawn? Therefore, the unicorn that has tasted blood is a dangerous creature indeed."

Durren dared a glance at Arein's downturned face. She was biting her lip and her face was scrunched, with the effort of not crying or not arguing, or perhaps both.

"Still," concluded Cullglass, "I have faith in you, my young students. I believe that together the four of you will be more than up to the task."

Suddenly it occurred to Durren that, as far as Cullglass was concerned, this was the matter settled. "Wait," he said, because no one else seemed about to speak up, "what exactly *is* the task?"

For an instant, Cullglass looked puzzled. Then, speaking deliberately slowly as though afraid that Durren might otherwise fail to comprehend, he said, "Why, to capture a unicorn, of course."

Cullglass had been right. For all the care with which he'd pronounced the words, Durren still wasn't certain he'd heard right. "You want us to…" he began. Then, realising that simply repeating what the storesmaster had said wasn't going to make the idea any more plausible, he shut up.

"The beast in question, you see," Cullglass finally explained, "has been behaving in a most malicious fashion. It has made repeated incursions upon nearby villages, goring and trampling their hapless residents. In short, it seems to have grown quite mad—or else, an infinitely worse possibility, grown wicked. Unpleasant though the prospect is, such things will happen. And perhaps we need not look too downheartedly upon the matter, for this gives the four of you a most unusual opportunity to prove your worth."

Abruptly, Cullglass hopped down from his stool, as though he'd decided he would come and help subdue the unicorn himself. However, all he did was stand and gaze distractedly at one set of shelves, eyes darting back and forth as though seeking a particular item.

"As you may imagine," he said, "unicorn-catching is a specialised business. I asked Head Tutor Borgnin if you might exchange your present equipment for something more appropriate to the task, but I'm sorry to say that he was not amenable. Rules, it seems, are rules, however grave the circumstances." Cullglass smiled, an expression his angular face wasn't altogether suited to. "Still, I have every confidence that you'll improvise successfully."

He took a step closer, raised both hands in a placating gesture. "There is, however, another minor difficulty—though one I've no doubt your combined ingenuity will be more than a match for. Your observer will not be able to transport back the four of you as well as a unicorn. Therefore, I'm afraid that you'll be walking."

Durren cringed inwardly. The prospect of spending a couple of hours with these three was quite bad enough, but who knew how long walking back from whatever distant destination they were being flung to might take? Were they talking hours or days? At this point, he'd hardly have been surprised if they were expected to spend the next few weeks blundering through the wilderness with a captured unicorn in tow. And all the while he would have to deal with Tia's stubborn silence, Hule's lunkheaded observations, Arein's crippling fear of the one thing that made her useful. By comparison, the idea of subduing a blood-crazed unicorn no longer seemed so bad.

Cullglass clapped, a sharp crack that startled Durren from his reverie. "I do believe that's everything," he said. "Unless anyone has any further questions or concerns?" His eyes lingered on Arein as he said this last.

Durren felt a bloody-minded urge to ask the storesmaster something really difficult. But it wasn't his fault that they'd been handed such an extraordinary and potentially fatal quest; more likely this was Borgnin's way of punishing them. And Durren sensed that, despite all his bluster and long-windedness, Cullglass was genuinely concerned for their safety.

Anyway, Tia and Hule were already halfway to the door. Durren fell into step behind them and Arein trailed after, her attention still focused entirely on her own feet. Moments later they were back in the corridor, the door thudding closed behind them. Unlike Dremm, Cullglass clearly didn't see the need to escort them either to the room where their rucksacks were stored or to Hieronymus's transportation chamber—and Durren hadn't the faintest idea of how to get back to either.

Fortunately, Tia seemed to have a better memory than he did, for she took the lead without waiting for discussion. A dozen turns later, just as Durren was beginning to doubt her confidence, she stopped at a door that he recognised and shoved it open. Within was the small room of high shelves where they'd first gained their equipment. There were even more gaps now, where parties that had come after had made their selections. And there was another difference, as well: the shelves of backpacks had been labelled with names. Durren hunted out his own pack, opened the flap to confirm that, yes, his coil of rope was still in there.

Only then did it occur to him that the room was unguarded. Aside from the other three, who would know if he should decide to change his useless first choice of item for another that was more practical—or at least lighter? But something about the notion of such blatant cheating made Durren uncomfortable, he wasn't certain he trusted the others not to report him, and anyway, mightn't this quest be the perfect opportunity to prove the rope's worth?

Before he could consider further, Tia was drawing their attention with a sharp clearing of her throat. Durren had no choice but to follow her once more, with a last, wistful glance towards the walls of potentially more useful items.

Minutes later and they'd come to Hieronymus's room. When Tia knocked, his reedy voice called back, "Come in."

Within, Hieronymus was sitting exactly where they'd left him. Did he sleep and take his meals in that chair, Durren wondered? At any rate, he did not look pleased. "You took your time," Hieronymus grumbled. "Do you think I have nothing better to do than wait on you, eh? I, a twelfth-level wizard?"

Durren was half ready to point out that they couldn't possibly have got there any faster, and in any case, it was Cullglass's verbosity that had delayed them. But before he could, Arein said meekly, "We're very sorry."

That seemed to appease the old wizard. "Just don't let it happen again," he grumbled, but this time there was no bite to the words. "Well, don't stand there letting the cold in. Do you want to go on this quest or not?"

No, Durren thought, *I've no desire whatsoever to go. In fact, I'd struggle to think of anything I'd less like to do.* But he trooped with the others down the single step to the lowered region in the centre of the room.

When he glanced back to Hieronymus, Durren was startled to notice that one of the pockets of the wizard's robe was wriggling. Plunging a hand into the baggy depths, Hieronymus murmured, "It seems that at least one individual is pleased to see you back here." When he withdrew his hand, his fingers were clasping an observer—presumably the same one as before, though how anyone was expected to tell one floating eyeball from another was beyond Durren's imagination.

Arein, however, appeared to have no doubts. "Hello, Pootle!" she cried out, with genuine pleasure.

Perhaps it was only Durren's imagination, but he felt that in turn there was something affectionate about the way the small creature blinked back at her. Pootle sped over and took up a position at the centre of their small group, rotating steadily as though attempting to watch them all at once.

"Are you ready?" Hieronymus asked, and had already begun to chant and gesture before they could possibly have replied.

Just as before, minuscule, dazzling lights began to flare, and to pop like greasy bubbles. Where they burst, the scene beyond looked softer, less clear. More and more the air sparked and smudged, until abruptly it was running like wet paint in a rainstorm, streaking in lush, nauseating purples and pinks and reds—and Durren was falling, though his feet insisted he still stood upon cold tiles.

No, not tiles: long grass, lapping about his ankles. Once again Hieronymus's chamber had vanished, and once again there was nothing to be seen in any direction but trees. Durren found himself wondering if all their quests would see them transported to dark forests in the middle of nowhere. Now that his vision was beginning to steady, his eyes reported a clearing much like the one they'd materialised in the last time: dark boughs all around and a solid canopy of foliage above.

As the scenery finally stopped swirling, however, and as the urge to regurgitate his breakfast passed, Durren began to notice that there were differences. For one thing, it was quieter here. Asides from his own laboured breathing and the faint sough of the wind, he could hear nothing. If he'd had to pick one word to describe that quiet, he would have chosen *deathly*—and the thought made him shudder.

Remembering their last quest, Durren sought for a patch

of clear sky above. Here, however, there were no telltale columns of smoke. He listened again, ears hunting for any distant sound that might hint at nearby civilisation; but he was met with only the same unfathomable silence.

Arein, too, was concentrating intently. "Didn't Cullglass tell us that the unicorn had been attacking villages?" she murmured. "I don't think there are any villages around here."

"He also told us that a unicorn's basically just a horse," Durren pointed out. "It could be travelling for miles around in every direction. Maybe it just wanders from place to place, attacking anyone it finds."

Arein looked doubtful. "A unicorn is much more than just a horse."

"All right, I know. It's a magical beast, and that makes it special." A thought suddenly occurred to Durren. "Does that mean you're able to find it? Can you...you know...*sense* its magic?"

"Probably," Arein admitted. But nothing about the way she said the word suggested she had any intention of doing so.

"Look," Durren said, "a quest is a quest. We don't get to pick and choose. You obviously have strong feelings about this, but if people are getting hurt, then don't we have a duty to do something about that?"

"I've never heard of a unicorn hurting anyone," Arein said. "They're afraid of people—and with good reason. A unicorn's horn is one of the most magical objects in the world. They must have learned centuries ago that they were a lot safer if they only stayed hidden."

"Cullglass had a point, though," Durren suggested. "In the end, magic or no, a unicorn's basically just another wild animal. Maybe it's sick with something? You know, like a unicorn version of rabies? A dangerous beast is still a dangerous beast, however magical or peaceful or timid it might normally be."

"I told you, it's much more than just an animal." But Arein sounded less sure of herself.

Tia had been watching their discussion from the shadows of her hood. Now she cut in, "We can't go home empty-handed. Either we find the unicorn or we spend the rest of our lives in this forest."

Durren, a little surprised that she hadn't already wandered off to track down their target alone, added, "I promise, Arein, we won't do anything hasty. We won't harm it if it leaves us a choice." He threw a sidelong glance at Hule, but if the fighter understood Durren's implication, then his face hid the fact well.

"All right," Arein said softly. "I'll find it. If I can."

She had already been standing still, but now she became utterly motionless. The moment passed. Then, eyes closed, Arein reached out her palms towards the ground, as though feeling for something that none of the rest of them could see.

Durren couldn't help thinking of how wizards were dismissed as charlatans back in Luntharbour. But he knew better than that now, for unless the rat-kind had set fire to their own roofs—and there was some perfectly rational explanation for how the four of them had travelled leagues in an instant—he had more than ample proof that magic was real and that it worked.

Without warning, Arein's outstretched hands began to rove. At first she appeared to be feeling out the shape of some unseen object. Then her head tilted upward, to gaze sightlessly into the distance, and she raised her left hand, palm rigid, as if pressing upon an invisible barrier.

Arein opened her eyes. "This way," she said.

"There's…something."

"*Something?*" Tia made no effort to hide the doubt in her voice.

"Magic," Arein corrected. "Magic that feels…strange. Not like anything I've known before. It's so *raw*. I think this might be the unicorn."

Tia didn't look any more convinced than Durren himself felt, but one thing was certain: Arein was their best, indeed their only, option. When she began walking, picking a course through the trees, Durren stayed close. Tia drifted away to one side, but kept her course in line with theirs, and Hule wandered along behind, giving no impression that he'd followed any of what had just taken place.

As they walked, Arein would pause every so often, to close her eyes and turn slowly on the spot until she once more seemed sure of her direction. These delays grew more and more scarce, as Arein became increasingly sure of herself. Eventually she announced, "I think we're close."

Only then did it occur to Durren that he hadn't thought beyond this point. In fact, he'd been deliberately trying not to contemplate what came next. "So how exactly do we go about catching a unicorn?" he asked. "I mean, presumably it's not just going to come with us because we ask nicely."

"Hule will punch it," Hule said, and slugged the air to illustrate.

"No, you won't. We promised Arein, remember?"

"Hule promised nothing," the fighter grumbled.

"I'll think of something," Tia said, as though there could be no question but that the task would fall to her.

"I have a rope," Durren pointed out. But no one paid him any attention, and he didn't feel like pressing the point. He thought about trying to tie a lasso in advance; hadn't they covered the correct knots in one of his lectures? Only, he couldn't quite recall the details, and he didn't much like the prospect of having the accidental strangulation of a magical creature on his conscience.

Arein had already begun walking again, picking her steps more carefully this time, drifting from tree to tree with at least the semblance of stealth. It seemed that once again they'd be going in without even the hint of a plan.

Because didn't that just work out brilliantly for us the last time? Durren thought.

The part of the forest Arein had led them to was particularly dense and ancient-seeming, the gnarled boughs coiled with ivy and mistletoe like garlands at a festival. However, Durren could see from the way the light grew stronger that somewhere up ahead the trees began to thin. For the first time, he could hear a sound other than the wind and their own muted footsteps: the steady tinkle of running water, from off to their left.

Arein slowed still further. Durren suspected that if she'd had any say in the matter she wouldn't have gone on at all. However, by then he'd realised that they were no longer reliant on her powers. He could see a shape through the trees, accompanied by a muted glow—and the shape was moving. As he watched, he was certain he glimpsed something long and pale and pointed, like a flicker of lightning between the trunks. Then it was gone.

When Durren glanced to check whether the others had seen what he'd seen, Tia put a finger to her lips. A moment later she'd vanished into the shadows of a patch of foliage. Arein, despite her obvious resistance, was moving forwards too, and so was Hule, though of all of them he was making the least effort to be quiet. Durren opted for a compromise between speed and furtiveness, by the logic that, unless the beast was stone deaf, it was sure to have heard Hule's crashing footfalls.

Surely it had, and surely the unicorn could have fled had it chosen to. But as the forest began to thin on all sides, revealing a broad glade with a rock-strewn stream closing its far edge, Durren saw that the unicorn was there waiting for them. The beast had taken up a position on the stream's near bank and was watching, its head at a slight tilt.

Despite everything Cullglass had said, no rational person could have mistaken the animal before them for a horse. If they had, however, it would have been the largest, fiercest charger ever to storm across a battlefield—and even that comparison barely did any justice. The unicorn was *huge*. And its bulk was made up solely of muscle, slabs of the stuff that shifted with every slight motion. Its flank and mane and elegant legs and head were all of the same colour, a white too bright for the shaded woodland round about, as though during the night the beast's hide had absorbed the moon's pale light and was now leaking that radiance back into the world.

Then there was the horn—and the horn was another matter entirely. Somehow, Durren had imagined a stubby, twisting thing, perhaps the length of a candlestick at most. The point aimed in his direction was certainly not that. It was at least twice as long as the unicorn's own head, the off-white of fresh milk, and curled in a spiral that began gently and sweepingly— before tightening to a point sharp as any needle.

The unicorn was the most remarkable thing Durren had ever seen. Looking at it, he felt awe and fear in equal measure. The animal was probably beautiful, but only in the way that a thunderstorm or a turbulent sea was beautiful. There was an impression of vast, raw power, just barely held in check but ready to be released at any instant. Certainly, what Cullglass had told them seemed infinitely more plausible now; here was a beast that could probably tear a village down to its foundations if it so chose.

Still, the unicorn was hard to be truly afraid of. Durren was finding it difficult, in fact, to think anything at all, or to do more than stare in dumbstruck awe.

Which was unfortunate—because, just as they'd seen the unicorn, so the unicorn had seen them. Its eyes were a pearly shade that contrasted strangely with the blackness at their centres, and Durren could have sworn the creature was appraising them. Perhaps it even knew enough to recognise the sword Hule had just wrenched from its scabbard.

The unicorn huffed from its nostrils, the air actually steaming. Now it was looking straight at Durren. He couldn't escape the sense that those pale eyes were staring into the very depths of him. The unicorn dug at the earth with its front hooves, tearing up earth and grass, and shook its head, with a whinny that seemed closer to human speech than a sound any horse would make.

Once again, the beast fixed its gaze on Durren—and he felt in that instant that it was trying to communicate something to him.

Then the unicorn charged.

6

Durren was so transfixed that only at the very last moment did it occur to him he ought to be moving out of the way.

By then, his one option was to fling himself full length into the grass. He moved barely in time; he was certain he felt the unicorn's hot breath as it passed, like steam from a bubbling cauldron.

Durren landed awkwardly and hard, the hilt of his short sword digging into his hip. It took a great effort to shrug off the pain and drag himself back to his feet.

He glanced round for the others. Arein had retreated behind a tree and was watching warily. Durren considered calling out to her; surely there must be some magic she could use to distract the rampaging unicorn? But he suspected he wouldn't like her answer, and this was hardly the time for a discussion.

Hule, meanwhile, had taken a stance in the centre of the glade, his sword still drawn and his buckler now upon his other wrist. He looked faintly perturbed, perhaps because the unicorn had chosen to target Durren rather than him.

As for Tia, Durren could see no sign of her—but then that

was hardly surprising.

Durren returned his attention to the unicorn. He'd half expected it to be already charging his way once more. However, as graceful as the beast might appear, it wasn't naturally suited for turning at speed amid the close-set trees. Having overshot by a considerable distance, it had taken a wide course and was only now picking up pace as it started back towards the clearing.

Durren considered nocking an arrow. But the prospect of shooting that elegant creature, even aiming only to wound, was simply too awful to imagine. On the other hand, he had no other ideas at all—and by then the unicorn had completed its arc through the underbrush.

Durren had just a moment to play through the possibilities in his mind. If he wasn't careful, Hule would try and put that sword of his to use. Then they'd find themselves trying to explain to Cullglass a dead unicorn, an impaled fighter, or perhaps both. Conversely, there was no reason to think Arein would use her powers as she had in their encounter with the rat-kind; clearly she considered the unicorn almost sacred, and it might even be that magic wouldn't work anyway, for even Durren could tell the creature was positively dripping with the stuff. As for Tia, he couldn't see how any amount of stealth was going to achieve much against a giant spike propelled by muscles and ill-will. Whichever way he looked at it, that left only Durren himself—and he still hadn't the faintest idea of what to do.

Nor was there any more time to think. Having finally corrected its course, the unicorn was heading back their way. Or rather, was heading *his* way. *What have I ever done to you?* Durren wanted to shout. For only a little distance away was Hule, still gripping his sword and clearly wondering if he was willing to try and turn its blade against a charging unicorn. Presumably he decided otherwise, but Durren didn't see— because by then he was hurling himself at the ground once more, the beast sweeping past like a pallid comet.

This time, Durren was quicker to regain his feet—and it was a good job, too, because here in the clearing the unicorn had a great deal more room in which to turn. Durren was beginning to doubt how long he could keep this up. If the animal was determined to kill him, he might not have a great deal of say in the matter. Really, all it needed to do was to stop this business of charging and bring its hooves into play, for each was as large as Durren's head and quite capable of cracking his skull like an egg. But even if the unicorn insisted on keeping to its current strategy, sooner or later Durren would be too slow— and if that horn should so much as clip him, he'd be finished.

A retreat was called for, Durren decided. He would be safer beyond the edge of the clearing, where the beast couldn't manoeuvre so easily. Perhaps, too, it would lose interest if it no longer felt he was trespassing on its territory. Durren took a step backward, another. The unicorn, having completed its arc, shook its head and eyed him with what could only be suspicion. Again, Durren felt that he could read some intelligence in its eyes, some message directed at him; not anger or hatred, but a warning of sorts. Durren took a third step, a fourth, and thought, *This is actually working.*

The unicorn charged.

Durren had just a moment to wonder at how it could move so instantly, so effortlessly. The beast had been perfectly still, now it was thundering towards him, and his eyes had registered no transition between the two states.

An interesting question—but now wasn't the time. Before

Durren had time to debate what his feet were up to, he was running. The edge of the clearing was near, yet felt like a league compared with how close he was convinced the unicorn must be behind him. His imagination insisted he could feel its steaming breath hot on the nape of his neck.

Having begun, Durren was now sprinting with all the strength in his body. What he felt wasn't panic but something purer and somehow worse: an utter single-mindedness to save his own life, and at the same time a certainty that nothing he did would be enough. His arms swung, his legs whirred, his breath came in fierce gasps. But, however hard he ran, he knew without question that the unicorn would catch him before he ever reached the nearing line of trees.

Then he was across the boundary, the light abruptly dimming as he plunged beneath the foliage canopy. Durren veered sharply to the right, felt the beast sweep past him, perilously close. He didn't slow down even slightly. He was alive, for a little while longer at least, and that was more than he'd allowed himself to hope for.

Durren dared a glance to his left. He'd thought he might have a slender advantage amid the trees; however, the unicorn was keeping abreast of him effortlessly, matching his speed and threading a course through the trunks that would soon cut him off. Perhaps Durren might stop and dodge, using the boles for cover. But then their conflict would come back to those hooves—and between them and its horn, the unicorn didn't lack for reach. No, a tree or two wasn't about to keep him safe.

From the corner of his eye, Durren saw the unicorn veer closer. He leaped a root, barely ducked a branch, and when he looked again the beast was out of view. A horrid certainty assured him that it was behind him once more—and close.

He veered left, lurched towards a tangle of thorny spineroot. Dropping to hands and knees, he scrambled through a gap, oblivious to the needle points slashing at his wrists and ankles. However, if he'd expected the unicorn to slow or turn aside, he'd underestimated the creature. The sounds he heard an instant later, the snapping of shattered foliage, suggested that it had simply ploughed right through the middle.

Frantic, Durren tripped to the right, barely avoiding a headlong crash into a gnarled old greywood. How could the unicorn follow so effortlessly when he himself had no idea where he was going? This was nothing like the chase with the rat-kind had been; that memory seemed almost appealing now. For what were a few people-shaped rats in comparison to this implacable horned monster?

At the last moment, Durren saw the bank descending before him. With no time to slow, he skidded down the steep decline, lost his footing and rolled, before struggling once more to his feet with a gasp. Another tree cut off his path and he bounced off it, changed course. A thud from behind told him the unicorn had negotiated the drop more easily than he had, most likely in a single bound.

Durren grasped his side, trying through pressure alone to still the fire building there. He wasn't going to last much longer. He'd been running at full tilt, running for his very life, and he simply hadn't the strength to keep going. He felt like a small animal being hunted by a huge predator—a rabbit, maybe, become prey to the fox. Just like that rabbit, his only choices were to be torn apart or to…

Or to go to ground.

He couldn't outrun a unicorn. Well, of course he couldn't. But he had at least some abilities that it lacked—and now, before his last energy was gone, was the time to put them to use.

Durren glanced around for a suitable target. At first he saw nothing, only trunks like pillars in an ancient hallway, smooth as polished marble. Then, swerving right, he spied just what he was looking for: a stunted spiderleaf, its branches pushing outward in every direction as though fending off the taller trees about.

Durren hurled himself towards it. Yet again he could feel the unicorn right upon his heels, its furnace breath warming his back. Durren could imagine its horn poised, readying for the killing thrust—and the thought was all the incentive he needed. He leaped.

He missed one branch, floundered, caught another. He'd never been much of a climber, but this one time his body seemed to know precisely what to do. His feet scrabbled upon near-vertical bark, propelled him upward. Somehow he clutched another branch, hauled, gained a footing and kicked off, striving to get yet higher.

The tree shuddered, with a crash like thunder.

Only by pure luck did Durren keep his hold. At that instant he was grasping a firm bough with both hands, and by instinct he flung his arms about it. Even then, the shock very nearly tore him free.

He knew, of course, what had happened. He'd expected the unicorn to steer aside, but it hadn't—because only a sane, benign animal would have done something like that. Instead, it had chosen to ram the spiderleaf tree at full force.

When Durren glanced down, he was appalled to see the beast just below him. He hadn't climbed nearly as high as he'd believed he had. Had the unicorn thought to raise its head a little further, it could probably have jabbed him in the foot.

Instead, it turned away. Durren felt a moment's foolish hope, until he realised that all the creature was doing was circling about for yet another onslaught. Below him, Durren could see the deep gouge the unicorn had carved in one side of the trunk; it looked exactly as though a woodcutter had been at work there. How many more such blows could the tree withstand before toppling to the earth, and carrying him along with it?

He hadn't thought this through at all. Certainly unicorns couldn't climb trees, he'd been right about that much; but then they didn't need to, not when they could tear them down instead. And that was precisely what the fiend was intent on doing. Already it was pawing at the ground, readying for its next assault, horn levelled like a javelin.

He'd jump, he decided—he'd leap before the unicorn struck. He just about had his breath back now. If he was lucky, he wouldn't twist his ankle. Then, once he was back on solid ground, he would run, and—well, he didn't know what would happen after that. Perhaps the unicorn would forget about him. Perhaps he could find a sturdier tree to climb. Perhaps the situation was hopeless, and all he was doing was delaying the inevitable. But anything would be better than this—for he understood perfectly now how that cornered rabbit felt as the fox closed in, and why even the most timid animal would flee rather than find itself trapped and helpless.

Durren manoeuvred among the branches, readying to spring, aware as he did so that the most he could realistically hope for was a controlled fall. The distance looked further than it had only seconds before. He glanced back to the unicorn. Still it hadn't charged. Was the creature taunting him? But even as the thought crossed his mind, it was in motion once more.

His plan seemed desperate now. As the unicorn closed the distance between them, Durren felt his muscles dissolve to trembling jelly. It was all he could do to keep his grip on the branch he clung to. He might well be able to fall out of the tree, but jumping? That was another matter entirely.

Then Durren saw Tia.

She had appeared, seemingly, from nowhere. Now she stood perfectly still at the base of the tree, close enough that Durren could almost have reached down to touch her hood. She had no weapon in her hands, no anything. In fact, she held her palms up before her, a pacifying gesture that the unicorn was ignoring utterly. Even if Tia should try to get out of the way, Durren doubted she'd make it in time.

Apparently her intention was to let the unicorn kill her. If so, the plan stood an excellent chance of succeeding. The beast plunged closer, closer. Durren wanted to scream at Tia, to demand that she move, but he knew he'd be wasting his breath. He'd never seen anyone so perfectly still in the face of danger. Even as the unicorn closed the final distance, its horn angled squarely for her breastbone, Tia didn't so much as flinch.

Then the unicorn stopped. It shouldn't have been able to; it was too large, travelling too fast, and even watching as intently as he was, Durren couldn't have said how the beast accomplished such a feat. He felt there should have been a screech of torn air, perhaps dirt geysering from its hooves. But all that happened was that one moment the unicorn was stampeding towards Tia, about to skewer her, and the next it was perfectly still, the tip of its horn no more than a finger's width from her chest. If Durren hadn't already known that the animal was entirely beyond the ordinary, that alone would have convinced him.

Then again, much the same could be said for Tia. Moving with inhuman patience, she reached out a hand and stroked the unicorn's silvery mane. The beast whinnied, shook its head; Durren felt sure that it must be readying to gore her. However, when Tia scratched behind its ear and murmured something Durren couldn't quite hear, it seemed to calm a little. Some of the fierceness went out of its movements. When the unicorn whinnied again, the sound was almost plaintive.

As unhurriedly as before, Tia reached to her waist. Durren remembered that she wore a sash there, bound tight around her stomach. Watching from above and at so abrupt an angle, he struggled to make sense of what she was doing. But then he realised she was unwrapping the fabric; a minute later and she held a great strip of night-black cloth. This she put around the unicorn's neck, until she had a sort of loose, improvised bridle. Durren was certain that at any instant the beast would realise what she was doing and respond accordingly. Yet it didn't—and even when she took a step, hauling gently, all it did was follow.

After the two of them had travelled a little way like that, Tia glanced back, acknowledging Durren for the first time. "You can't stay up there all day," she said, "we've a long way to go." Then she set off walking again.

Durren had almost let her slip out of sight before her words penetrated. His mind was working sluggishly; everything he'd just witnessed had an air of unreality. Finally he realised that he risked being left alone here, stuck up a tree in the middle of nowhere. Hurriedly, he clambered down; doing so proved harder than going up had. At the foot of the trunk, he noted the deep gouge the unicorn's horn had carved. With a shiver, he started in the direction Tia had headed.

He spied the unicorn first, as a splash of brilliance amid the forest gloom. Next he saw Tia and Arein; the dwarf girl had caught up and was pacing along on the beast's far flank. Lastly, Durren noticed Hule, over to their left and keeping a careful distance. Hule was staring at Tia and his face was plastered with the most absurd grin Durren had ever seen.

"What's so funny?" Tia asked him sourly.

"Taming a unicorn," Hule called. "Everyone knows that's something only virgins can do. So that means you're a virgin."

The look Tia gave him would have turned the finest wine to vinegar. "That's right, I am," she said. "And so are you. The difference is that you'll stay that way."

Before Hule had had time to think that one through, she'd marched on, unicorn in tow.

Durren did his best to suppress a snigger at Hule's expense. Then, watching Tia's retreating back, a thought occurred to him: how exactly were they meant to find their way back to the academy? Theoretically the responsibility should fall to him as the party's ranger, and he hadn't the faintest idea of where they were or of what direction they were travelling in.

Fortunately, it seemed that Cullglass, at least, had given the matter some consideration. For, at that moment, their observer dropped into view and began to zip and twirl, as though mapping patterns in the air. After a few seconds of that, Arein suggested, "I think Pootle wants us to follow."

The observer nodded, or rather bobbed, and then sped off ahead. An instant later it was back, though still keeping its distance, floating backwards in a constant line. It didn't seem concerned that it couldn't see where it was going; whenever a tree threatened to block its path, the little creature would slip aside at the last instant and continue on its way.

After a few minutes of following along in silence, Arein blurted, "I think we should call him Blackwing."

In response to their puzzled expressions, she explained, "The unicorn...I think we should call him Blackwing. When I was little, I had a giant bat named Blackwing."

Durren hadn't the heart to point out that Blackwing was the most ridiculous name he could imagine for a unicorn, or that there was no good reason for them to give the beast any name at all when in a day or two they'd be rid of it for good. "Why not?" was all he said.

The going was hard through the deep woodland. In theory, Durren's particular training should have made him most suited to negotiating the maze of low branches, treacherous stubs of rock and roots placed perfectly to catch unwary feet. As it was, the others all seemed more confident than he felt. Tia stepped almost as lightly as the unicorn itself did, treating the rough ground as though it were no more cluttered than a royal highway. Hule, meanwhile, simply barged his way through, as though the thick woodland was a busy tavern and he was trying to force his way to the one empty table. Even Arein was managing, by staying close to Tia and the unicorn and following in their wake.

Watching them, Durren wasn't certain who he was more intimidated by, the rogue or her new pet—*Blackwing*, insisted a voice in his head that sounded a lot like Arein. However, finally he decided that he'd worked up the courage to ask Tia the question that had been bothering him all this while.

Durren sidled as close as he felt he could without drawing the beast's ire. When Tia glanced his way, he asked, "Tell me, how did you know it wouldn't just kill you?"

She considered him coolly, those pale eyes of hers impossible to read. "I didn't...not for sure. Only, after the second time he charged you, it seemed to me that if he'd wanted you dead, then you'd have been dead."

"And you thought you'd test your theory by standing in front of a charging unicorn? How did you know it would even be able to stop in time?"

Tia shrugged. "I had a hunch. If I was wrong, I was confident I could get out of the way in time."

Durren couldn't help thinking that for once her self-assurance was misplaced; she couldn't possibly have cut her brush with oblivion much closer. "Well, you scared me half to death," he complained.

She gave him a crooked half-smile. "I didn't know you cared."

He was surprised by the heat that flushed his cheeks. "We're never going to get promoted if one of us dies," he muttered.

Tia's smile vanished as abruptly as it had appeared. "I promise you," she said, "if any one of us should die, it certainly won't be me."

Durren had no answer to that, except to acknowledge that quite probably she was right. So he dropped back again, returned his attention to the challenge of walking in a straight line without being whipped by branches or stumbling over every dip in the uneven ground.

Whenever his concentration wasn't occupied with not tripping, however, Durren kept one eye fixed on the unicorn. He was finding it harder and harder to believe that the beast was the same one that only minutes ago had been intent on taking his life. With Arein next to it, sometimes patting its flank, and Tia guiding it by her improvised bridle, the unicorn seemed utterly content. Maybe, he thought, there was some truth to what Hule had said in jest. If nothing else, the creature certainly seemed to prefer the company of women to that of men; whenever he or Hule strayed too near, it soon began to grow skittish again.

So the day passed, with Pootle leading and the five of them tramping behind, through what Durren was beginning to imagine as endless tracts of forest. Had there been anyone to see, they'd have made a curious sight: four teenagers, a floating eyeball and an inexplicably tame unicorn. Even Durren had to shake himself sometimes to escape the sense that this was all some odd dream he'd eventually wake from.

Once or twice they realised they were nearing a road or a village. But Pootle seemed to understand enough to adjust its route accordingly, even if that meant leading them through dense underbrush or, on one occasion, a shallow river. Eventually Durren became aware that the air was growing cool and the shadows large. When he looked up through a gap in the canopy, he could see that the sun was close upon the horizon.

"I think we should stop," he proposed. "It's going to get dark soon, and we don't even have tents."

The scowl Tia gave him suggested that she'd rather walk all through the night than spend even a minute camping out here with him.

"Also," Durren added, "we're not going to be able to follow Pootle once the light's gone."

He wasn't sure how true that was; it was hard to miss a large flying eyeball, and in any case there was that faint glow coming off the unicorn, which for all Durren knew would be sufficient to see by.

However the point seemed enough to persuade Tia. "I suppose you're right," she said grudgingly.

Still, she kept on for a while longer, and Durren didn't have the heart to argue. He was grateful, though, when he realised she'd simply been hunting for a sheltered spot in which to make their camp. *That should have been your job, ranger,* he pointed out to himself, but Durren wasn't at all convinced he'd have chosen better. She'd discovered a narrow glade, sheltered on all sides, and he could hear the chuckle of a stream running nearby.

Only as they came to a halt did Durren fully appreciate how weary his feet had grown. They'd been walking for almost the entire day, with only a brief stop early in the afternoon to eat some of the supplies Arein had discovered were in their rucksacks: dried meat and fruit, and biscuit so hard that he'd been fearful of breaking a tooth.

Durren had been wondering what unicorns ate—perhaps some mysterious substance he'd never so much as heard of—and was a little surprised when Blackwing seemed satisfied to lower its head and begin cropping the long grass. The beast appeared to have grown completely accustomed to their company now, or at the least to have absolute trust in Tia and Arein; Durren still had his doubts as to how it would react if he or Hule got too close.

Watching the unicorn eat, Durren noticed something he couldn't believe he'd missed before. The creature was standing with its left flank to him, and he could see now a pattern of marks beneath its pallid coat, some fine and silvery, others broad and faintly pink. They could only be scars, the vestige of wounds long since healed. Maybe they were claw marks, inflicted by some savage forest creature; however, it seemed to

Durren that they could as easily have been the work of men. Was that why the beast had grown hostile? Had it once been hunted? That would explain a great deal.

"Make a fire," Tia demanded of no one in particular, shaking Durren from his thoughts. "I'm going to find us something for dinner." And with that she had vanished back into the trees.

Glancing about, Durren saw that Hule had already made himself comfortable against a trunk and apparently settled down to nap, while Arein was tending to Blackwing. Clearly, the task of firewood-gathering fell to him.

Fortunately he didn't have to go far before he found a ready supply. He stumbled back to their makeshift camp with arms laden. And fire building, at least, was one task Durren's lectures had prepared him for. Minutes later, when Tia returned, carrying two large hares by their ears, he already had a good blaze going—enough that Durren thought he read a hint of grudging approval in her expression as she set about skinning her unfortunate prizes.

Night had fallen in earnest by the time their scanty dinner was prepared, spitted and roasted. The little glade was a bubble of warm amber light, with utter darkness about its edges and an awning of scintillating stars overhead. Blackwing's bulk was visible by its own faint glow, like another patch of moonlight, and every so often the unicorn would remind them of its presence with a snort or a pensive whinny.

Durren was half convinced that they'd spend the entire night in silence until Arein piped up, her voice wavering with nervousness, "So what are everyone's plans for after we graduate? Why did you all come to Black River?"

Obviously it had taken her a great deal of courage to ask

the question, and Durren felt sorry for her as it became apparent that no one was willing to answer. He'd have liked to say something, but at first he could think of no response that wouldn't reveal far more than he was willing to. Then, as the hush grew painfully long, he blurted, "What about you, Arein? What are you going to do?"

Durren realised immediately that all he'd accomplished was to make her feel even more uncomfortable. "Oh," Arein stammered, "well, I mean...it's complicated."

He thought she meant to leave her answer there, but, with a deep breath, she began again. "The thing is," she said, "there just aren't dwarf wizards. Or at least, occasionally there are, perhaps one every fifty years or so. But in general we're just not a very magical people. And, you see, no one really knew what to do with me back home. I think maybe they were even a little afraid." A shadow crossed her round face. "I mean, nobody ever said anything, but..."

Her words trailed away to nothing, and once again Durren realised it fell to him to coach her into conversation. "So what will you do once you graduate?"

"I'd like to go back home," Arein replied earnestly. "Just because dwarves have never been wizards, that doesn't mean they *can't*. It's a hard life up in the high mountains, and maybe magic could make things easier. And then, if someone else happened to turn out to be attuned, well, they wouldn't have to be alone. So," she concluded, "that's what I'll do."

Feeling that this time Arein had reached a genuine end, Durren glanced towards Tia instead. He found himself suddenly curious as to what her answer would be. "What about you?" he asked, half certain she'd simply ignore him.

She did at least look his way, though the shadows never left her face. "What about me?"

"Why are you here? What is it you want to be?"

"I'm a rogue," she said, as though that were all the answer he could possibly need.

Durren nearly left the question there, but his curiosity gave him unexpected courage. "I know what your class is," he said. "That's not what I meant. You've come a long way to be here; I'd heard that dun-elves never left Sudra Syn without a good reason."

"You know your geography."

Durren almost said, *My father often traded with the southern continent*, caught himself at the last moment, and instead muttered, "I liked to listen to sailors' tales as a boy, that's all."

The way Tia looked at him gave Durren the uncomfortable impression that she'd seen right through his clumsy lie. But all she said was, "When I graduate I'm going to the capital, to work in politics."

Durren understood her meaning. *Politics* was the trade all the best rogues wanted to end up in, and the word meant something very different for them than to practically everyone else. Between the wealthy families, the various military factions, the guilds, the wizard communes and the king's court itself, there were no end of opportunities for someone willing to steal, cheat and blackmail on command—or worse. Many a body had been found floating down the river because of politics, and many an academy trained rogue had dealt the blows that put them there.

But was that really what Tia intended for her future? Durren didn't know her, of course, not even slightly. Yet he struggled to imagine her slitting innocent throats in dark alleys just because some rich lord told her to. Maybe she was simply posturing then. However, he wasn't convinced that was something she'd do either; it wasn't as though she seemed to care what anyone thought of her. Then again, the only other explanation was that she simply didn't want to tell the truth. Either way, Durren could think of no more questions to ask. There was just no tactful way to enquire how someone felt about the possibility of killing strangers for coin.

Again it looked as though the conversation had come to its end. But then, out of nowhere, Hule declared, "Hule's family are warriors back to the twentieth generation. Hule's kin has the blood of trolls in it."

On the one hand, Durren could readily believe that. On the other, from what he understood of trolls, he wasn't certain how such a thing would work; nor did he want to give the problem more consideration than he had to. Either way, he didn't see how Hule's response answered Arein's question. "But what is it you want to do?" he asked. "These days, you can't just fight for no reason."

Hule looked smug. "It will be the Brazen Fist for me. Once I leave the academy, I can enter as an officer."

The Brazen Fist was the king's own military order, a group that theoretically existed to defend the capital but in fact ranged far and wide, even going so far as to hire out its services to earn a little extra gold. In truth, the Fist was a curious mix of national defence force and mercenary army, and Durren could see Hule fitting in well—though certainly not as any kind of officer.

Still, Durren was willing to allow the fighter his delusions, if only because they hardly seemed worth arguing over. "That's a good living," he acknowledged.

"The best!" Hule asserted. "Who wouldn't want to be paid to wield a sword?"

Durren couldn't bring himself to debate that point either. He was willing to let the conversation drop altogether when Arein cut in, "So what about you, Durren? Why did you come to Black River?"

Durren froze. He realised he should have been anticipating the question, should have prepared a plausible answer. "Oh, you know," he mumbled.

But he wasn't going to get away with that. Arein was staring at him attentively, the firelight glinting from those oversized glasses of hers.

"I don't really have any definite plans," Durren tried. "What I mean is, I'm just glad to be at the academy. I haven't thought too much about what happens next."

"Ha!" Hule scoffed. "Of course you'd say that. What use would a Flintrand have for honest work? Once you graduate, your most taxing labour will be to choose which cushion feels softest beneath your overfed rump!"

There was nothing confrontational in Hule's tone. Durren got the impression, in fact, that from his perspective he was simply stating facts. Still, Durren felt his blood boiling. The urge to plant his fist between the fighter's eyes was nearly uncontrollable, and all that held him back was the certainty that Hule would probably be quite happy with that. Even if he wasn't actively trying to provoke a fight, Durren had no doubt that he'd make the most of an opportunity should one arise.

So instead, Durren took a deep breath. "As I've said, I'm not one of those Flintrands. They're cousins...*distant* cousins."

Hule only laughed, as though the notion of a Flintrand that wasn't obscenely wealthy was too absurd even to consider.

"Maybe I'll join the Brazen Fist, too," Durren muttered.

"I hear that if you only pay enough, you can enter as a

provincial general."

"I wouldn't know about that."

Hule chuckled, obviously pleased with himself to have made Durren so uncomfortable.

The fighter would keep baiting him for as long as Durren allowed him to. So, rather than respond, he yawned exaggeratedly. "Anyway, I'm worn out," he said. "What with being chased up a tree by a unicorn and everything. Goodnight, everyone."

And before Hule could think up any more snide comments, Durren had rolled over in his blanket and travelling cloak and had closed his eyes.

7

To say Durren woke early was to suggest that he'd actually slept—and though he felt sure he must have, at least for brief spells, both his body and mind were doing their best to persuade him otherwise.

As he untangled himself from his cloak and struggled to his feet, he saw that, though Arein and Hule were still both fast asleep and snoring, Tia was missing. Durren's first thought was that he wouldn't put it past her to have gone on alone with the unicorn, perhaps intending to claim all the credit for herself. He was annoyed to realise that she'd only be telling the truth if she did.

However, the unicorn was where he'd last seen it, loosely tethered to a tree. The animal didn't appear to have moved at all, leading him to wonder if it had slept either, and if so whether it did so standing up.

Then, as he glanced around, Durren saw Tia too. She was approaching through the trees, bearing an armful of firewood. She must have registered the surprise in his face, because her own look was questioning in return.

Not able to express what he'd been thinking—that he was surprised to see Tia helping others—Durren mumbled instead,

"Have you been up long?"

Tia's response was to place her pile of wood beside the fire and a finger to her lips, with a nod towards the two sleepers. Another surprise; Durren would have imagined she'd have been the one insisting they set off with the first light.

He crouched beside her. She was already teasing at the embers, stirring them into fragile life. As he watched, she drew her hood back and leaned forward to blow softly at the fire's base. After a moment, tender flames began to lick about the twigs she'd placed.

Durren, however, found that he was paying more attention to Tia than to her handiwork. This was the first time he'd really seen her face up close, without her hood drawn up. For that reason, he'd never entirely realised how striking her features were. He wouldn't have used the word beautiful, and pretty was hopelessly unsuitable, but there was something about her that made him struggle to look away.

It was her intensity, he thought, at least in part. Even with this trivial task, Tia seemed utterly focused. Then there was the way that her dark grey skin resembled stone come alive, so that every slight movement surprised him. The word he was looking for, Durren decided, was *interesting*; here was a face he couldn't imagine ever growing bored by.

Tia's eyes flickered his way—and Durren looked aside quickly.

"You could try helping," she suggested.

Of course, Durren reminded himself as he began hurriedly feeding wood onto the reviving fire, finding someone's face interesting wasn't at all the same as thinking they were attractive, let alone liking them.

The others woke soon after that. Tia didn't seem inclined

to go out hunting again, so they breakfasted on their rations, which were every bit as dry and unappetising as they'd been the day before. As soon as they'd all finished eating, they set out, Pootle dancing ahead, Blackwing still happy to troop along with them so long as Arein was by its side and Tia leading it by the nose.

By early afternoon, Durren could tell that they were drawing close to their destination. The mountains beyond Black River had been growing steadily clearer all day, and by then he could also make out craggy foothills, at the base of which the academy lay. Tia, who seemed to know the area better than any of them, confirmed that they were less than an hour away.

Durren watched as the huge old fortress rose beyond the treetops, its back set to one rugged cliff. The building looked every bit as ancient as that precipice; indeed its stones had surely been quarried, long ago, from the rock face.

And, Durren thought, to call it a building was misleading in itself: the Black River Academy looked more as though a dozen edifices of various functions had been thrown together, castles and libraries and temples and halls tumbled one upon another. Wings had been built and rebuilt, entire sections had changed hands or purposes, and no new Head Tutor felt that they'd made their mark unless they'd added a tower here, a spire there.

The closer he drew, the more Durren felt a surge of pride. What an extraordinary place this was! Luntharbour might have more than its share of grand architecture, but nothing there conveyed such a sense of raw and teeming history, of stories and grand deeds stacked from floors to rafters.

However, as they drew near, a more troubling concern presented itself. Durren hadn't given much thought to what would happen when they finally got back, but it struck him now that they could hardly just march through the front gates. If nothing else, he had difficulty imagining the unicorn staying so calm if they tried to drag the beast through the main courtyard. What if one of the classes was training? Given the creature's hostility towards all things male, such an encounter could easily end in a bloodbath.

Fortunately, though Cullglass's instructions had been vague on the matter, it seemed the storesmaster was nevertheless watching over them. Today as yesterday, Pootle had been charting a route that kept them well clear of inhabited areas and major roads. Now, the observer began upon another diversion, drifting in a direction sure to avoid the academy's main entrance.

There was no choice but to trust the diminutive creature and follow. Eventually Pootle's route brought them to the long shadow of the walls. Close up, Durren could see where a narrow path ran off to the right, in the direction of the river that gave the academy its name. Soon they found themselves on a rocky outcrop, with the high walls ascending to one side and on the other a steep drop to the dark water below, which coursed in falls and flurries along its ebon bed.

Just as Durren was beginning to wonder where the path could possibly lead, they arrived at a small door set into an archway. The portal was bound with strips of iron, and would probably have required a battering ram and an afternoon's solid labour to open had it been locked—which, fortunately, when Durren tried the handle, it turned out not to be. The door opened onto a small courtyard that he'd never seen before.

From their route and what he could see of the nearest wing, he reasoned they'd arrived somewhere in the rearmost corner of the academy. The yard gave the impression of being rarely used; a few empty barrels were stacked in one corner, some filthy straw heaped in another.

Presumably here was a back way to Cullglass's stores—for Pootle was already hovering near another door on the far side. Durren was about to follow when he realised Arein had stopped ahead of them, her arms folded across her chest.

"Are we really going to do this?" she said.

"Do what?" Durren asked—though he thought he had a good idea of what she meant.

"Are we really going to hand over Blackwing? We know he wouldn't hurt anyone."

"I don't know that," Durren told her. "I know it tried to run me through with its horn and nearly chopped down a tree to get at me, that's what I know."

"That was a *misunderstanding*. He was scared."

"Certainly," Durren agreed, "that would explain it. I must have been an intimidating sight to a giant horse with a spear on its forehead." He realised even as he spoke, though, that the words didn't sound half as biting as he'd intended. His heart wasn't altogether in this argument. He couldn't help remembering the sight of those scars lacing the beast's pearly flank; probably it really was afraid of people, and had learned to be so in the worst possible way.

But Durren should have realised he had no say in the matter. "Yes," Tia said, "we're handing over the unicorn." Her voice was steely. "We're going to complete our quest, and the three of you aren't going to hold me back from reaching level two."

And with that she was leading Blackwing past Arein, without so much as a glance at the dwarf girl.

Three passages later, they turned a corner to find Cullglass waiting for them before yet another door, this one standing open in anticipation of their arrival.

Seeing them, the storesmaster clapped his hands gleefully. "Well, well!" he said. "The conquering heroes have returned—and with their prize in tow."

At that, Blackwing whinnied nervously, and scratched at the slabs underfoot with its front hooves.

Here was another problem that none of them had anticipated. Was Tia going to stay with the unicorn forever? If not, then someone was likely to get hurt, and sooner rather than later. Durren found that he'd already tensed, ready to spring aside if the beast should return to its old habits and charge back down the narrow corridor.

However, Cullglass didn't appear overly concerned. "Bring him here, my dear," he addressed Tia.

Though she didn't look impressed at being called *my dear*, Tia did as she was told—and so did Blackwing. The unicorn kept near to her, its eyes huge and white. Durren found it strange to see the animal, which only a day before had nearly impaled him, behaving so meekly. However, the closer they got to Cullglass, the more the unicorn looked as though at any moment it might try to bolt.

Yet it didn't. And as they drew within reach, the storesmaster revealed an item that until then he'd been concealing behind his back. It was a length of cord, fine as braided hair and glowing with a pale light not dissimilar to that cast by the unicorn. The cord ended in a loop, which Cullglass proffered to Tia. "If you'd be so kind…"

Realising what was being asked of her, Tia took the loop and lowered it first over Blackwing's horn and then around its neck. Immediately the beast grew still; its eyes took on a dreamy aspect and the tension left its body.

Cullglass breathed a faint sigh of relief. In answer to Tia's questioning look, he said, "As I told you, there are a very few items in existence designed solely for the purpose of catching unicorns. Would that our Head Tutor had acceded to letting you use this; no doubt your mission might have been accomplished at considerably less risk."

Cullglass gave the cord a tentative tug, and Blackwing took an unresisting step closer. Satisfied, the storesmaster led the unicorn towards the open door. Glancing over his shoulder at Pootle, he added, "Please guide our young friends upstairs, won't you?"

The observer appeared to understand. It veered away again, and the four of them hurried after. Durren couldn't but notice, though, how Arein dragged her feet and kept peeking back towards Blackwing, even as Cullglass manoeuvred the unicorn the last distance through the doorway.

Soon they were at the main entrance to the stores. There must be even more to their layout, Durren realised, than the one huge room they'd seen. Tia knocked, but there came no answer. When a minute or more had passed, Durren found himself wondering whether Cullglass hadn't fallen foul of Blackwing's temper after all, magical cord or no. However, when Tia knocked again, he heard the muffled rap of footsteps and the great portal swung inward.

Cullglass beckoned them with a wave of a hand. He looked immensely pleased—with himself or with them, or both. Rather than lead the way to the portion of the room that served as his office, the storesmaster began talking almost before the four of them had had time to enter.

"Let me begin by saying how very proud I am, not merely of your success but of the courage and fortitude with which you accomplished it! I will consider it an outrage if the Head Tutor doesn't look more fondly on our little party from now on. In fact, I'd be surprised if all of your statistics haven't improved by the end of this week. And after that, promotion must surely be close."

Pleasing though it was to hear, Durren couldn't help wondering if such effusive praise was altogether deserved. After all, what had they really accomplished? His contribution had been to nearly get skewered, Hule's to wave his sword about, and Arein's to hide behind a tree. Just as in the rat-kind village, Tia was the only who'd actually done anything, and even then only by acting alone and endangering herself. On the whole, Durren felt that their success owed a great deal more to luck than judgement.

Still, there was no denying that they'd brought the unicorn back, or that all of them were still in one piece. And if they hadn't exactly managed to work together, they'd at least succeeded in having something approaching a civil conversation. Compared to the utter disaster of their first quest, that still felt like an achievement of sorts. Anyway, if Cullglass wanted to be impressed by mediocrity, if he wanted to commend them to Borgnin for it, then certainly that was no bad thing.

"What's going to happen to Blackwing?" Arein asked. Her voice was quavering, but there was a stubborn note there. However, the words were barely out of her mouth before she realised that Cullglass had no idea what she was talking about. "I mean," she stammered, "to the unicorn? What's going to happen to him? Will he be hurt?"

"Hurt?" repeated Cullglass. "Why, my dear girl, of course he won't be hurt. A unicorn, even a mad and violent unicorn, is a rare, precious creature."

"He didn't seem very mad or violent," Arein pointed out.

Cullglass fixed her with his gaze. "With all due respect, there are many poor villagers who would tell a different story." The storesmaster steepled long fingers before his nose and looked grave. "Those who lived to tell any tale at all."

Durren was certain that would be the end of the discussion, and nothing could have surprised him more than the fact that Arein didn't back down there and then. "But maybe," she suggested, "we got the wrong unicorn?"

Cullglass shook his head. "The chances, I'm afraid, are miniscule. Anyway, the beast you delivered matches the description given to the academy perfectly."

"Then," Arein said, "perhaps they were lying? Did you see those scars? Someone's hurt Blackwing; perhaps it was the villagers, and now they want him out of the way to hide what they did. Maybe he just never knew until now that there were any kind people in the world. Or…"

Cullglass held up a hand, and Arein reluctantly let her sentence fade. "My dear young lady, I admire your compassion; rest assured that my own is barely less. No harm will come to your precious Blackwing, I assure you of that. And if a way exists to rehabilitate the beast then I'll take full responsibility in finding it. Or, if there *has* been a mistake…" The storesmaster looked troubled. "Well, I won't pretend that such things have never occurred. If such is the case then there too I'll hold myself responsible. In fact, I will take your concerns this very afternoon to the Head Tutor. Would that suffice to put your mind at rest, Areinelimus?"

Arein didn't look altogether reassured. Nevertheless, she nodded and said, "Yes, thank you."

"I'm glad," Cullglass told her, with a fond if rather plaintive smile. "Well," he continued, turning to the rest of them and brightening immediately. "It seems that once again our time together must conclude. I hope to see today's success reflected in your individual performance. And rest assured that I'll have another challenge worthy of your burgeoning abilities before too long."

The next few days were as busy as ever, if not more so. It seemed to Durren that, in the eyes of their tutors, learning a new skill meant only that you needed to be taught five more. Even when he felt he understood something, there was always a new subtlety to grasp, a fresh complexity that invalidated half of what he thought he knew. More and more, his memory teetered with the weight of fresh insights and techniques. By evening he was invariably exhausted, both physically and mentally, full of dread for the morrow and yet at the same time thrilled by its possibilities.

Given all that, Durren was surprised by how often he found his thoughts drifting, almost against his will, to Tia and Arein. There were times when he even felt he might have been glad to see Hule. It wasn't that he'd enjoyed their last quest, exactly; he still had the bruises to remind him of just how unenjoyable certain parts had been. Nevertheless, he'd liked the freedom of being out in the endless-seeming wilderness, and, if he was honest with himself, he'd even appreciated the experience more for having company. Of course Tia was standoffish, Arein was hard work with her outbursts and her clumsy attempts of friendliness, and Hule was simply an idiot—

but Durren had known worse people in his time. In fact, compared to the types who'd hung around his father's estate, the sons of merchants and wealthy lords he'd been forced to feign friendships with, he found that he almost liked them.

More, though, Durren found that he could imagine a situation where the four of them might actually succeed in working together. What would it take, after all? Only for Tia to start communicating, for Arein to grow less distrustful of her own power, for Hule to pay attention and do what he was told. After all, they'd managed to capture a unicorn; not everyone could have done that. Perhaps their party might even be capable of something extraordinary, a grand quest that would go down in Black River's annals, to be gossiped about by generations of students for decades to come.

And that would be disastrous for Durren.

Even the thought made him feel trapped all over again, just as he had when their party was first announced. Maintaining a steady level of mediocrity had been difficult enough when he'd only had himself to think about; with the four of them together, the prospect seemed nigh impossible. And the worst thing was that a part of him *wanted* it to be impossible. That part liked the idea of them succeeding together, of wiping away the dismal memory of their first failure with some spectacular show of prowess.

The more Durren thought, the more he wondered if perhaps his approach hadn't been wrong from the start. Having set such a low standard, even a merely good performance would stand out now. Yet he was going to have to improve, or else he'd end up being the one to hold their entire party back. Already he could imagine the look Tia would give him, her disdain and annoyance. And Arein? Disappointment, probably, though she'd try her best to hide it. As for Hule—well, Hule would probably just punch him.

The only possible solution, so far as Durren could see, was to begin discreetly improving. So that was what he set his mind and body to over the following days. He began with archery, since that was the activity he'd always found most difficult not to excel at. In the next practise, he placed every shot on target, and even a couple within the centre ring—though each time he was careful to look surprised. He had to fight the temptation to land one in the bull's-eye; he promised himself that in a week or two he would, once everyone had had time to accept his dramatic improvement.

Sword and knife fighting were easier. He was genuinely no more than good at either, and the gap between his real ability and the pretence he'd been making was correspondingly narrower. It was no great effort to try a little harder, and he even found that he was enjoying himself. He won about half his practise bouts, but even his losses were close-run, and correspondingly exciting.

In lectures, meanwhile, Durren made a point of paying more attention. He took diligent notes in place of the scraps he'd scribbled before, which half the time he'd been unable to decipher when it came time to write them up by candlelight. He began to ask questions as well, and was shocked by the extent to which subjects that had seemed dry and futile began suddenly to catch his interest.

At the end of the week, Durren was surprised to find himself summoned into another meeting with Eldra Atrepis. He shouldn't have been due to see her for another three weeks. His first thought was that his worst fears had finally come true—though it was hard to think of anything he'd done either so unusually good or extraordinarily bad as to warrant special attention.

When he entered Atrepis's office, a nondescript room in a corner of the wing given over to the rangers, she was busy reading from a pile of papers and didn't look up. Durren wondered if he was supposed to sit, decided he didn't dare. Instead, he stood patiently waiting, and took the opportunity to discreetly study the Head Ranger.

The sharpness of Atrepis's features, which made her face severe even in repose, made Durren wonder if there wasn't elf blood in her ancestry somewhere. Her black hair, cut short just past the level of her eyes, was barely flecked with grey, the only real clue towards her age. Merely from looking at her, Durren suspected that she must have been a remarkable archer in her day.

In fact, likely she still was. One of the few pieces of decor was the bow mounted above her desk, a beautiful weapon of black wood and graceful curves; moreover, the moss-green robes Atrepis wore were cut like a ranger's rather than an academic's, designed so as not to impede her motion. Durren found it easy to see how she'd have attained so high a position in the academy. Indeed, he'd heard talk among the other students that she might succeed Borgnin as Head Tutor one day, and he could readily believe that too.

Finally Atrepis slipped the papers into a drawer of her desk, looked up. "Ah, Durren Flintrand. A student whose name promised great things and whose performance has so far failed to deliver."

Durren found himself wanting to ask her why coming from a rich family should be any special guarantee of ability. But common sense told him that provoking Atrepis was the least astute course here. Unable to think of any more useful reply, he stayed silent instead.

"Perhaps," she suggested, "you're never going to live up to such potential."

This Atrepis phrased as a question, and Durren wondered what response she was expecting. Both yes and no both seemed like equally wrong answers. "I think maybe," he said, "that I could do a lot better than I have been doing."

Atrepis left just long enough before answering that Durren had time to think through all the things he should have said instead. Had he been too vague? Perhaps not vague enough? Was it sensible to claim he could do a *lot* better? Mightn't he have been wiser to hedge his bets? Then again, the last thing he wanted was for the Head Ranger to suspect he'd been purposefully underperforming.

"Yes," Atrepis said finally, "I do believe you're right. Certainly the reports I've had from your tutors these last few days note a marked improvement, enough that I felt it worth my time to meet with you especially and commend your efforts. Tutor Ashbless has proposed that we acknowledge a rise in your intelligence. Three more points and you'll be worthy of advancement to level two, and to publicly use the title of Trainee Ranger of the Black River Academy—a considerable honour in itself."

Durren was so taken aback that he barely knew how to answer. In the end, he settled for, "I'll do my best."

Atrepis nodded. "I do hope so," she said. "Well, that's all. You may see yourself out."

Only afterwards did it occur to Durren how good he'd felt to be commended by Atrepis. Praise had been a rarity at home, and when it had come was invariably for achievements he took no pride in: smartness of dress, neatness of person, or staying silent at gatherings where his presence was a necessary inconvenience. And since coming to Black River, he'd deliberately avoided doing anything praiseworthy. In fact, the more he thought, the more he was convinced that his meeting with Atrepis represented the first time anyone had applauded his efforts for something he actually cared about.

Durren knew he was on the cusp of a significant decision, and still he had no idea what choice to make. Did he dare risk doing his best? Could he bear not to? He realised that the thought of disappointing people—Atrepis, Arein, even Tia—bothered him. Yet the prospect of what might happen if he didn't troubled him equally if not more.

Durren was still tormenting himself with those same questions the next morning, after a long and restless night, when the summons for their next quest came from Cullglass.

8

This time, Durren was third to arrive, with Hule tramping down the passage only a few steps behind him. Tia and Arein, however, were both waiting by the door. Arein offered a tentative smile, while Tia seemed her familiar, perpetually hostile self.

Though actually, as he drew nearer, Durren noticed that she looked even surlier than usual. "Is something wrong?" he asked, before his brain had had time to point out what a terrible idea the question might be.

"Is something wrong?" Tia echoed. "I suppose it depends on your perspective. I've been promoted to level two, which you'd think would be good news. Except that I can't be, because none of the rest of you have. So, whatever this quest is, we're going to do a perfect job of it. I'm not going to let any of you get in my way." She jabbed a finger his way. "Especially not you."

Durren was taken aback. "What's that supposed to mean?" he managed.

"It means you're not trying. It means you're going to be the last of us to level up. It means that I don't know what you're up to and I don't care, but you're not going to stop me doing what

I came here to do."

He wanted to argue, he really did. But what could he say? She was right and they both knew it, and the worst thing was just how easily she'd seen through him. In fact, rather than be angry, Durren wanted to tell her about the efforts he'd been making all week, and about his commendation from Atrepis.

But Tia had already lost interest in him, and now she rapped hard upon the door.

This time Cullglass opened all but immediately. "Ah, there you are, my young accomplices. Greetings, greetings."

However, for all his show of enthusiasm, Cullglass's expression was businesslike and glum. He led the way without further word to the office portion of the room, which seemed more cluttered and unruly than ever. There he turned on them and, with the sombre fervour of a tragedian, pronounced, "Magic."

Just as Durren was beginning to wonder if that was all he had to say, the storesmaster picked up his own dangling thread. "Magic is a cornerstone of our civilisation. In the right hands it can achieve great good. However, in the wrong hands..." Cullglass gave a slight but visible shudder. "In the wrong hands, magic is a fearful thing."

Durren was coming to suspect that the storesmaster possessed an inclination towards drama. In this instance, however, his anxiety seemed genuine—and that alone was reason enough to be nervous. For if Cullglass was worried, then surely they should be doubly so; whatever the threat, they'd be the ones to face it.

"It has been brought to the Head Tutor's attention," Cullglass went on, "that a priesthood in the hills east of Fort Jargen, formerly famous for their good deeds and responsible use of magic, have grown somehow corrupted. Where in the past they strived to heal the unbalance, now they seem actively to be exacerbating it, abusing their power without the least concern or accountability."

Remembering all that Arein had told him, Durren looked to see her reaction. Sure enough, her eyes were wide with horror. This quest had already become personal for her, and he wasn't at all certain that was a good thing.

"We further believe," Cullglass said, "that this change in their behaviour may have something to do with the item with which they've been channelling their power. It's a stone, no larger than this"—and he clenched his fists together to illustrate—"known as the Petrified Egg. We've been unable to ascertain precisely what it is, for its nature has always been closely guarded by the priests. Suffice to say that it's sure to be dangerous, and that your task will be to recover this so-called Egg and return it here."

Cullglass stepped back to consider the four of them gravely—as though, Durren thought, he was committing their faces to memory in case he should never see them again.

"I won't lie to you, students…this is a gravely dangerous quest. If I were to be absolutely honest, I'd have to admit that I begged Head Tutor Borgnin not to give it to you, arguing that a higher-level party would be better suited. Sadly, the Head Tutor was not sympathetic; he told me that he's eager to see whether your recent success was an anomaly. Nevertheless, if you should ask me to, I'd gladly repeat my apprehensions. Frankly, to do so would be a weight removed from my conscience."

Durren knew what answer Tia and Hule would give. *Yes, of course we'll steal a magical doodad from an entire monastery of crazed priests intent on the destruction of reality.* And though Arein might have her concerns, she'd go along with it anyway, purely out of timidity. That left only Durren himself to give the cowardly but sensible answer: that this was entirely above their level, and perhaps even beyond their ability to survive.

Only, he couldn't. Not after what Tia had said, and not after his meeting with Eldra Atrepis. He couldn't be the one to let them all down.

Cullglass nodded solemnly. "Then know," he said, "that I'll be watching over you, ready to intervene in an emergency. And know too that, when you succeed in this—as I'm certain you shall!—your tenacity is sure to be rewarded."

Hieronymus seemed indifferent to their return, but Pootle at least was pleased to see them—or at least to see Arein. The observer flew close to her and then completed half a dozen rapid circuits around her head, while she chuckled with delight.

"Now then," Hieronymus said, "I'd hope that even you four understand how this works by now."

Tia led the way down into the shallow pit at the centre of the chamber and, without further ado, Hieronymus began his incantation. Once again there came the sparks of light, the sense that the room was beginning to run and smear like melting butter. Then walls, floor and ceiling were gone altogether, replaced by whirling gold and purple and the sensation of falling without falling.

The next Durren knew, there was mossy stone beneath his feet and a cool breeze ruffling his hair.

As his vision and swirling stomach began to settle, he saw that for once they'd arrived in view of their target. A low valley ran beneath the hillside they'd materialised upon, a river flowing languidly along its base. The slope descending at their feet was overgrown with thorny ambergale bushes and great spreads of the delicate blue flowers called wolf's toe. The monastery, meanwhile, was on the river's far bank. Presumably the priests ground their own flour, for a millwheel jutted from the building's near side, through which the water plummeted to a pool below.

The monastery itself was evidently ancient, as old perhaps as Black River. And like the academy, it had been rebuilt and modified over the years, left to ruin in parts and added to in others, so that newly carved stones nestled against blocks that might have been cut a dozen generations ago. The structure was imposing—particularly the high tower jutting from its middle—and eccentric in design.

However, the place didn't entirely emit the sense of brooding malevolence Durren had been expecting. In fact, with its whitewashed walls, many small windows and gently curving arches, the monastery appeared quite peaceful. He was reminded of the grand market halls further along the coast from Luntharbour, of the fishing villages they'd occasionally visited when he was a child.

Tia pointed to the tower. "That's a focal point. It's where this Egg thing's most likely to be." She studied the sheer walls for a moment. "I think I can climb up."

Durren had barely absorbed what she'd said before she'd begun to march downhill, towards where a narrow bridge arched across the river.

He had to run to overtake her. "Wait," he said, "just wait a minute."

Tia scowled at him, looking half ready to simply shove him aside. "What is it?"

"This is what you always do!" he said. "If you really want us to level up, then it's time you admitted that you're as much a part of the problem as we are. You decide on a plan, you go off on your own, and you couldn't care less what the rest of us are doing in the meantime."

"And," Tia said, "it's worked every time."

"If you call the four of us almost getting captured by angry rat people working. If the goal was for me to be nearly stabbed to death by a furious unicorn. Anyway, you're missing the point! If you do everything yourself, then of course you're going to level up and we won't. You're not giving us a chance."

Durren was so busy preparing himself for her rebuttal that it took him a moment to realise she hadn't spoken. Whatever he'd been expecting, it certainly wasn't the look of earnest deliberation that Tia wore.

"Fine," she said. "My suggestion is that I climb up to the tower, break in and steal whatever this Petrified Egg is. I'd find that a lot easier if I had a diversion. Do you think you three could provide one? I'll need about, oh, ten minutes. Is everyone happy with that? Does anybody have a better suggestion?"

The other two had caught up by then, and Tia looked from face to face. Arein shook her head, while Hule was preoccupied with scratching behind one ear and appeared not to have heard the question.

Finally, Tia's ash-grey eyes fell on Durren. "Well?"

"It sounds like as good a plan as any," he admitted. "But do you really think you can climb that tower?" The ascent looked impossible from where he was standing.

"I can climb it," she said.

Suddenly remembering, Durren pointed out, "I have a rope. I mean, if that would help."

Tia looked at him as though he'd offered her a wooden spoon to scale the wall with. "I'll manage, thank you."

This time, when she started down the slope, Durren followed after. He scrutinised the building before them, wondering if anyone might be on guard and have seen their arrival—but if there were eyes watching, then their owners were well hidden. In fact, the scene was altogether tranquil. All he could hear was the steady song of water coursing over stones and the twittering of small birds from among the ambergale bushes. Close up, the monastery retained its air of quietude; it was hard to imagine any wrongdoing occurring within those brightly whitewashed walls.

Which made it the perfect hiding place, Durren insisted to himself. Or did he believe the priests should have painted their home in blood and hung skulls from every jutting beam, just so that passers-by would be left in no doubt as to how evil they were?

The four of them tramped over the footbridge at the base of the slope. They were almost upon the building now, the nearest wall only a few paces away. Abruptly, Tia sat down in the damp grass and began to rummage through her pack.

At first, Durren took the four items she drew out for weapons, for that was what they looked like: each ended in a broad metal spike of about a thumb's length. Only as she slipped one over the toe of her left boot and drew a strap tight did he begin to understand. The second went on the other foot, and the remaining two—which were of a subtly different design—she slid around her outstretched hands and gripped tight.

The result was that each hand and foot ended in a vicious-looking point. These must be the items Tia had selected from the storeroom on that first day, implements no doubt designed specifically with her nimble, sneaky class in mind.

Now Durren understood the reason for her confidence. Still, the spikes would not be much use in and of themselves, not without the experience to pick the right route and the strength to hammer those blades into the slender gaps between stone blocks. Even with the tools of her trade, Tia still had a daunting task before her.

If she was at all concerned, she certainly hid the fact well. Reaching the wall, Tia stared upwards for the better part of a minute, as though memorising every detail for future reference. Then she placed one foot, experimentally. Almost quicker than Durren's eye could follow, she flung up a hand and dug her fingertips into a crack, not even relying on her climbing spike. Already her entire body was off the ground, suspended by one foot and the tips of three fingers.

Tia glanced back at them. "Well, what are you waiting for?"

Durren would have liked to wish her good luck, but he suspected she'd find a way to take the comment as an insult, and in any case she was no longer paying them any attention. Instead, he led the way onwards, towards the front of the monastery and where he assumed the entrance to be. When they reached the corner he glanced back, to find that Tia was already halfway up the wall and still making steady progress. She made the work look simple, though Durren had no illusions that it could be.

This time, however, he wasn't convinced that their own part would be significantly easier or less dangerous. All well and good for Tia to tell them to cause a distraction, but what exactly was that meant to entail? The last time they'd drawn attention away from her, it had nearly ended badly for all of them—and mad priests bent on the corruption of reality were an infinitely more intimidating prospect than a bunch of irate rat folk.

"We need a story," Durren proposed. "Some plausible reason to be here."

"Hule says we should just fight them."

"We're not fighting anyone," Durren said, and was surprised when Hule let the point drop. "Arein, this is more in your area of expertise than ours. Do you have any suggestions?"

Arein looked uncomfortable. "There's nothing worse a wizard can do than deliberately aggravating the unbalance. Even just refusing to take responsibility for your own magic use is awful. If the people inside are as bad as all that, I'm not sure any story we make up is going to be much help."

Durren sighed. He knew she was probably right, but he'd hoped for a little more reassurance. Suddenly Hule's plan—or at least the plan of letting Hule charge in on his own—seemed almost sensible. Still, they needed something, and it looked as though the task of coming up with a suitable fiction would fall to him. At least, Durren thought, lying was a subject he had practical experience in.

"Arein," he said, "will they know you're a wizard? I mean, just by looking at you? Is there a thing where wizards can sense other wizards, like how you knew where Blackwing was?"

Arein considered. "No, not really. I mean, nothing like that. Wizards aren't magical, not the way a unicorn is. We just have a certain aptitude for using magic. It's more of an instinct than anything."

That was a start, Durren supposed. There was, of course, the fact that she was wearing a cloak and carrying a staff, which amounted to a wizard's uniform. But maybe Durren only thought that because he'd spent so much time at the academy, where each class dressed basically the same. After all, many people wore cloaks to travel, and staves were hardly uncommon either. Arein's was a cheap enough thing, not like those of some of the higher-level students; it wasn't engraved with metal or carved with mystic sigils or topped with a crystal orb.

"All right," Durren said. "We're travellers, on our way to Fort Jargen, where we're supposed to be meeting our parents. They're expecting us by this evening, and they're important people…important enough to send someone looking for us if we don't arrive. But Arein, you've twisted your ankle, do you understand? That's why we borrowed that staff for you in the last village we passed through."

"That could work," Arein conceded. "I mean, they probably don't want to draw attention to themselves. Yes, I think it's a good idea, Durren."

"And what about you, Hule?" Durren asked.

Hule looked puzzled. "What about me?"

"Do you understand what we're going to tell the priests when we get inside?"

"Hule still says we should fight them," the fighter grumbled.

"But do you understand?"

Hule nodded moodily.

"Okay. Good." Durren didn't sound half as confident as he'd have liked, for it had only just occurred to him that the problem with having come up with a plan was that they'd now have to put that plan into action. Talking about tricking mad priests was one thing, actually doing so quite another.

He turned his attention once more to the monastery. There was a doorway set into a large portico, its border inlaid with glinting fragments of pottery in red and blue and gold. But there was no door, only a short, broad passageway leading to a smaller entrance within the building, beyond which lay deep shadows.

"Hello?" Durren called, as loudly as he dared.

There was no answer—but then he hadn't really expected one.

"I suppose we'll just have to go in," he said, hoping against hope that one of the other two would contradict him.

Instead, Arein addressed the observer, which had been zipping back and forth between them and Tia and currently was hovering above her left shoulder. "You'll have to stay back, Pootle," she said. "I'm sorry, but you're bound to give us away."

The eyeball bobbed uncertainly, as though weighing her words. Then it shot off, back in the direction they'd come from, and this time didn't return.

Since he seemed somehow to have elected himself their temporary leader, Durren went first. Out of the sun, the passage wasn't so gloomy as it had appeared from outside. Reaching the end, he found that it opened onto a far longer corridor. This one must run the entire length of the building, and was illuminated by slants of light from high slit windows. There were further arches in either direction, none as large as the one they'd entered by, but all just as open; Durren was beginning to suspect that there were no doors in the place anywhere. From their left he could hear faint sounds of activity and voices, so he led the way towards them.

Beyond the next opening was a colossal hall, huge enough that it must have filled an entire third of the monastery's central portion. The decor and furnishings were simple to the point of minimalism, with only a few long tables and benches at one end and the rest of the floor left bare. What light there was came from apertures carefully placed to correspond with windows in the outside wall, and fell in slanting beams of dusty yellow.

Durren's heart thundered as he counted perhaps thirty priests scattered about the room. A few were sitting at the tables, but most were kneeling on the floor of the open area. At a glance, their numbers appeared to consist more of men than women and more the elderly than the young. Other than that, however, they made for a remarkably varied crowd, with skin tones of yellow, white, brown, grey and black hinting at a multitude of different races. Their only uniformity was in their robes, which were of a greenish blue that made Durren think of the waters of the Middlesea on an overcast day.

Seeing the four of them, one of the nearby priests wandered over. "Can I help you, my young friends?" he asked.

The priest, like many of those in the room, carried a long staff not dissimilar to Arein's. He was younger than Durren would have expected, and amber-skinned as Durren himself was, likely from somewhere upon the coast or else a traveller from the far shores of the Middlesea.

"I hope so," Durren said. "We've been walking for hours, and my friend has hurt her ankle."

He motioned to Arein. Her limp looked overdramatic to his eyes, but if the priest felt any suspicion, he hid it well.

"You're certainly welcome to rest here," he said. "We don't have much, but what we have we're glad to share." His brow creased in puzzlement. "But, if you don't mind my asking, how is it that you came to be all the way out here?"

So Durren told the story he'd prepared, placing special emphasis on just how important their parents were and how they'd probably be worrying, even now, about their absent offspring. All the while the priest listened sympathetically, and without any obvious indication of having realised he was being fed a string of lies.

"Ah," he said, when Durren had drawn his rambling tale to a conclusion, "that would certainly explain it. Well, I only have a little skill at doctoring, but I'm sure I can bandage an ankle. Won't you come along with me?"

The priest began to move away, towards an opening on the opposite side of the hall—and Durren realised he had no idea what to do next. Their distraction was working, so far as it went; those priests who weren't kneeling and deep in concentration seemed at least aware of their presence, and no one had left the room since they'd arrived. But if the four of them were to go now, then they'd be no use at all to Tia.

How long had it been since they'd left her? Durren realised he had no way to judge the passage of time. What felt like hours was probably far less than the ten minutes she'd asked for.

The priest was waiting now, his expression enquiring. Arein and Hule were both looking to Durren as well, as though it was his responsibility to find some solution to their predicament. But he had nothing—and at any moment the priest was sure to query his hesitation, to notice the gaps and implausibilities in the tale he'd spun, and would drop this facade of pleasantness. Durren racked his brains, frantic to think of something, anything, to break the mounting tension.

However, when a distraction came, it had nothing at all to do with him—and he was as startled as everyone else. For just then the air was torn by a scream, long and heartfelt.

The voice was a woman's, Durren felt sure—just as he was certain he'd recognised it. And the sound had come from above, in the direction of the tower.

9

Hard as it was to tell one person screaming from another, Durren had no doubt that the voice had been Tia's. And he had never in his life heard such raw fear.

He wanted to run to help her—but the priests made that difficult. Many of them were on their feet now, a few drifting hesitantly towards the exit on the far side of the hall. Some were glancing with suspicion towards Durren, Arein and Hule. Among their number was the acolyte that Durren had told his story to.

Durren tensed. There was just a chance he could slip past all of them. He picked his route: veer right past the young priest, duck sharply left, then weave through those two and dash straight ahead, feint left, slip right instead. Yes, he thought he could make it.

Then Durren heard the scrape of metal on metal.

In its wake, silence fell like a hammer blow. Durren could hear not even the rustle of cloth or the shuffle of feet.

Hule, he thought, *you damned idiot.*

"Hoy! Foul sorcerers!" Hule bellowed, as though on cue. "Defend yourselves, if you dare."

The young priest looked more puzzled than afraid. Perhaps

that was understandable; one minute he'd been quietly corrupting the unbalance, the next people were screaming and a sword-wielding ruffian was howling insults at him. Even so, he levelled his staff before him, and a few of the others followed his example. Though none of them seemed quite sure what to make of the situation, they began moving to surround Hule.

That meant they were surrounding Durren too. Already his route to the far archway had closed. He glanced to Arein; she was retreating towards the entrance through which they'd arrived. Durren couldn't blame her, but he had seen no sign of stairs leading upwards in that direction, so nor did he feel he could follow her.

Hule darted forward, swinging his heavy sword. There was a crack, and then one of the priests was holding two short staves rather than one long one. With a yelp, he dropped both and took a quick step back. Another, braver priest took the opportunity to swipe at Hule's left side, but Hule brushed the blow aside effortlessly with his buckler, followed with a jab that left another opponent hastily retreating.

Durren nearly went for his own short sword, thought better of it. Nor was the decision altogether squeamishness; a fight here would only bog them down, and the numbers were overwhelmingly in the priests' favour. Anyway, the moment one of them decided to bring magic into the equation this would all be over.

Hule glanced his way. "Well?" he muttered. A sweep of his sword sent two priests stumbling aside. "Get going, why don't you?" With a tilt of his head, he indicated another exit, this one at the nearer end of the room, where the kneeling priests had been.

It was still the wrong direction, but at least it was closer;

perhaps Durren could find a way around. Rather than second-guess him, or even pause to wonder at the fact that Hule had apparently come up with something approaching a plan, Durren made his break. He flung himself at a gap between two priests, narrowly avoided getting the end of a staff in the ribs, skidded and caught himself and dashed onward. No one else tried to stop him; between the strange youth waving a sword about and the one running away, clearly they considered Hule the greater concern.

Durren made it to the smaller archway. Beyond was a short corridor and then an elongated bunk room. There, a priest was hurrying on her way, no doubt drawn by the commotion. When she saw him, her mouth formed into a questioning O. Rather than slow, Durren leaped onto the nearest bed, sprang from that to the next, and was past her before she'd even realised what was happening. He charged towards the far end of the room, and she made no attempt to follow.

The next passage had doorways off to either side, but they led only onto washrooms, the bathing pools there no doubt fed with ice-cold river water. Durren ran on instead to the next junction, turned left and left again. By his reckoning, that brought him out on the opposite side of the monastery from the one at which they'd entered. His flank was already beginning to ache, but he gritted his teeth, kept going.

When he passed the large arch that led back into the main hall, Durren dared a glance. Hule was still surrounded and still keeping the priests at bay; apparently none of them had yet thought to incinerate him or turn his blood to smoke. Hule seemed to be trying to force a path in Durren's direction, but the priests had him hemmed in as tightly as they dared.

For a moment Durren considered staying to help. But even

now the memory of Tia's scream still rang in his ears. So instead he pressed on, grateful that, thanks to Hule, not one priest was looking in his direction.

Just beyond the archway, the passage gave way to a flight of steps, which Durren started up three at a time. At what he judged to be the corner of the building, the staircase turned sharply, then grew noticeably steeper. Immediately he almost stumbled into someone: an elderly priest who scowled in confusion. In fact, there were four of them, Durren saw, making none-too-quick progress up the precipitous stairs; apparently all of the older priests had gone to investigate Tia's scream, while their younger brethren stayed to deal with the intruders.

Durren elbowed his way past, staggered onward. A couple of the aged priests protested as he barged by, but neither tried to stop him. Round the next corner were yet more stairs and more elderly priests. Durren gritted his teeth, kept moving, dodging and shoving and slithering.

The next flight of stairs was significantly shorter and terminated in a narrow landing, beyond which a broad ingress finally opened upon the tower. Durren could see no more than that, however, since the foremost priests blocked his view: above and ahead, the leaders were disappearing through the entrance. Durren heard gasps, of surprise or alarm, and then much muttering among them.

He pushed his way through to the landing. From there, Durren could just see through the vault and the crush of bodies to the space beyond.

The tower was octagonal, with further arches on every second edge, open to the outside and revealing gently sloping rooftops. The structure's ornamentation was simple, the floor tiled in a crude diamond pattern, and the columns and domed ceiling decorated only with unpainted plaster, yellowed by the passage of years. Further, the room contained nothing but a pedestal at its very centre, a square pillar of stone carved with runes and pictographs. Upon the pedestal, balanced improbably on its rounder end, was what could only be the Petrified Egg.

It was indeed egg-shaped—but that was as far as the similarity went. The object was about twice the size of Durren's clenched fist, and its surface resembled fine pottery, though something told him this treasure had never been manufactured by the hand of man. For the Egg possessed a strange depth, as though its outer skin was faintly translucent, and within he could perceive dim shapes jostling against each other.

However, strange though it was, Durren found concentrating on the Petrified Egg impossible—for by then he'd seen Tia. She might no longer be screaming, but her mouth remained open improbably wide, as though the cry had simply grown too large for her to express. She was crouched at the far side of the room, one hand clutching the wall, as if she was afraid that at any moment she'd be swept away. Durren had never seen anyone look so afraid, and it was all the more strange and shocking for being Tia, whose face normally gave away so little.

At the sight of her, something in Durren snapped. "What have you done to her?" he roared at the milling priests, and began to shove his way forward, his one thought to reach Tia and somehow to help her.

However, Durren had barely crossed the threshold before he stumbled to a halt. From nowhere he felt a sense of the most unfathomable dread. Though he couldn't have said why, he knew that soon, very soon, something terrible was going to happen—and that he was powerless to stop it.

Distantly he noted a ruckus from the stairwell. Someone shouted, and Durren was certain the voice was Hule's. The fighter must have finally fought his way free of the main hall. Durren should have been glad, but he understood now that Hule was every bit as helpless as he was; nothing he did could possibly save any of them. And sure enough, as Hule finally tumbled into the room, he progressed no further than Durren himself had. Then his sword slipped from his fingers, rattled upon the tiles. Hule made a gargling sound, threw an arm across his face, and cowered.

Normally that would have surprised Durren. Just then, he barely noticed. Whatever was wrong with Hule, he'd have to take care of himself. Even Tia hardly seemed important anymore. Because Durren was sure now that, whatever had terrified him so, whatever had rooted him here, it was behind him at this very moment.

He didn't want to look. Only, not seeing was worse. To know that what he feared was nearby and yet out of sight brought back jagged fragments of childhood nightmares.

Then the voice came, from close at his back. "So this is where you've got to."

In that moment, Durren was certain his heart had stopped beating. His body felt cold and distant, not a part of him at all. Yet somehow he found himself turning towards the voice, as though all alone it had the power to control him like a puppet. He knew what he was going to see.

Sure enough, there before him stood his father.

He was taller than Durren remembered. His eyes were darker, like chips of coal. And though he'd always trimmed his beard to resemble a blade stabbing from his long chin, the black hairs appeared even sharper than before, as though to touch them might draw blood.

There were questions Durren knew he should be asking, but all of them seemed hazy and remote. All he could bring himself to say was, "Sir?"

His father took a step nearer. He was every bit as imposing as he'd been when Durren was small. And it would always be that way, Durren thought: he'd never outgrow this man, never be able to look him in the eye—because his father would always find a way to become taller.

"I suppose you're proud of yourself? That you believe you've found a way to punish me? Yet all you've done is shame me, Durren. Just as you've shamed your mother's memory, and every Flintrand through the ages. You disgrace your name and your heritage."

Durren wanted to defend himself. He wanted to say that he didn't care—because the things he desired, the person he wanted to be, had nothing in common with his father's intentions. He didn't give a damn about piling up gold he'd done nothing to earn; he had no wish to grow wealthy off the sweat of strangers. All that mattered was that he use the skills he had, and perhaps one day do some good with them.

Yet Durren said none of that. How could he? The terror was paralysing. It wasn't only that his father was here, but that his presence made no sense—yet, at the same time, seemed inevitable. This was the moment that, from his first day at Black River, Durren had known would come. And if he couldn't explain why it should be here or now, then surely that was only another failing to be ashamed of.

"You thought to rebel," his father said, "but that rebellion is done. No more wasting your time at that grubby academy of imbeciles and paupers; no more playing with bows and arrows. Soon you'll forget that these past months ever occurred. We'll go home now, Durren. And this will be the last you'll ever see of the world outside my walls."

Durren knew his father's words were true. As badly as he might wish to resist, he would be dragged from here, back to his miserable former life, to train for a career he already despised. Nothing he did would change that fate. He'd been a fool to imagine even for an instant that he could control his life, that anyone but the man before him might dictate his future.

Except that something was distracting him. Something in the corner of his eye threatened to draw his attention. A part of Durren insisted that, whatever it might be, it couldn't possibly matter. Probably it was to do with those three companions he'd had briefly, that futile quest they'd been on—and what was all that but a dream he was now waking from?

Still, Durren found himself looking. Perhaps he was only trying to buy an instant's reprieve from the moment when his father would haul him from this room and all his hopes would evaporate forever.

A number of the priests still stood about, none of them appearing quite sure of what was happening or how they were meant to respond. Tia was still curled in the corner, her jaw locked rigidly in a silent scream. Hule was flailing and babbling at something only he could see. And Arein was walking towards the pedestal in the centre of the room.

She crossed the floor as calmly as though she were in the great dining hall of Black River. Reaching the centre, she placed a hand on either side of the curious stone perched there and lifted it free.

In the moment she did so, Durren felt as though a vast

weight vanished from his shoulders. He found that he could breathe properly once more, and only realised then that he hadn't been able to before. Too, he could move again. Of course none of that meant he'd be able to talk his father round, but perhaps he could flee, maybe come up with some scheme to—

Wait, his father? How could his father possibly be here? What had made perfect sense only instants before now defied all explanation. And sure enough, when Durren glanced back, the person nearest to him was a stooped and grey-haired priest. Urden Flintrand was nowhere to be seen.

Something strange had just happened, that much was clear. But there was no time to consider. The priests were muttering among themselves, only now seeming to grasp the fact that one of these young interlopers had snatched away their precious Egg. Arein, meanwhile, having secured the prize they'd come all this way for, was simply standing there, staring at the stone and rotating it between her hands.

At least, she was until Tia—on her feet now and apparently fully recovered—caught hold of her sleeve and heaved her towards the leftmost arch. Seeing them go shook Durren from his reverie. "Come on!" he bawled at Hule, who was still eyeing the room warily, as though at any moment something might leap from a corner.

Together they dashed past the pedestal, towards the exit through which Tia and Arein had vanished. Only as they drew close did Durren see the drop to the monastery's slanting rooftop. Barely hesitating, he took the fall at a run and landed with a jolt, only just keeping his footing on the mossy tiles.

Ahead, Arein and Tia had already reached the building's end. Only as he and Hule hurried to join them did Durren think to wonder where Tia's plan went from here. Yes, they had the Egg, and yes, they'd escaped from the tower, and that was all fine and good—but it still left them trapped on a roof, the ground a distant blur below.

The priests, having clambered down after them, were spreading out in a line that cut off any hope of escape back into the building. Yet, having done so, they kept their distance. In fact, aside from the fact that the younger acolytes had now caught up with their elder brethren, they didn't make for a particularly intimidating crowd.

Then again, the thing about being an order of corrupt wizards with no qualms about abusing your power, Durren supposed, was that you didn't *need* to look intimidating. After all, it hardly matter what impression you gave when you could melt the flesh from someone's bones with a few words and the wave of a hand.

Still, that didn't mean they couldn't be reasoned with—or that it wouldn't be worth trying, when the alternative was an unwinnable fight. "Maybe," Durren said, "if we give the Egg back they'll let us go. I mean, they don't have any reason to kill us, do they?"

"We're not giving the Egg back," Tia said.

She spoke with such adamant certainty that Durren wondered if the two of them were really in the same situation. Did she understand that they were high on a rooftop with a horde of murderous priests before them, a fatal plummet at their backs?

"Tia…" he began, but didn't know how to continue.

"The mill pool," she said. "The water's deep there."

By then, Durren's thoughts were so muddled that he could barely piece together the significance of what she'd said. Why was she talking about mill pools? What did it matter how deep some water was? Then he saw how she was gazing over the edge of the roof, how she was taking half a dozen quick steps back, and finally he understood.

"There's my rope—" Durren tried.

But by then Tia had already jumped.

Gulping down his shock, Durren stumbled to the edge. He'd never exactly been afraid of heights, but that wasn't to say he wasn't afraid of falling from them, and it took all his courage to glance over.

At first he could see no sign of Tia. Then her head breached the surface of the large pond beyond the waterwheel. A moment later and she was swimming with confident strokes towards the far bank.

Durren turned back, ready to tell the others that Tia was all right. However, it seemed that Hule had read as much from his face—or else hadn't the sense to wonder—for the fighter was already making his own run-up. An instant later and he was dashing past, with a triumphant bellow that continued until the very moment he hit the water far below.

That left only Arein. She was a few strides from the edge, and eyeing it as though it were the rim of some fathomless abyss. "I don't know if I can do this," she said.

"There's no choice," Durren told her. He spoke the words as persuasively as he could, because he was also trying to convince himself.

The priests were finally beginning to advance—though uncertainly. Perhaps they imagined that their uninvited guests were now flinging themselves to their deaths. In mere instants they would reach Arein, and then this would all be over. Durren wondered if he should lead by example, but he couldn't shake the conviction that if he left her alone, Arein would stay just where she was. And would she be so wrong to? Just because Tia had survived, that wasn't to say either of them would.

Then Arein was running, and he realised he'd misjudged her yet again. For he'd never seen such naked terror in a face, not even Tia's back in the tower, and still the dwarf girl didn't hesitate. She flung herself from the edge, arms and legs scrabbling at empty air.

Durren could see no choice but to follow her example. He retreated four swift paces, ran and leapt.

The fall was worse than he'd expected. It seemed to go on for longer than it had any right to, long enough for him to understand with perfect clarity that he was plummeting from a great height. Everything was a blur, he wasn't even sure he was the right way up, and the first point when he was certain he was falling towards water and not solid ground was when his feet struck the mill pool. Then he was sinking—and sinking fast.

He could see nothing, could hear only a colossal rushing like a cataract. The water, dark and heavy, closed upon him like a coffin lid, intent on pushing him to its deepest depths. Only as the last air was squeezing from his lungs did he remember which was up, which was down. Then, with barely a thought, he was thrashing towards the surface. As he broke through, Durren gasped, at the same time sputtering foul-tasting water.

Jumping off a building might not be something he had much experience of, but swimming was another matter; he'd spent enough time in the warm waters off the coast near Luntharbour. As soon as he had his breath, Durren started towards the bank with assured strokes. But he'd hardly begun when he realised that the commotion to his left was Arein, floundering; she paddled like a three-legged dog. So as he passed, Durren caught hold of her arm and drew her with him.

The mill pool wasn't wide. Even with Arein flapping behind, it didn't take Durren long to reach the far bank. There he helped Arein haul herself onto the slippery stone and then clambered up himself. Hule was energetically ringing greenish water out of his undershirt, while Tia was watching Arein intently, oblivious of her own dripping clothes.

"Tell me you've still got it," she said, her voice tense with forced calm.

Arein reached into her sopping robe, rummaged around. When her hand returned, she was clutching the Petrified Egg. Durren's heart lurched at the sight, and for an instant he found his eyes darting, certain he'd see his father approaching. But no, there were just the four of them. Clearly, whatever had happened before, the phenomenon had been tied not just to the Egg itself but also to the pedestal, or even the entire tower.

Durren looked back towards the monastery. He had half expected the priests to come leaping after them, but apparently none were quite that determined. A few of the most elderly adherents were watching from the rooftop; the rest were surely hurrying even now back down those many stairs. It was a decidedly long way around, and they'd have to divert even further to cross the river via the bridge. For all that, they were sure to catch up in a minute or two.

"We need to go," Tia said. She pointed back up the hill in the direction they'd arrived from, towards where the ground broke into slabs of jutting stone amid knotted clumps of ambergale.

Tia led the way and the rest of them fell in behind her. When Durren glanced back, the first priests were just rounding the corner of the monastery. He could hear their cries as they called to their companions. They didn't seem to be much for running, but there were a lot of them, and they surely knew this area better than Tia did. Not only that, but who could guess what dark magics they had at their disposal? After what had occurred in the tower, Durren's respect for sorcery was at an all-time high. Had the sky abruptly begun to rain fire or the ground opened to swallow him, he would barely have been surprised.

Beyond the brim of the hill, the landscape grew inhospitable: a plain of broken ground split by chasms and great, jumbled boulders, with among the wreckage a few stubby trees and bushes grasping at the sky. It was the sort of terrain where the priests might easily overtake them, especially if they knew routes that weren't immediately obvious.

"I think we might do better to hide," Durren suggested. He didn't entirely like the idea, not when for all he knew there were spells that could be used to sniff them out, but it was still more appealing than the thought of spending the next hours being hunted through that labyrinth. And if they were going to find a place then now was the time, while the hillside still hid them from view.

Nevertheless, he'd thought Tia would argue. Perhaps it was her sopping robes that made her mind up rather than any respect for Durren's opinion. "I'll find somewhere," was all she said.

They carried on, picking their way carefully over loose shale. Durren found himself unable to keep from peeking over his shoulder, certain each time he'd see the priests closing in. Then, just as he was convinced that any chance they might have had was gone, Tia called, "This way."

She had spied a narrow channel, slanting to cut a deep gash

through the ground, and had already scrambled halfway to its bottom. Hule and Arein followed, though without such ease or grace, and Durren brought up the rear. He could immediately see Tia's logic. Not only did the gully hide them from view, at its end it tunnelled beneath a cluster of huge rocks that had toppled together in ages past, offering cover from the ridge behind.

Seconds later, after much difficult clambering, Tia said, "Here." Then she was vanishing into a narrow triangular fissure in the rock wall.

The hole she'd found was larger than Durren would have expected from the outside, and larger, too, than its barely navigable entrance suggested. By any other definition, however, it was tiny. The space was just sufficient for the four of them, and even then was more intimate than he would have liked. Jamming himself into a gap just within the opening, he had Arein's foot against his thigh and Hule's elbow wedged into his side.

Still, Tia had certainly found them a hiding place, and— unless there really were magical means by which to track them down—one that wouldn't be easily discovered.

Durren could just see, too, that Pootle had taken up position at the centre of their tangled group and was rotating steadily. "Homily, paradigm, lucent," he tried. However, the observer only considered him gravely. Evidently it was true that the spell would only work when they were completely free of danger. That policy seemed back to front, in Durren's opinion; at best it suggested that the tutors were more concerned with the safety of the academy as a whole than that of any individual students.

At any rate, they were trapped. There'd be no escaping by

magical transportation, and the obvious drawback with hiding was that they were sure to be cut off soon, if they hadn't been already.

Certainly, Durren could hear the priests moving around outside. Sometimes it was the rattle of pebbles skittering; sometimes they called back and forth to each other. They sounded worried, but Durren was unable to make out individual words. Every time he convinced himself that they'd given up, he would catch a distant shout, or a clatter of falling stones that might represent someone clambering nearby.

Durren did his best to make himself comfortable, while at the same time moving in perfect silence. But his attempts proved futile. Any space that might have eased the cramp in his limbs was taken up by some part of one of the others. There was nothing to do but endure, and to wait—until they could be sure the priests had finally called off the hunt, or until they were discovered.

10

Outside, the light was fading. Evening was drawing in. But within the small cave, darkness had already fallen, and all Durren could make out of his companions was shapes amid the gloom.

He had been straining his ears for hours now—hours that felt like days. Twice he'd tried whispering the recall spell, but to no effect. Perhaps Pootle hadn't heard, but more likely the observer was still aware of danger close by.

Yet a long time had passed since Durren had heard anything other than the most distant and ambiguous sounds. Perhaps that shrill hoot minutes before had been a signal, but more likely it had been only a bird call; maybe that rattle of gravel had been set loose by a careless foot, but just as probably it was the ancient stones above them settling. In the deep silence, every small noise was all too easy to misinterpret.

"I think they're finally gone," Arein whispered. She sounded both relieved and exhausted.

"I'm going out to look," Durren decided. He had reached a point where murderous, magic-abusing priests seemed preferable to one more agonising moment of confinement.

Before anyone could argue, he was crawling back through

the hole. Outside, the sun was gone from view and the sky a glowering red. Durren could see no one, and when he listened, all he heard was the sighing of the wind and the back and forth whistles of small birds in a patch of nearby bushes. So far as he could tell, the four of them were alone.

When he glanced back, Arein's head and shoulders were halfway through the gap. The opening beyond the cave was far from large, walled as it was by monolithic rocks to every side, but after his hours of constraint, the space seemed immense. Durren perched on an outcrop, and after they'd each slithered free of their hiding place, the others picked their own spots and sat massaging outstretched arms and legs.

Durren knew that the thing to do now was to pronounce the transport spell and get the four of them back to the academy as swiftly as possible. Yet he couldn't find in himself any real sense of urgency, and none of the others seemed concerned either. It was pleasant to be outside, breathing fresh air, stretching limbs confined for far too long. More than that, though, he felt that a great deal had happened in the last few hours, and only now did he have the opportunity to consider those events with a clear mind.

He looked at Arein, who had sprawled on the ground with her back to a sheet of rock and her legs stretched before her, and was now busily polishing her glasses with an edge of her robe. "What happened up there, to Tia, Hule and me..." he began.

Arein squinted at him, and then slid her glasses back onto her nose. "It was a spell," she said—confirming what Durren had already come to suspect. "But it must have been powerful; I never knew something like that was even possible. From the way you were all acting, I'd guess the enchantment was designed to confront you with your worst fears."

"Spiders," Hule muttered, half beneath his breath.

"*Spiders?*" Arein echoed.

"Hule *hates* spiders," the fighter insisted, and the disgust with which he spoke the words left no doubt of how serious he was.

"I saw my father," Durren said, before he could stop himself. The memory of what had happened up in the tower had been haunting him through every moment of their imprisonment in the cave, and he realised only now how badly he needed to share the experience with someone. As much as he'd been shaken by encountering his father like that, by hearing the words he'd dreaded for so long, the revelation that the entire episode had been only the conjuring of his own frightened mind had made it somehow worse.

After a moment, he realised how the three of them were looking at him. "I mean...I saw..." But none of the lies that came to mind were at all persuasive.

"What do you mean," Tia said, "you saw your father?"

He was caught. Somehow Durren knew that even from that small clue she would work out the rest, sooner or later. You didn't decide to study as a rogue unless the instinct to pry out secrets was a significant part of your nature. Yet the truth felt like a stone in his throat, too large to cough loose.

Only they were staring at him now, and his pause had gone on for a very long time, the silence it left growing unbearable. "I saw my father," Durren said, "coming to take me home."

"What," Arein asked, "like, for a holiday? Are you scared of holidays? I don't get it."

It was her obliviousness more than any desire to admit the truth that dragged the words out of him. "Look—I'm not supposed to be here, all right? Do you really think that Urden Flintrand, the wealthiest merchant in all of Luntharbour, would allow his son to go off and train to be a ranger? Let alone at the lowliest, most notoriously dangerous academy in the entire kingdom?"

"It's not that bad!" Arein said.

Durren frowned at her, confused.

"I mean, maybe Black River isn't the best academy, but I'm sure it's not actually the worst. And it isn't *that* dangerous; I've heard it's much safer than it used to be. They say nearly eight out of ten students only ever suffer minor injuries—"

"Arein," Tia said patiently, "I think you may be missing the point."

Arein paused, blinked. "Oh. Am I?"

Tia looked to Durren, and he felt that those pale eyes of hers could see right through him. "The point," she said, "is how Durren is here without his parents' permission, when having that permission is a prerequisite for enrolling in the academy."

Arein's brow furrowed. "That's true," she agreed thoughtfully. Then, to Durren, "So, how *are* you here?"

"I forged my father's handwriting," Durren said. "I wrote a letter pretending to be him and asking for the admittance paperwork. Normally they don't let anyone enrol without a visit first, but because the person asking was the great Urden Flintrand, and because the letter said he'd pay all the fees in advance, it turned out they were more than happy to bend the rules. When the answer came, I stole the parcel from my father's office before he had a chance to look at it and filled the papers in myself. Then I stole the gold I'd need to pay for my tuition and came straight here."

Arein looked as astonished as though he'd claimed to have

grown wings and flown all the way from Luntharbour. "But didn't they think that was strange?" she asked. "I mean, you arriving with so much money like that?"

"Probably they did," Durren admitted. "But then, five years' worth of tuition fees is an awful lot of gold, and maybe they decided not to question too hard."

"I'm still not sure I understand," Arein went on. "Why are you so afraid of your father coming to get you? Surely, for all he knows, you could be anywhere?"

Having come this far, there seemed no point in hiding any of what remained. In fact, it felt good to be finally telling someone the truth. "The thing is," Durren said, "that my being here only stays secret so long as no one from the academy writes to my father. And they write to a student's parents under two circumstances: when they've done something terribly wrong or something exceptionally right. Once I realised that, I knew the only way I could stay here until I graduated was to be the most average student they'd ever seen."

"But you must have realised that word was going to get back to your father sooner or later?"

Durren shrugged embarrassedly. He hadn't. But he could see now that he should have, could see too just how much effort he'd made to hide the truth from himself. "I suppose I thought that after a while he'd just forget about me. I mean, he was always forgetting I existed, even when I was at home; there didn't seem any reason to think he'd pay more attention when I wasn't around. Anyway, all I need is a couple of years and then I'll be of age. Maybe he can try and make me pay his gold back, but he can't make me go with it."

At that, Hule laughed loudly. When Durren glared at him, the fighter declared, "Your scheme is stupid and you sound like a child."

Durren would have liked to protest. But Hule was their resident expert on idiocy, and if even he thought a plan was stupid, then there could be no doubt that it was. Durren had felt so brave at the time, walking away from everything he'd ever known. Yet what use was half a plan? Especially one that left you in perpetual fear of discovery? No, Hule was right; he'd behaved like a child, and a foolish one at that.

"I didn't feel like I had any other options," Durren mumbled, sounding sulkier than he'd have liked.

"At least you've finally admitted the truth," Tia said.

Her tone of voice surprised him. "You say that you like already knew."

"I knew there was *something* off about you. Nobody tries so hard to be useless, not without good reason. I'd have worked it out eventually, but I'm glad you saved me the wasted effort."

As so often seemed to be the case, the fact that Tia was blunt beyond the point of rudeness didn't actually make her wrong.

"Look," Durren said, "you have to promise me…no one can ever know about this. I realise I haven't come up with the best solution. I need to put a lot more thought into it. And I know I've been making things difficult for the rest of you. I won't do that anymore, I promise; I can keep my head down without being entirely worthless. Only, if word of this got back to Borgnin, if my father found out where I am…"

He shuddered. For an instant, the memory of his vision had been painfully clear: Urden Flintrand towering over him, the disdain dripping from his voice. And only then did Durren realise that the encounter hadn't altogether been a product of his imagination. Rather, his mind had assembled his father's words from a dozen occasions, a dozen times when he'd been told off, or ordered about, or made to feel small.

"I won't tell," Arein said quietly.

Durren smiled. "Thanks, Arein."

"Neither will I," Tia told him. "You have my word."

"Thank you, Tia." Then, abruptly reminded of how this conversation had begun, Durren blurted out, "So are you going to tell us what you were so frightened of back there?"

"No. I'm not." Tia sounded angry at the mere suggestion—but, more, she sounded afraid. Whatever she'd seen, it had obviously shaken her badly. Durren struggled to believe that anything could scare her so, but her expression was enough to dissuade him from pressing the point.

Hule stood up, stretching and cricking his neck. "Hule says it's time we got back."

"He has a point," Durren agreed. Now that he'd had a chance to stretch his own deadened limbs, he was beginning to notice the nip in the evening air, and the fact that he hadn't eaten a thing since that morning. Anyway, there was every chance that the priests were only taking a break from their hunt, perhaps returning to the monastery to gather lanterns. Durren couldn't persuade himself that they'd abandon so precious a treasure without the utmost effort.

"Wait," Arein said. Her voice was small and cautious, yet at the same time determined. "There's something else. Something important. And we can't go back, not until we've discussed it."

Durren sighed inwardly. Was this like her fixation with the unicorn? What was she caught up on this time? "We can't return the stone," he said, "if that's what you're thinking. I know that strictly speaking we stole it, but only in a good cause."

"No, that's not it." Arein's cheeks reddened. "I mean...maybe partly it is."

"Arein," Durren said, "The academy wouldn't send us on a quest just for their own amusement. And they certainly wouldn't have us take something if they weren't confident it was in the wrong hands in the first place."

"I know all that," she told him. "Only—why could I take the Petrified Egg? Why didn't its powers work on me?"

That stopped him in his tracks. Hadn't he briefly wondered the same? But the question had seemed less than important when he'd been expecting to be turned inside out by the mad priests, and by the time he'd plummeted from a building and almost drowned, he'd forgotten altogether.

"It was probably some magic thing," Durren tried, though he knew as he spoke what the answer would be.

"Magic isn't...it just doesn't work like that. It's not some special key that fits every lock. And I told you, *I'm* not magical just because I can do magic."

"All right then," Tia cut in. "Obviously you have an explanation. So what is it?"

Arein looked suddenly shy. "It's to do with fear," she said. "It's to do with what I'm afraid of, and what I'm not afraid of."

Hule grunted irritably. "Hule is bored and cold and wants to go home! Will you give a plain answer, dwarf girl?"

"I'm trying to! Look—it's like I told Durren. The one thing that scares me most is the unbalance, and the thought of something I did making it worse. That's why I try not to use magic unless I absolutely have to. And I think that was what allowed me to take the Petrified Egg; I think that was its protection. Only, if that's the case, then why weren't the priests themselves affected?"

Hule opened his mouth to answer, but Arein cut him off. "Yes, I know, magic! And I told you, magic doesn't work that way. Even if there was some kind of a counter-spell to resist the Egg's effects, I was watching them and nobody cast anything. They were just as vulnerable as the rest of us, yet all of them seemed fine. I've been thinking, and as far as I can see, there's only one explanation."

Durren understood. He wished he didn't, but he did. "They're afraid of the same thing you are."

"Exactly!" Arein looked pleased that he'd worked it out. "It's the perfect defence mechanism; the only ones who can go near the Petrified Egg are wizards who appreciate how terrible it is to abuse the unbalance."

"Or ones who just don't care," Tia suggested—though there was doubt in her voice.

"That wouldn't work. We know the Egg picks up on your darkest fears, so not caring wouldn't be any defence at all."

"So what you're saying is…" But Durren let the sentence trail away. He understood precisely what Arein was saying, Tia's scowl made it clear that so did she, and even Hule looked mildly contemplative.

"We'll talk to Cullglass," Tia said. "That's all we can do." If her tone was firm, she still sounded less certain than usual.

"She's right," Durren put in. "Just maybe it's possible that the academy made a mistake, that this was all somehow a misunderstanding. But we can't just assume, Arein. And we can hardly wander back into the monastery and hand them the Egg as though nothing's happened."

"No," Arein agreed, "I understand that. Only—" Though she looked sheepish, Durren was coming to learn that she wouldn't let her anxieties stop her, not once she had her mind set. "We have to promise, all right? That we'll do the right thing, if it comes to it?"

Durren's heart sank. Already today he'd revealed the secret he'd intended to admit to no one, and now here he was, being asked to commit to something with the potential to cause no end of problems. Of all the possibilities likely to draw attention, he had no doubt that openly contradicting a member of the academy staff was high on any list. Still, he knew Arein wasn't about to take no for an answer—and he wasn't sure he blamed her. "I promise," he said.

"You have my word," Tia agreed.

"Fine," Hule said. "But surely we're done now?"

Arein merely nodded. Durren could tell that being the centre of attention for so long had taken a great deal from her.

He tried to examine his own thoughts. It was as though what Arein had said had scraped at a healing wound he'd previously been able to ignore, and now the itch was inescapable. One thing was for sure, there was more going on here than the facts they had could explain. Were it not for Cullglass's warnings, Durren would never have imagined the priests were other than what they seemed: a secluded commune given over to pursuing their good works in peace. So either Arein was right and this entire quest had been a mistake, or the priesthood was up to something even more insidious than Cullglass had led them to believe—a plot monstrous enough to warrant such a grand charade.

Durren found it hard to say which possibility unsettled him more. However, there was no use worrying now, and for once Hule had a point: it was high time they headed back.

Glancing round for Pootle, Durren discovered the observer perched high upon the rocks above and watching the four of them steadily. Only then did it occur to him that he was glad the creature had no ears; though, now that he thought, the observer did seem to respond to spoken commands. Yet even if it had heard his secrets, surely it had no means to transmit them back to Hieronymus. At least, Durren had to hope that was the case.

"Come here, Pootle," he said—and sure enough, the observer understood enough to descend towards the centre of their group.

Durren glanced from face to face. Was it only his imagination or had something changed between them over the course of the day? For the first time, they actually felt to him like a party, rather than simply four people pressed unwillingly into each other's company. Despite everything that had happened and all he now had to worry about, Durren found the idea appealing.

He nearly asked if everyone was ready, but Tia and Hule's expressions of impatience and the way Arein was shivering against the evening chill answered that question.

"Homily, paradigm, lucent," Durren said, and the world began to melt.

11

Durren had never thought he'd be so glad to see Hieronymus's transportation chamber. The day had been long and arduous, and only now did his body seem to be registering those facts. Suddenly he wanted nothing more than to curl upon his hard, straw-crammed mattress in the rangers' dormitory, and sleep until the worst aches had abandoned his body.

That wasn't going to happen, though—at least not yet. Their quest wouldn't be done until they were rid of the prize they'd been sent for.

It occurred to Durren that they might have asked Hieronymus about the Petrified Egg. But nothing in the old wizard's expression of drowsy disinterest suggested he'd be likely to know anything useful or, knowing, be prepared to share. Maybe they'd be better to start with another wizard then, one with specialist knowledge on the subject of enchanted items? There was sure to be such a person among the faculty, and likely Arein would be familiar with them from her lectures.

Only, how would that look? If instead of returning to Cullglass with the object of their quest, they were to start interrogating the academy staff about its secrets? No, Cullglass was their mentor, and it wouldn't do to go behind his back.

Anyway, the choice was already out of Durren's hands. Tia, having muttered a brief "Thank you" to Hieronymus, was heading towards the door, and the other two were following in her wake. With a final glance back at the old wizard, Durren hurried after.

Tia led the way through the corridors, guided by her unerring sense of direction. Soon they were at the entrance to Cullglass's stores and she was rapping out three sharp knocks upon the blackened planks.

"Come in!" came the muffled reply.

When Tia tested the door, sure enough, it was open. Cullglass was perched on his stool, within the central area that served as his office. A lantern hung from a stand close by, but other than that the room was sunk in shadow, so that it seemed as if the storesmaster was the lone shipwrecked survivor upon an island of light amid a sea of darkness.

Cullglass waited patiently as they threaded their way through the maze of shelves and tables. When they were close, he steepled his long fingers before his even longer face and announced, "Here you are, my young friends. What a long and no doubt trying day of adventuring you've had. But a successful one also, I do believe. Let me see what your diligence has won."

Arein stepped forward. She didn't look at all comfortable as she reached into her robe and drew out the Egg. Durren was certain he could see her fingers shaking as she placed the curious object into Cullglass's outstretched palms. And was it Durren's imagination or did it seem that, just for the barest instant, the Egg reacted? He could have sworn the swirling patterns within its surface sped up as though agitated.

"Ah!" murmured Cullglass. "So this is what a Petrified Egg

looks like. My, but what a curio! An object of dark and wanton power, to be sure."

There was a wooden box on the nearest table, lined almost to the brim with straw. Abandoning his stool, Cullglass placed the Egg within, as carefully as though he were handling a newborn baby.

"And what an achievement," he continued, "to snatch so remarkable an item from beneath the very gaze of its masters! My pride in you knows no bounds." Cullglass clapped his hands. "Well, I can only imagine that the four of you must be exhausted. As much as I'd like to hear the day's events in your own words, I won't be so thoughtless as to keep you from your rest."

Arein shuffled her feet. "The thing is," she began, "those priests...they weren't quite what we were expecting."

It was hardly the most persuasive of beginnings, and Cullglass certainly didn't look impressed. "Is that so?"

"Only," Durren cut in, before he was able to restrain himself, "they didn't seem all that evil at all. In fact, they were just like perfectly normal priests."

"But is that so surprising?" the storesmaster asked. "Should anyone gain the faintest inkling of what they were truly up to, reprisals were certain to be forthcoming. Had this academy not been first to investigate, it would have been the Brazen Fist, or else interested parties from among the wizard communes. At any rate, their only hope of continuing their fiendish practices unmolested was to maintain the persuasive illusion of innocence."

"That's true," Arein agreed. "Only, there's more to it than that."

Cullglass hesitated. "Is that so?"

"The Egg was projecting a fear spell. The only ones it didn't affect were those whose deepest fear meant they'd never try and abuse its power. That's the only reason I managed to touch it. But if that's the case, then how could the priests be evil? Unless their intentions were pure, they couldn't even enter the same room as the object they used to focus their power."

"Hmm," Cullglass mused. "Yes, I see your argument. However, it's not without its potential flaws. For a beginning, you're relying all but entirely on supposition; we have as yet only the crudest understanding of what the Petrified Egg is or of how it works. And with all due respect, Mistress Thundertree, perhaps what you encountered wasn't a fear spell at all, or worked in some altogether different fashion to those you're familiar with. I hope you'll take it as no criticism if I point out that these priests were possessed of vastly greater magical knowledge than you yourself."

"I know that," Arein said. "Only, it *was* a fear spell."

There was such certainty in her voice that Cullglass couldn't fail to hear it. He frowned, picked at the fingernails of his left hand with those of his right. "If you're right," he said finally, "and I'm willing to accept that you may be..." The frown deepened. "That would certainly be cause for concern."

"We were hoping," Durren said, "that you'd look into it. That maybe there's been a mistake." And as he spoke, he couldn't help remembering the similar conversation they'd had only days before, after they'd returned here with Blackwing.

Perhaps Cullglass's mind was working along similar lines, for he looked grave now. "Yes," he said, "yes indeed. I'm persuaded that this matter warrants further investigation. After all, what could be worse than for us to inadvertently darken the reputation of our prestigious academy? I could never forgive myself if through some error I'd had you act as common thieves. I assure you, this matter will receive my utmost attention."

Cullglass lowered his voice, leaning forward so as to bring his mouth closer to their ears. "In any case, I confess that I now feel the need to set my own mind at rest. There's a most unsettling possibility here. Unlikely, certainly unlikely, but if it were true—"

"You mean," Tia said, "that someone in the academy might be manipulating quests for their own ends."

Cullglass looked pained. "I'd hoped not to hear the matter phrased so bluntly."

"But that *is* what you mean."

The storesmaster nodded heavily. "Yes. It is."

But, Durren thought, Cullglass had said that he received their quests directly from the Head Tutor himself. Was it conceivable that Borgnin was somehow being manipulated? The alternative was almost too awful to contemplate, let alone put into words: if Borgnin himself was abusing his authority then all of Black River, everything Durren believed in, was corrupt to its very core.

Cullglass hadn't said as much, but Durren felt strongly that the storesmaster was entertaining the same terrible conclusion.

"I must ask," he said, "that you behave with the utmost discretion—if only to ensure your own safety. By the time we next meet, I sincerely hope that I'll have some answers for you. But until then, let us keep this matter among ourselves. I'm quite certain that there's an explanation, and a perfectly innocent one. Still, we would none of us be worthy of our places at Black River if we hoped for the best without at the same time anticipating the worst."

Cullglass's eyes flickered from face to face, and it seemed to Durren that he was hunting for something: agreement, certainly, but perhaps also reassurance. Durren offered a hesitant nod; he saw no choice now but to hope the storesmaster was as good as his word. Anyway, the longer he'd spent standing in this oasis of light amid the gloom, the heavier his eyelids had grown, and the more his aching body reminded him of the demands he'd made. He was ready now for the day's events to become somebody else's problem.

Whatever Cullglass had been seeking, he seemed to have found it, for he clasped his hands together with a resounding slap. "As for the four of you," he said, "you must let the matter trouble you no more. You did exceedingly well, and have every reason to be proud of your efforts. I've no doubts that such hard work will bear fruit in the not-too-distant future. Now, be off with you! Go fill your stomachs and rest your weary limbs."

Those were precisely the words Durren needed to hear, and Tia and Hule seemed to feel the same way; already they were turning towards the door. Only Arein was hesitating, her gaze apparently unwilling to release the Petrified Egg, where it lay in its nest of wood and straw.

When Durren gently touched her arm, she flinched, and then looked up at him. It seemed to him that she was asking his permission: *Am I really all right to leave it here?*

Though Durren wasn't at all sure of the correct answer, he gave her a smile he hoped was reassuring. And sure enough, when he started after the others, Arein followed.

Durren felt aimless. He had been glad to see the back of Arein, Hule and Tia, but without them he felt oddly lonely. As he wandered through the passages, he heard the first bell of the evening sound. There would be no more classes or lectures today, but dinner wasn't for another hour. In theory, he was free to go back to the dormitory and try and rest. In practise, he felt full of a useless energy that made the prospect of relaxing seem impossible.

Instead, he wandered towards the library—the small one reserved for the rangers rather than the main one, which was intimidatingly grand—and selected a book he had no intention of reading, simply to waste a little time. He chose a manual on knife fighting, a subject he'd never had much aptitude for; he couldn't understand why anyone would want to get so close to an opponent, not when there were such things in the world as bows and arrows. Durren pored over the illustrations until the dinner bell sounded, absorbing nothing except a further conviction that anyone who considered a knife the best means of defending themselves was likely an idiot.

Evening meals were the only occasion when all the students of Black River came together as one. Within the vast dining hall, they were divided according to classes, and then again by levels. Nevertheless, Durren found himself straining to see if he could pick out Arein, Tia or Hule from amid the sea of downturned faces. He thought he recognised Arein at the end of one bench—not many wizards were small and stout— but he couldn't say for sure.

The food at Black River wasn't actively bad, though it was a long way from what Durren was accustomed to. His father had never been a glutton or even a generous host, but there was a certain basic level of luxury expected of a wealthy Luntharbour merchant. Here, the worst that could be said of the dishes was that they were plain and unvaried. Sure enough, tonight's meal consisted of overcooked rice and some sort of stew: the sauce was thick and brown, the chewier chunks were definitely meat and the mushier ones most probably vegetables, and it tasted of not much of anything. Still, the meal was likely nutritious enough, and Durren was sufficiently hungry not to care about trivialities like flavour. He kept his eyes locked on his bowl and ate with steady determination.

For that reason, Durren only realised something unusual was occurring by the steady murmur rising from his classmates. When he finally looked up, it was to discover that he was the only one still paying any attention to his nondescript dinner. All the other student rangers were gazing towards the far end of the room, or else leaning to whisper in friends' ears.

It happened that the rangers were in the furthest corner from the main entrance and that Durren was close to the aisle end of the table. His position gave him an unimpeded view all the way to the colossal doorway, with its ornate coats of arms and intricate carvings. He could see that a figure was approaching with rapid strides and, after a moment's concentration, that it was Eldra Atrepis.

He understood now why there was so much muttering and gasping going on; that the head of the ranger class should come here was surprising indeed. Staff didn't eat with students, and even the serving of food was the responsibility of the apprentices themselves. In fact, Durren couldn't think of another occasion when he'd seen a member of the faculty here in the dining hall.

As she drew closer, Atrepis's gaze began to rove across the gathered rangers. Much too late, it occurred to Durren that she must be looking for someone in particular. But his fear had barely begun to form when Atrepis's eyes found him and pinned him to his seat.

"Durren Flintrand."

She was here for him. Her face, the barely controlled rage there, told him this was nothing good, and surely something very bad indeed. In fact, he felt he knew exactly what she wanted. And for an instant Durren couldn't escape the sense that his waking nightmare from up in the monastery tower had come true—or else had been a kind of prophecy.

Yet all Atrepis said was, "Follow me."

Durren wasn't sure that his legs would work, and he surprised himself when he actually managed to stand up. Rather than acknowledge him, Atrepis spun on her heel and stormed back the way she'd come, and Durren saw no choice but to hurry after.

Just as he felt that he knew why she'd come for him, Durren knew, too, where they were going—at least from the moment it became clear that Atrepis wasn't leading the way to her own office. He couldn't but wonder why he was trailing along behind her, marching willingly towards his own destruction. Was he fooling himself with some cruel illusion of hope? Did he expect a last-minute reprieve? Yet more likely it was only that the one alternative his mind had to offer, of fleeing like a frightened child, was too ridiculous to consider seriously.

Then they turned a corner and there before them was a doorway much like any other in the academy, except that upon the capstone was carved in jagged script HEAD TUTOR. Seeing those words, all Durren could think was, *I should have run.* For surely that would have been better than what was coming.

Atrepis knocked twice, waited, and then opened the door and ushered Durren through, with a glare so penetrating that he felt it deep in his bones. Borgnin's office was not much more impressive than Atrepis's had been. The desk at one end, behind which the Head Tutor sat, was the only hint of extravagance. It was carved from a black wood such as Durren had never seen, the legs engraved with designs of shields and mythic beasts entwined with ivy. There were more shields mounted on the walls, with the heraldry of the four classes and an appropriate weapon—a sword, a bow, a wickedly curved dagger, a staff—mounted above. But, so far as decoration went, that was the sum total of Borgnin's indulgence. The only other furnishings were sets of drawers and shelves, all cluttered with books and scrolls that surely detailed a thousand matters relating to the running of Black River.

Turning his attention back to Borgnin, Durren realised that the Head Tutor was now holding up a document in one hand.

"Do you recognise this?" Borgnin asked.

Durren squinted at the sheet of parchment—and his heart turned to lead in his chest. Yes, he recognised it. There at the bottom, he could even see his own handwriting—though the name he'd scrawled wasn't his own.

Urden Flintrand. The forgery was perfect, if Durren did say so himself. But that hardly mattered anymore. Those hours upon hours he'd spent practising each line and curve weren't going to save him now.

"I see that you do," Borgnin answered his own question. "I trust you aren't about to try and persuade me that this document was in fact authorised by Urden Flintrand?"

"No," Durren said, "I'm not." He felt unreasonably proud of the fact that he'd managed to keep his voice from shaking.

"You're prepared, then, to admit that the handwriting is yours? That the document is, in effect, a forgery?"

"Yes," Durren said. "That's right."

Borgnin nodded. There was no particular emotion in his

face, not even irritation. Durren suspected that he was handling this matter with precisely the degree of concern and interest that he would handle anything, from the most minor of acquisitions to the entire academy unexpectedly bursting into flames.

"There are a few further questions I'll need you to answer," Borgnin said—and behind the words, just as clear though unspoken, *But understand that nothing you say will save you.* "First, is your name really Durren Flintrand? Are you really Urden Flintrand's son?"

"I am."

"Are you able to prove it?"

Durren considered. "Probably not."

"Well. For the moment I see no choice but to take your word; we'll know the full truth soon enough. I assume, then, that your father is unaware of your presence here at the academy?"

"He doesn't know I'm here."

"Does he believe you to be somewhere else? Does he know that you're safe?"

Would he care? Durren wondered. "He doesn't have any idea where I am," Durren said. "Or even if I'm alive." It felt strange to say out loud like that; he'd never considered the matter so bluntly before. Perhaps at this very moment there was an empty tomb in the family crypt bearing his name.

"And," Borgnin continued, "this isn't a matter for the record, but I find myself curious nevertheless. I wonder, do you fully understand the import of your actions?"

Durren wanted to say that not only did he understand, he could see nothing wrong in what he'd done. Oh, of course he'd stolen, strictly speaking, but the money he'd taken from his father was little more than a drop in the oceans of his gold—and anyway, shouldn't any parent with the means to do so be willing to pay for his son's education? If Durren had had to rely on deception, then it was only because that was the one choice he'd had left.

However, he knew that wasn't what Borgnin wanted to hear—and that he was far past the point where arguing could possibly achieve anything. "Yes," Durren said, "I understand."

"You must realise, then, what the consequences will be?"

"I'm being expelled," Durren said. The words were like acid in his throat, but he was determined that it should be he who spoke them and not Borgnin.

"If it were within my power to do more," the Head Tutor said, "then I certainly would; this matter is likely to cause the academy a great deal of embarrassment. Not to mention—since we will surely have to return the funds you misappropriated to pay your fees—a great deal of money. Perhaps most frustrating is the fact that, according to Mistress Atrepis, you were beginning to show some genuine promise as a student."

That last remark caught Durren utterly by surprise. And abruptly he felt a lump of pain welling inside him that, if he were to show even the slightest hint of weakness, was sure to turn to tears. Rather than surrender, he grasped for the most vindictive of the many thoughts clattering around his mind. "My father would never ask for the money back," he said. "So you could probably keep it if you wanted to."

For the first time, Borgnin actually looked annoyed—though still not quite angry. "I've tried to show you respect, Master Flintrand, by discussing this matter civilly instead of having you exit the academy on the toe of someone's boot. I ask you, please show this institution the same courtesy. I think you know perfectly well that Black River would never choose gold over its reputation."

Not like my father, Durren thought. *My father would choose gold over just about anything. Over his wife, over his son, over other people's lives, even over his own happiness.* And once again, the tears threatened. He wanted to tell Borgnin that he was sorry, but the words seemed too useless to justify the effort. Being sorry wouldn't change what he'd done, or that he'd been found out, or what the results were to be.

"What happens now?" Durren asked instead.

"I will write to your father for instruction," Borgnin said, "and send my letter by the morning post—which means that, given a prompt response, we shall know where we stand within twelve days at the most. Until then, since I can hardly treat you as a prisoner, you may continue your pretence of being a student of Black River, if you so wish."

"I'd like that," Durren said.

"Very well then." Borgnin turned his gaze to Atrepis, who Durren realised only then had been waiting patiently by the door all this while. "Mistress Atrepis, perhaps you might show Master Flintrand back to his dormitory?" His eyes drifted back to Durren, and they were dark and hard as ebony. "And though it won't be necessary to post a guard on him, I hope he'll understand that his behaviour for whatever time he remains here will be expected to be beyond reproach."

At first, all Durren could feel was a numbing pain rooted somewhere in the region of his heart. It was heavy, almost too heavy to bear, and made the possibility of moving seem impossible.

He thought that perhaps if he could cry, then the weight

would go away, but he couldn't—partly because he was surrounded by other students, but mostly because he couldn't find the energy. Nor did he want to look, to listen, even to smell, because anything his senses reported would be a reminder of what he was soon to lose. If they had seemed valuable before, now the academy and his life here were the most precious things he could imagine.

Even those aspects of his existence that he'd never much cared for, even the ones he'd actively disliked, made the pain in his heart throb. Like this dormitory itself: he'd never slept well here, kept awake by the snores and whimpering night terrors of his fellow students. Yet the knowledge that in a few days this prickly straw mattress would be left vacant, or else given over to another student, made him want to cling to it as though it were a raft on a stormy sea.

And that was the very least of what he was losing. The truth was that every last part of this life he'd struggled so hard and against such odds to carve out for himself was about to be taken from him. He wasn't leaving, he was being thrown out. And the more Durren considered that fact, slowly but surely, the more his sorrow gave way to anger.

Though he hadn't said as much, it was clear Borgnin hadn't discovered Durren's subterfuge on his own. Nor could Pootle have been the one to reveal his secret; if the observer had reported back to Hieronymus or Cullglass, then surely Durren would have been marched to Borgnin's office the moment he materialised back at the academy.

No, someone else had told the Head Tutor—and there were only three people who knew. Durren couldn't believe that Arein would do such a thing, nor see any possible motive for her doing so. Hule had probably forgotten the entire conversation the moment it ended. That left only Tia. Tia, who was so determined to reach her second level that she'd risked all their lives to do so. Tia who had as much as told Durren she wanted him off their party, who'd made no secret of how she felt he was holding her back. And what class did she belong to? Only the rogues, whose entire job definition relied upon being devious and underhanded and achieving goals by any means necessary.

There could be no question, and he was only surprised that it had taken him so long to reach the obvious conclusion—and that Tia had made so little effort to cover her tracks. Then again, she'd probably imagined there could be no possible consequences for her. What, after all, could Durren do?

He could confront her, that was what he could do. He could tell her to her face that he knew she'd given him up, and what sort of a person that made her.

It was the kind of foolhardy plan that he could easily have talked himself out of. Durren could feel, in fact, the counterarguments already buzzing about the corners of his mind like angry wasps. All else aside, hadn't Borgnin explicitly cautioned him against just such an act?

Rather than risk paying attention to those dissenting voices, Durren jolted to his feet. He didn't care what was sensible, or even what was right. All he wanted was to hear from Tia's own lips why she'd betrayed him—and he wasn't about to let anything stand in his way.

12

There was no specific rule to say that students from one class couldn't go into areas set aside for the other three. On occasions, in fact, as when Durren went to Hieronymus's transportation room, doing so was unavoidable. However, there was without doubt an unspoken agreement against entering certain areas, those deemed private or personal. And, of those, the dormitories were the most implicitly restricted.

So maybe it was just a spirit of bloody-mindedness that made Durren start there of all places.

Except that, because he had no idea of the layout of the rogues' wing, things weren't quite that straightforward. For a start, it soon became evident that the place had been designed for rogues by rogues: there were no signs, no names on doors, no directions of any kind. Nor was there anybody around to ask. Though Durren occasionally heard faint sounds of activity, he saw no one. It was as if any students he might have encountered faded away an instant before he could set eyes on them.

Luck, then, more than sense, brought him finally to the room he'd been seeking. And though there *were* clear rules against students harming other students, nevertheless Durren felt a moment of alarm as he glanced around the dormitory and saw so many lean, cloaked figures, each of them watching him back.

"What do you think you're doing, Durren?"

Tia's voice came from behind him. Durren spun, words spilling from his mouth before he'd even set eyes on her: "I think you know damn well why I'm here."

Tia considered him coldly. "No, I don't."

Would she really deny the truth? That made it worse, somehow. "You told Borgnin about me," Durren snapped. "You told him my secret."

"Of course I didn't," Tia said, as though her innocence was the most obvious thing in the world.

Durren paused, mouth gaping. Of all the possible outcomes, he simply hadn't considered that she would refuse to admit what she'd done. All he could think to say was, *Yes you did*, and he had just enough sense left to realise that the two of them standing here contradicting each other wasn't about to achieve much.

Fortunately, Tia broke the stalemate. "Follow me," she demanded.

She brushed past him and led the way out of the long room, leaving Durren no option but to follow. In the passage, she opened the first door she reached, which happened to belong to a storage cupboard filled with pails, mops and brooms. When Durren only stared at the cramped space in puzzlement, Tia caught hold of his sleeve and hauled him inside, dragging the door closed behind them.

It crossed Durren's mind that he was trapped in a closet with a rogue, and that similar situations had ended badly for many across the centuries. Then, when no blade sank into his guts, he recalled that the particular rogue he was trapped in a closet with was Tia, who, as much as he hated to admit it, was definitely attractive—and all the more so at close range. Durren was annoyed to realise that his heart was beating more rapidly, that his palms felt clammy. He insisted to himself that he should be anxious to get out because the girl before him was training to dispose of people in precisely such circumstances, not because she was a *girl*—but insisting didn't much help.

"Durren," Tia said, "listen to me carefully, because I don't want to have to say this more than once. Whatever you think I've done, I didn't. If someone told on you, then it wasn't me. And I think that if you'd take a minute to calm down, you'd realise that."

Durren did his best to bring his errant thoughts to order. "But if it wasn't you…" Only, he realised, he already had the answer to his question. "Why would he do it?" he asked. "I mean, I know we don't exactly like each other…" Once again, Durren trailed off. Fine, he and Hule weren't entirely friends, but he'd never have imagined that the block-headed fighter would do something like this.

Tia was watching him steadily. "Do you pay attention to anything besides yourself?"

"What's that supposed to mean? Of course I—"

"I don't think so," she interrupted. "If you did, you'd have known a long time ago just what Hule's up to. And you'd also have realised that there are more important things going on here than whether or not you get expelled."

Durren didn't understand. What could possibly be more important than that? Did she really not appreciate what being here meant to him? No, it was only that she didn't care. His presence at Black River didn't matter to her, so of course Tia couldn't realise how much it would matter to him.

As for what she meant about Hule, that was another mystery—and another knot Durren had no interest in unravelling. Hule was an idiot, and worse, he was an idiot who didn't know when to keep his mouth shut. Well, that was one lesson Durren could teach him, at least. Maybe a fist to that square jaw of his would make him think twice the next time he was about to destroy someone's life out of sheer stupidity.

"I'm sorry I blamed you," Durren said grudgingly. Then, not waiting for an answer, he pushed past her, was through the door and marching down the corridor beyond in what he judged to be the direction of the fighters' wing.

He hadn't expected Tia to follow, so he was surprised by the tap of her feet upon the flagstones behind him. "Durren, will you listen to me for a minute?"

What could she possibly want? Was she really going to try and dissuade him from giving Hule the beating he so richly deserved? Well, Durren wasn't about to let her. Instead, he stared straight ahead and picked up his pace.

"No," Tia continued, "obviously you won't. Still, I'm telling you this anyway. There's something not right about these quests we're being sent on, and I think you know it. That unicorn wasn't some murderous beast; those priests weren't conspiring to corrupt the unbalance and bring about the end of the world. One of those might have been a mistake, but two? No, something's badly wrong here."

Hearing her words, Durren felt that there were two versions of him warring inside his mind. One had heard what Tia had told him and knew that probably she was right: yes, there were questions to be asked about the quests they'd been sent on, and probably he should be trying to reason out the answers. Yet the other Durren insisted that the academy's problems had nothing to do with him, because after all he'd been expelled, and the reason he'd been expelled was named Hule Tremick, and so how could anything be more important than planting a fist right between Hule's eyes? Moreover, that version of him was by far the louder; there was no ignoring it, even had he wanted to.

Tia sighed. "Do you even know where you're going?"

Durren hadn't the faintest idea. He was choosing corridors at random, but he wasn't about to admit as much.

Regardless, Tia strode past him. She turned into a side passage and beckoned for him to follow. "Then let's get this over with," she said, "and maybe once you've got it out of your system, you'll listen to some sense."

Veering after her, Durren struggled to fathom how one minute he'd been trying to lose his temper with Tia and now here she was, leading him through the maze that was Black River. Still, there was no denying that she knew her way around a hundred times better than he did. She seemed to have no trouble picking her route, and after a while, Durren began to suspect that she must have taken time to study and memorise the academy's entire sprawling layout—presumably from maps and charts, since a lone rogue wandering the halls would surely have drawn attention.

Just who was this strange girl? What could have driven her to do such a thing? Durren had spent a great deal of time with her over the last weeks, and only now did it occur to him that he barely knew the first thing about her—really, nothing more than her name.

Not long after she'd taken charge, he realised that at some

point they'd transitioned from the rogues' wing into the fighters' block. The walls, which had been unadorned, were now decorated with an assortment of shields and weapons, some of types Durren had never seen before: strange variations of flails and glaives, and axes with altogether too many heads.

Just as there had been something alarming about intruding into an area filled with students trained to sneak and backstab, so here Durren was uncomfortably aware of an air of suppressed aggression—as though at any moment these passages might erupt with bellowing warriors and senseless violence.

Tia stuck her head into one room, and then another. They passed a couple of fighters, a tall boy and a burly girl, and it struck Durren that the thing to do might be to ask if they knew where Hule was—but Tia only ignored them and pressed on. Though Durren doubted she'd ever walked these corridors before, her sense of direction still seemed certain. She turned a corner, marched to the end of that passage, where a heavy door stood open. The word DORMITORY was carved into the lintel.

Unlike the sleeping quarters of the rogues or rangers, the fighters' dorm had bunk beds and a broad central aisle. Most of the room's occupants were clustered into groups and shouting over each other about one subject or another. Some were taking the opportunity offered by any patch of clear space to practise wrestling, boxing, or even duelling with wooden swords. A few of the more studious—the minority by far—had books spread over their knees.

Only Hule seemed to be alone and unoccupied. That fact made him all the easier to pick out. He was sitting on his bunk, eyes half closed, and didn't look round at their arrival until Tia said, "Hello, Hule."

Hule's expression told Durren everything: if he'd needed a confession then there it was, plain to see. It took all of Durren's self-restraint not to hit him in that very moment, and if Tia hadn't been there, then perhaps he would have. Yet even the briefest glance around the hard faces suddenly watching from about the room told him that to attack one fighter would be to attack them all—perhaps not because they cared about Hule himself, but as a matter of principle, or maybe just as an excuse for a good ruckus.

Hule's mouth was slowly opening and closing, making him very much resemble a snared fish puzzled at the sudden lack of water.

"Outside," Tia told him.

Hule looked as though he'd have liked to argue, perhaps to be indignant at being ordered out of his own dormitory. Instead, he nodded sheepishly and trailed after as she led the way.

Here there were no convenient storage cupboards that Durren could see. Instead, Tia carried on, taking turn after turn. Durren felt certain that at any moment Hule would finally resist, would refuse to go any further—but he didn't, and nothing could have persuaded Durren more of his guilt.

They came out, finally, in one of the many small open areas that littered the academy's interior. This one appeared to be an herb garden, crammed into a narrow rectangular space by windowless walls, and with the door they'd entered by serving as both entrance and exit. Unsurprisingly, no one was tending the garden at this late hour.

Before Hule could descend the three narrow stairs to the path that wound among the beds, Durren rounded on him. He caught the fighter by the scruff of his shirt and shoved hard. Hule managed to keep his footing, but only by colliding hard with the wall; the breath left his body in a loud huff. However, that didn't stop him getting his fists up before his face. Rather than try and grapple with him, Durren snarled, "Tell me why, Hule."

"Hule doesn't have to answer you." But he sounded less defiant than he'd obviously intended to. Perhaps it had occurred to him that the odds were two against one, and that—with Tia having closed the sturdy door behind them—no one would be coming to his aid.

"You can stop that now," Tia said.

The look of surprise on Hule's face turned rapidly to something that bordered upon panic. "Hule doesn't understand—"

"Hule," she said impatiently, "no one really refers to themselves by their first name all the time. And, frankly, it's long past the point of becoming annoying. You can start talking normally, or I'm going to let Durren settle this with his fists. Maybe I'll even hold you down for him."

The mix of emotions in Hule's face grew more complex. So far, Durren had never seen the fighter's expressions range much beyond bored and aggressive. Now, however, he appeared genuinely conflicted, as though weighing up the odds of some difficult conundrum.

Eventually Hule gulped hard and said, "All right look, I'm sorry."

"Are you apologising to me for being annoying," Tia said, "or are you apologising to Durren for ruining his life?"

"Well...both."

"Because if you're apologising to Durren, then you should

165

say so to his face."

Hule looked as though, if he could have escaped by crawling out of his own skin, he gladly would have. Yet, his eyes drifted towards Durren. "I'm sorry," he said. "Telling on you was a terrible thing to do. I knew the moment I left Borgnin's office. I think I even knew at the time. It was lousy of me, and I'd take it back if I could."

Durren had no idea how to respond. Hule's was by far the most earnest apology he had ever received, and what made it all the more strange was that he barely recognised this version of Hule who'd given it. Could he really be the same person who'd barely been able to string a sentence together mere minutes before?

"Fine," Durren said, "you're sorry. But being sorry doesn't change anything. I'm still going to get expelled. And why would you do it? Do you really hate me that much?"

"I don't hate you," Hule said. He sounded surprised at the very suggestion. "I mean, I don't particularly like you, but I don't hate you. I just…there was an opportunity and I took it. It didn't have anything to do with you."

Durren had been beginning to calm a little, disarmed by Hule's penitence—but that set his blood boiling once again. "Explain to me," he growled, "how you telling the Head Tutor that I tricked my way into Black River doesn't have anything to do with me."

For the first time, Hule appeared genuinely nervous. "I didn't mean it like that! I just mean, I hardly gave you any thought. Like I said, I see now how wrong that was, and I'm sorry. But it seemed like such a good chance, and I knew that if I thought too hard, I'd never be able to go through with it."

Durren felt a hand on his shoulder, drawing him back—

and only then did he realise just how close he'd been standing to Hule, how he'd been leaning in with clenched fists. Reluctantly, he took a step back, forcing some of the tension from his body. Tia gave him a look that said, *That's better*, and stepped into the gap between them.

"Hule," she said, "I think Durren would like a proper explanation for what you did. And I'd like to hear it, too. After all, we're supposed to be a party."

Hule, having begun to relax when Tia hauled Durren away, had clearly had time to realise that having her interrogate him was no improvement at all. "I don't know where to start," he mumbled.

"Perhaps with why you've been referring to yourself by your own first name all this time, and now, just because Tia called you out on it, you've stopped?" Durren suggested. Objectively he knew that there were more important matters to be addressed, but that was the one currently bothering him the most.

Hule sighed. "Do you know what it's like to grow up in the Borderlands? I don't mind a good scrap every so often, but where I come from, it's the only thing that matters to anyone. Once, when I was six years old, I lost a fight with a boy from a neighbouring household and my father refused to speak to me for a month. A month! And you know what I said about having troll blood? There are people in my family who really, genuinely believe that. I mean, have you *seen* a troll? The smallest ones are twice the size of any human, and they're about the ugliest things imaginable. Just looking at one for five minutes would make you want to poke your own eyes out; you certainly wouldn't be thinking about taking it home to meet the grandparents. But some great, great ancestor started the rumour and no one ever thought to ask the obvious questions, and so here we are—and everyone just accepts it for a fact. And *that's* what it's like to grow up in the Borderlands."

"None of that explains," Durren pointed out, "why you've been calling yourself by your own name all this time."

Hule gave a broad shrug. "It was just something I started on the first day; it seemed like a thing that a trainee fighter from the Borderlands would do. I had a cousin who talked that way. His name was Thunk. It was always *Thunk wants this, Thunk says that*—and all he ever had an opinion on was who or what needed punching and how hard. Anyway, once I'd been doing it for a while, I realised I couldn't just stop." Hule looked disconsolate. "And can you imagine what that's been like? I mean, I've never claimed to be the smartest of people, but acting like a total idiot really starts to get you down after a while."

"I hope you don't expect me to feel sorry for you," Durren told him. However, he found that he couldn't put much bite into the words. Hule's self-inflicted plight was so ludicrous that it was hard not to feel at least a little sympathy.

"Fine," Hule replied. "There's no reason you would. Still, maybe you can at least see how difficult these last few months have been. The thing is, this character I'd made up…it turns out that's not even what you need to be a good fighter. Within a week I'd persuaded everyone that I hadn't a thimbleful of brains.

"But then I discovered how much they expect you to know, to read and study and—well, what was I meant to do? Either I admitted I'd been faking all the time and they thought I was mad, or I kept on the same way and hardly got a single question right. I knew it was too late to confess, so that just left failing half of my lessons."

"That still doesn't explain," Durren said, "why you had to stab me in the back." He was finding it more and more difficult to hang onto his anger in the face of Hule's increasingly absurd confession.

"Doesn't it?" Hule asked. "How else was I ever going to come to Borgnin's attention? I thought perhaps he'd raise my level as a reward, and then maybe that could be a new start. I could use the opportunity to begin doing better at my classes."

Tia had been silent all this while, her gaze levelled upon Hule, her face unreadable as always. Now, however, she said with weary amusement, "Hule, for someone who's spent three months pretending to be an idiot, you really are an idiot."

Partly it was her words and partly the look on Hule's face, but regardless of everything that had happened and of how furious he'd been just minutes ago, Durren couldn't help but laugh at that. Tia was smiling too, and when she saw that Durren had noticed, she finally lost control. Hule, meanwhile, looked as if he might happily have strangled the pair of them. Yet the more helpless their hilarity became, the more his frown drifted into a smirk. Then abruptly all three of them were laughing helplessly.

Durren was the last to stop. He'd almost grown hysterical by the end, and now his sides were aching and his eyes watering. The entire situation was too preposterous. All this time that he'd been pretending to be the most average ranger in the academy, Hule had been feigning idiocy. Now Durren was being kicked out, not through any malice on Hule's part but only because, like Durren, he had backed himself into a corner he could see no way out of. That was such a stupid reason for all of Durren's dreams to come crashing down that he could hardly take it seriously.

Hule, though, now that his own fit of laughter had passed, did look grave. "Durren," he said, "I really am sorry. It was a lousy thing to do. And it didn't even work; Borgnin just scowled at me after I'd told him, like it was the worst thing I could have done."

"Because it was," Tia pointed out.

Hule hung his head. "I know."

Durren hunted for the last dregs of his anger, realised they were nowhere to be found. This was as close to forgiving Hule as he was likely to come. "I'm not saying it's all right," he said, "but I suppose the truth was going to come out eventually. I couldn't possibly have gone five whole years without being discovered somehow. And I suppose I can understand what it's been like for you, living a ridiculous lie all this time. So, not that it matters, because I won't be here in two weeks' time, but…" And he offered Hule his hand.

The fighter clasped Durren's outstretched palm, gave a cautious smile. Hule even looked less stupid now; he was hard to recognise for the same person Durren had known over the last few weeks.

Tia cleared her throat. "All right. Now that that's done with, perhaps the two of you can start thinking about something other than yourselves."

Durren released Hule's grip and turned to her. "You do understand that I've been expelled, don't you? I mean, that's quite serious."

"I'm sure you'll survive," Tia told him dismissively. "And like you said, it was sure to happen sooner or later. But in the meantime, I could use your help—all the more so since you don't have anything to lose."

That didn't exactly sound promising. Whatever Tia's opinions to the contrary, Durren felt that he had a great deal left to lose. Still, he had no desire to incur her scorn—and after today, he realised, he owed her one. She'd shown more forbearance when he'd falsely accused her than he'd ever have expected, and were it not for her, his confrontation with Hule could have gone very differently.

At any rate, Tia seemed content to take his silence for agreement. "That's good," she said. "Because I'm going to prove that there's something suspicious going on here at Black River. I'm going to get to the bottom of these quests we've been sent on, and I'm finding out who's to blame. And as much as it pains me to admit it, I can't do any of that without your help."

13

Hule and Durren waited in the herb garden, amid growing darkness and uncomfortable silence. Tia seemed to have been gone for an age. All she'd said by way of explanation was that this was a conversation the entire party needed to be involved in.

When she returned, it was with a timid-looking Arein in tow. The dwarf girl looked as though she'd been summoned with no explanation at all, and seemed shocked to see Hule and Durren waiting in this out-of-the-way spot. "Oh, hello," she said.

Tia had also acquired a small lantern from somewhere, and she set it down in their midst, so that its glow illuminated all their faces from beneath. They looked, thought Durren, like a group of conspirators in a play, perhaps gathered to plot the murder of some fiendish king. It was an exciting notion, and went some way to dispelling the nervousness he felt at the strange situation. For all that he was beginning to trust Tia, she certainly had a roguish way of going about things.

"You all know what we're here to discuss," she said.

Hule put his hand up. "Um, I don't."

Tia sighed. "I thought we were past all that?"

"No," Hule told her, "I really don't know what you're talking about. And if I don't get back to my dormitory soon, then I'm going to be in real trouble."

"I told you before," Tia said, sounding even more exasperated. "There's something not right about these quests. Honestly, Hule, are you sure you weren't just pretending that you've been pretending to be stupid?"

"I'm sure." Hule sounded genuinely hurt. "All right, look, I know you had some questions about that last one. But Cullglass has said he'll look into it, and I don't see what more we can do."

"He said the same about Blackwing," Arein put in, "and nothing came of that."

"Maybe it did. Maybe he just didn't get the chance to tell us because you were already pestering him about something else." This time it was Hule's turn to sigh. "I'm just saying, we should give him a chance. Perhaps in a few days we can go and talk to him, and then with a bit of luck he'll have some answers, and these things you're worrying about will turn out to be one big mistake."

"There's more going on here, Hule," Tia said, "and I think you know it."

"I'm not saying there isn't. I'm saying, we're just four students, and this is an academy, and there are ways of going about things. I don't need any more trouble than I have already, and I'm sure Durren feels the same."

The way Tia rounded on Durren, you'd have thought he was the one who'd doubted her. "Do you?"

"No!" Durren replied hastily. He would have liked to leave his answer there—but he couldn't, he realised. He genuinely didn't know which of them was right. Yes, their last two quests had left him wondering, and yes, it bothered him that they might have kidnapped an innocent unicorn and stolen from a bunch of perfectly well-meaning priests. Yet Hule made a good point; he really was in more than enough trouble as things were. "Only..." he began, and then had no idea how to continue.

The look Tia gave him didn't help in the slightest. "Only?"

"Only," he tried, "we have to be realistic. I mean, it's just possible that Black River isn't everything we expected it to be. Maybe, sometimes—well, maybe this is just what quests are like."

Durren glanced round at the others. He'd expected Tia's barely subdued crossness, but the disappointment he saw in Arein's face was much worse.

"You don't mean that," she said.

"I don't know if I do or I don't. Look, I think that Black River is basically a good place, or I wouldn't be here. Certainly I always believed that they try to help people. But...well, this is the real world. Tia, you know that better than anyone. How many rogues are going to find their way to the capital, and what sort of things will they be doing there? And you, Hule; won't most of the students from your class end up in one army or another? That might mean the Brazen Fist, but it might also mean mercenaries fighting out past the borders. Even wizards, Arein—not all wizards are as good-hearted as you. Magic can be a weapon, and that's precisely how some of your classmates will end up using it."

He'd said more than he'd meant to—more than he would willingly have admitted to himself. The way he'd described the academy was nothing like the way he'd always thought of it, and he much preferred the idealised version his past self had believed in.

"You're right," Tia said, "Black River isn't perfect. It isn't meant to be. I know what this place is, Durren, better than most. Still, it's one thing to train people in skills that they might use to do harm, quite another to encourage them to. And to the best of my knowledge, the academy has never sent students out on quests that actually broke royal law, or suggested they pursue anything but the more upstanding careers. So if it should turn out that we wrongfully stole from that monastery then we really do have a problem. After all, it was our faces they saw, not Adocine Borgnin's."

"That's a good point," Hule admitted. He sounded less than comfortable with the notion.

"Now," Tia continued, "I'm going to find out what's behind these last two quests. If everything turns out to be aboveboard then I'll be as happy as anyone, and likewise if Cullglass keeps his promise. But in the meantime, I don't see any reason why we shouldn't ask a few questions ourselves. I can't make any of you help me, but I'm also not asking you to break any rules, so there's no good reason you shouldn't."

"What do you have in mind?" Durren asked. He realised that he really did want to help Tia; but that desire didn't make his trepidation go away. What troubled him, he saw now, was the prospect of leaving Black River under an even darker cloud than he was already. But, perhaps more than that, it was the thought that what he'd said before might be right. What if the academy wasn't everything he'd believed it to be? What if Borgnin wasn't the honest and upright figure Durren had thought—or Atrepis even? He had wanted so badly to believe that these people, this place, were better than his father and the world of greed and unkindness he moved in.

"First I want to know if you're in," Tia said.

Durren nearly asked her what she was so suspicious of. But if today had proved one thing, it was that the four of them couldn't altogether trust one another. "All right," he said. "If you promise we'll stay within academy rules then, yes, I'll do what I can."

"Me too," Arein said quickly, with a glance towards Hule.

The fighter shrugged dejectedly. "Fine," he said. "I suppose things can't get much worse."

Tia nodded—and something in the gesture told Durren that those were the answers she'd been anticipating all along. "Then what we need is information," she said. "Arein, I'd like you to study the magical side of this. Find out whatever you can about the Petrified Egg: what it really is, where it came from, why anyone might want to steal it. Look into unicorns, too, and see if there's any kind of a connection."

"I can do that," Arein agreed.

"Hule," Tia said, "I want you to investigate our first quest. Was that treasure the rat-kind were hiding really hijacked from a merchant caravan? If so, who were they and how did they lose it? And what came of the matter, if anything? Was the chest ever recovered?"

"Fine," Hule acknowledged, without much enthusiasm.

"As for you, Durren, you get the easiest job: I want you to talk to some of the rangers and get an idea of the sorts of quests that other first-level parties have been sent on. We need to know if anyone else has the same concerns we do. Maybe none of us want to believe that this is how Black River secretly does business, but if it is, then it's better we find out sooner rather than later."

"All right," Durren said. Since he'd failed to make a single friend from among his classmates in the time he'd been here, that mission wasn't half so easy as she'd made out—but he wasn't about to admit that to Tia.

"Good. Then let's give it—what?—four days. I'll send word about when and where we'll meet. In the meantime, it's probably best that none of us speak to each other."

"Wait," Durren said, "what about you? What are you going to be doing while we're asking all these questions?"

"You don't need to know that." Tia bent to pick up the lantern. "I'll be in touch." She opened the hatch, licked her fingers, snuffed out the wick—and darkness flooded in upon them.

By the time Durren's eyes had adjusted to the starlit gloom, Tia was gone.

Only after he, Arein and Hule had separated, as he was wandering back through the dimly lit passages, did Durren begin to consider what he was getting himself into. He'd thought his situation couldn't get any worse after his meeting with Borgnin, but he was beginning to see how wrong he'd been. Borgnin had a great many punishments at his disposal, and even if Durren was only going to be here for another few days, the Head Tutor had the means to make that time particularly dreadful. Maybe asking inappropriate questions was all it would take to draw the wrong attention—especially if there really was some sordid secret just waiting to be discovered.

Still, Durren had given his word, and he wasn't about to break it. Now more than ever, keeping his promises seemed important. Perhaps he wasn't going to be a ranger for very much longer, but that didn't change the values he'd set for himself.

However, he didn't make any headway that night. Durren

strongly suspected that word had already got around about his expulsion. Even if it hadn't, the other students had seen him being marched out by Atrepis, and he didn't at all like the curious looks he was attracting.

But by morning, after a night involving much feeling sorry for himself and little actual sleep, Durren had decided he didn't much care what anyone thought. After all, the one advantage of expulsion was the knowledge that, in two weeks' time, no one's opinion of his character was going to matter a great deal.

That still left the problem of just how he was meant to go about the task Tia had assigned him. Perhaps it was that he'd been afraid of drawing attention, or maybe just that he'd rarely met anyone he'd liked enough to talk to back in his old life at Luntharbour, but whatever the case, Durren had made little effort to be friendly with his fellow rangers. Now, after three months, and though common sense dictated that it was far too late to do so, he was going to have to at least try.

That first day, he focused on basic pleasantries. He said hello to as many people as he could, and in archery practise and wrestling class threw compliments and commiserations around with wild abandon. He grasped any opportunity to help out if it meant a chance to swap words with one student or another, and laughed at every joke that anyone made, no matter how unfunny. Probably they all thought he'd gone mad, but Durren decided he could live with that.

At any rate, he found that he was enjoying himself. This new, sociable persona was significantly more fun than his old one had been. And at least half the time, his attempts were met with good humour. By evening, he realised the day had been among the best he'd spent at Black River. He felt full of energy, his mind already working on what he might say tomorrow and to whom. As he lay in bed, waiting for sleep to claim him, those thoughts were almost enough to distract him from the sword of expulsion descending by degrees towards his neck.

Over the next couple of days, Durren shifted his approach towards the lines of enquiry Tia had told him to pursue—and his questioning grew cannier. You could learn a lot just from listening, he discovered, and then still more by applying what you'd learned. Overhearing a conversation between two students allowed him to ask around about a particularly successful quest to rescue two stranded children from a fangspider warren out past Thornfurrow. That in turn led to discussion of a mission into underground ruins to recover rare ancient artworks. And the more interest Durren expressed, the more people seemed willing to share. Once you knew how to broach the topic, gossiping about quests was something students didn't need much encouragement at all to do.

Finally, the evening of the fourth day came around. Durren had seen nothing of Tia, Arein or Hule, and had resisted the impulse to look for them in the dining hall. In terms of Tia's assignment, that day had been by far the most productive. The other rangers were growing used to his questions now, and the friendlier ones seemed to have interpreted his sudden inquisitiveness as a thinly veiled attempt to make up for his earlier standoffishness.

Maybe they weren't altogether wrong. As well as the details Tia had set him hunting, Durren had also learned a few salient facts about himself and his soon-to-be curtailed life at Black River. For the most part, his fellow rangers were nothing like the brattish, self-absorbed youths that his father had foisted on him back in Luntharbour. Rather, they were smart, interesting people, eager to learn and excited about their class of choice.

Now Durren knew that, along with all his other regrets, he could also reproach himself for having missed the opportunity to make new friends. It would be all the harder to feign pleasantness with callow merchants' sons, and he doubted he'd even try.

At any rate, he'd done what Tia had asked of him—and, so far as he was concerned, had done it well. But by the time the first evening bell sounded, there was still no word from her. Perhaps, he thought, she'd been showing off when she'd said she would contact them, only to realise later that getting messages to three students in three different wings of Black River was no easy matter, even for a rogue.

With the day's classes done, Durren wandered back to the dormitory. Having exchanged a few words with a couple of students he was getting on particularly well with, he flopped onto his mattress and fished out the book he'd borrowed from the library. The tome was a manual on fletching, and he was finding it surprisingly interesting. Back home he'd always made his own arrows, and now he had vague, impractical thoughts of a career in that direction when his time at Black River was up.

He flicked through the pages to the point where he'd left off—and was surprised to find there a bookmark he didn't remember placing. It was a neatly folded rectangle of paper, and now that he thought, he definitely hadn't put it there. Durren reached with trembling fingers and unfolded the yellowed sheet. In two columns of precise handwriting were the words, NORTHEAST TOWER. SIXTH BELL.

Durren didn't know whether to laugh or to be horrified. Both urges were equally strong. There was something gravely funny about the thought of Tia going to so much effort to convey so simple a message. On the other hand, he wasn't at all comfortable with the notion that she'd somehow crept in here without anyone noticing, or that she'd known he would pick up this book at this particular time. Had she been spying on him? Might she be watching even now?

Then again, the more he considered, the more Durren realised that she had probably just slipped a couple of coins to one of his fellow students and asked a few discreet questions about his habits. She needed only to have pretended to be an infatuated admirer wanting to convey a love note; such things happened all the time. Durren felt pleased with himself at having reasoned out her trickery—and it really *was* funny that she'd gone to so much trouble.

Sixth bell was the penultimate bell of the day, the one rung to signal the end of the dinner hour. He could eat a rushed meal and still have time to get to this northeast tower, wherever it might be. He knew which was the northeast corner of the academy, of course, but there were so many minarets and spires, most serving no function at all and half not even accessible. Simply searching in that region of Black River, especially in the dark, would be an exercise doomed to failure.

He thought about going to the library, perhaps hunting for a map—but then he remembered that he was now the new Durren Flintrand, the one who spoke to people and asked questions. So instead, he got up and sidled over to a cluster of students talking near the doorway.

After five minutes of idle chatter, mostly on the topic of a particularly excruciating lecture from the day before, Durren realised there was no easy way to turn the conversation around to what he wanted to ask. Finally, seizing on a moment's silence, he blurted out, "Listen, has anyone heard of the northeast tower?"

Someone had. A boy named Arlo Mainbrow turned out to have an interest bordering on obsession in the academy's architecture. By the time Durren had his directions, he'd realised that probably everyone there now thought he was planning a romantic liaison. Still, there were worse misconceptions they could have, and at least it was partly true; there was no denying that he'd received a note from an attractive girl eager to meet him.

Durren rushed through his dinner and was among the first out of the hall. Then, instead of heading back towards the dormitory, he set about following the directions Mainbrow had given him. Tia had chosen her spot well: it was possible to reach the northeast tower without going through any of the frequently used portions of the academy, and he passed no one on the way.

Finally, Durren came to a low, narrow door that he felt relatively confident was the one he sought. The fact that it stood open a crack was more evidence in its favour. Was it always left unlocked, or was this more of Tia's handiwork? Durren slid through and closed the door behind him, leaving it just as he'd found it, in case Hule or Arein should be following behind.

With the door closed, however, the gloom was unyielding. Durren found that the only way to ascend the narrow stairs was by feeling his way along the outer wall. He hoped Mainbrow hadn't sent him to the wrong place; it even crossed his mind that perhaps the mysterious message hadn't come from Tia after all. In the deep darkness, he could easily imagine that those brief words had been written by someone else, someone who didn't like that Durren had been asking so many indiscreet questions.

Durren did his best to remind himself of how unlikely that

was. In any case, there was no turning back now. And after a couple of turns, he began to realise that after all the blackness wasn't as pitchy as he'd first thought: a dim glow of lamplight filtered from above him, and grew steadily as he ascended.

Eventually, a last turn gave way to an opening in what could only be the floor of the tower's summit—and there were the others, waiting. The room was small, circular, and of no obvious purpose; metal rungs in one wall led up to a hatch high above. In the middle of the paved floor was the lamp whose cheerful radiance Durren had seen from below.

Tia was standing as far from the light as possible. Hule sat cross-legged before the lantern and already looked bored. Arein, meanwhile, though she was clearly out of breath, was practically hopping from foot to foot. When she saw Durren, she gaped and made a strangled noise, as though there were fifty words in her throat and she was trying to sputter them all at once.

Before she could cough up whatever was on her mind, however, Tia got there first. She had her hood drawn up as usual, and her face was invisible within its folds, leaving her voice eerie and disconnected. "Good, you made it. Did you find out what I asked you to?"

Durren, annoyed to receive not even a hello, said, "I think so."

"And Hule? Did you learn anything about our first quest?"

"I did," the fighter confirmed breezily.

"What about you, Arein?" Tia said. "Any answers regarding the Petrified Egg?"

Arein couldn't have looked more relieved if she'd finally reached the front of the privy queue after waiting all morning. "Yes! Yes, I've found out all about it. But none of that matters right now. Because on the way here I realised what connection there is between a unicorn and a magic stone. And it means we have to go, right this minute."

Tia held up her hands. "Just wait," she said. "Arein, whatever this is, whatever's so important, we need to discuss it first."

"No!" Arein cried—and now there was real desperation in her voice. "Tia, listen to me. There's no time for any of that. Before we do anything else, we have to rescue Blackwing."

14

I don't understand," Durren said, when no one else seemed about to respond. "Are you saying we were sent to catch Blackwing just because someone wants to hurt it? That doesn't make much sense."

"Durren, you remember how I've told you that there's nothing inherently magical about wizards? But that there is with magical creatures such as unicorns?" Arein was obviously striving to stay calm, and only just succeeding. "Well, in a way, what Cullglass said was the truth: if it wasn't for all the magic its ancestors absorbed, a unicorn would just be a big horse. The part where all of that power is concentrated, that's also what makes Blackwing different from the animal he would have been."

For once, Durren felt he understood. Perhaps he was finally beginning to get his head around this magic business. "You mean its horn, right? You're saying Blackwing's horn is a magical object, like the Petrified Egg?"

Arein looked grateful. "Exactly. They're both objects full of raw power."

Then Durren really did understand—not only what she was trying to convey, but why she was so upset. The answer was obvious, though he could see how it was also the last one that somebody as kind-hearted as Arein would arrive at. "You mean that if all you wanted was a unicorn's horn, there'd be no reason to keep the unicorn itself."

At that, Arein's face fell. Her bottom lip began to tremble. "So we have to find him, don't you see? We have to find him and get him away from here."

"I think there are other things we need to do first," Tia said.

Arein gazed at her in horror. "What could be more important? Maybe whoever's behind this is hurting Blackwing right now."

"Listen to me," Tia said. "I hate to say this, but if someone set us up so that they could kill Blackwing and cut off his horn, then that means he's already dead and has been for days. But if he's still alive, there's no reason to think he won't stay that way. However you consider it, Arein, and as much as this may not be what you want to hear, we have other priorities. So will you try and calm down?"

As usual, Arein looked half ready to argue—and as usual, Tia's logic was hard to refute. "All right," the dwarf girl agreed.

"Thank you," Tia said, with more sincerity than Durren would have expected. "Now, we need to know what you found out about the Petrified Egg."

Arein took a deep and shuddering breath. By the time she let it out, she seemed just about back to her usual self. "To be honest, I couldn't learn much. That Egg, whatever it is—I get the impression it's awfully old, and that the monastery must have had it for a long time. But there are records of other similar objects, ones designed to store and magnify magic. And some of those had potent spells built into them, too, to keep them from being stolen. Most people think they must have been made by ancient wizards, but there are some stranger theories as well: that dragons gave birth to them, or that they were made by shapeshifters to be weapons in a war. At any rate, no one knows how to create them anymore, and most of the famous ones were destroyed decades or centuries ago."

"That doesn't prove anything either way," Tia said thoughtfully. "If the priests had been hiding such a powerful object all this time, it's possible they really were up to no good. On the other hand, it's just as likely that someone at the academy found out what they had and wanted it for themselves." She turned her hooded gaze on Hule. "How about you, Hule? What did you learn?"

The fighter stood with a flourish, clearing his throat as though he were an orator on a stage. "The casket we were sent to recover contained jewels and ornaments, which were being transported by a firm named Harper and Kosh. They had an outbreak of the runs among their guard company, the night before they were due to leave, and had to set out light-handed. They still managed to fend off a rat-kind attack, but when they were adding up the damage afterwards, they noticed that one chest was missing."

"But how do you know all that?" Arein asked, plainly impressed.

Hule grinned. "For the same reason I know that the casket was eventually recovered. Borgnin sent a level four party in after us and they managed to get it back without the rat-kind ever so much as realising they were there. The fighter on that party was a braggart named Ordus; he was only too glad to tell me every last detail so long as I acted suitably impressed."

"Then that quest was legitimate, at least," Tia said.

"It looks that way," Hule agreed.

"Fine. You next, Durren. What did you discover from talking to the other rangers?"

So Durren briefly conveyed what he'd managed to find out—which, after Arein and Hule's speeches, didn't seem like all that much. "As far as I can tell," he concluded, "none of the other rangers have the sort of doubts we do. All the quests they've been on were reasonable and lawful."

"Then it's just us," Tia said.

Durren couldn't tell whether she sounded pleased or disappointed. Either way, now was his opportunity to ask the question he'd wanted to raise since he'd arrived. "So what about you then? What have you been up to while we've been running around on these missions you set us?"

Durren couldn't see Tia's eyes within the folds of her hood, yet he could feel how they settled on him. "I've been following Cullglass," she said.

Durren gaped at her. "You've—?"

"I've been spying on Cullglass. Ever since he was first assigned to us, but more so these last few days."

"Wait," Durren said, "what do you mean? In what way, spying on him?"

Tia sighed, as though that were the most ridiculous question he could have asked. "I mean just what I said. Our tutors encourage us to pick out targets and trail them in our free periods, so it was barely even breaking any rules. And since Cullglass had a large part to play in whether I ever got to level up, I thought it might be useful to know just how he spends his time. Then, after that last quest, it occurred to me that maybe someone's manipulating him. Maybe somebody else on the faculty, or even from outside of the academy, has been using him and us. So I started paying more attention."

Durren couldn't decide if he was more shocked or impressed—which, he was coming to realise, was a common reaction to anything Tia told him. "And what did you find out?"

Tia held up a hand and counted off points on her fingers. "That he likes his own company. That he rarely speaks with other members of staff. That all doors to the stores have excellent locks on them and that, even if they didn't, Cullglass keeps them barred on the inside at night. And that twice a week he leaves the academy with a large parcel and comes back empty-handed."

Durren felt almost let down. The first three weren't remotely strange, and as for that fourth..."Maybe he's sending a gift to a relative," he suggested. "Maybe it's to do with the stores, trading items that are no longer needed, something like that."

"Yes, I thought so too," Tia agreed. "When I followed him as far as Olgen, I almost gave up. Only, he didn't go to the traders' offices, where parcels and letters are couriered from. He kept on to the far edge of town, and then I lost him. But the direction he was heading in was away from any of the main roads, and even from the woodsmen's trails. Not only that, but he was gone for the entire afternoon."

"That *does* seem strange," Arein put in. "But how come you lost him?"

"I'm damned if I know." Tia sounded uncharacteristically peevish; clearly she'd been tormenting herself with the same question. "He was there one moment, gone the next. At first I thought he'd spotted me, but there was no possible way he could have. Anyway, if he had, then I'm sure he'd have said something by now—and probably Durren wouldn't be the only one being expelled."

"So he likes to go for a walk in the woods," Durren said, annoyed by the casual reference to his personal disaster. "All right, it's not exactly normal behaviour, but there are no end of reasonable explanations."

Tia stepped closer to the lantern. For the first time that night, Durren could see the outlines of her face—and how she was scowling at him.

She said, "It's not only that he walks in the woods. It's that he takes something into the woods and comes back without it. Anyway, we don't have any other leads, and if Cullglass is being extorted somehow, then we can hardly rely on him to come up with answers. So whatever you think, I'm going to follow him again. But after what happened last time, I'm not sure I can do it alone. The four of us together would stand a far better chance."

"I think Pootle might help us," Arein piped up. She spoke as though she hadn't so much as considered that Hule or Durren might be unwilling to go along with Tia's plan.

"That thing?" Hule asked. "Why would it? Anyway, how would you get it off Hieronymus?"

Arein couldn't have looked more indignant if he'd insulted a close personal friend. "It's a member of our party, isn't it? I'm sure it would want to help, and I'm fairly sure I can cast the scrying spell that's used to see what it sees. As for Hieronymus, he doesn't keep Pootle with him all the time. There's a sort of coop in the wizards' wing—or whatever the equivalent is for floating eyeballs. I'm sure nobody would notice if one were borrowed for a few hours."

"All right," Tia said. She sounded pleased. "Yes, that could work. If Cullglass keeps to the same pattern, then he'll next be going three days from now, just before third bell. Can the rest of you sneak out by then? He uses that small side door we brought Blackwing in by. If we were to meet in the courtyard there just after second bell, we could be outside and waiting for him."

"This all seems like a waste of time to me," Hule grumbled. "But I've a lecture on metallurgy scheduled for that period that I was going to have to pretend not to understand a word of. So, yes, I'll be there."

Only then, as Tia's enquiring stare fell upon him, did Durren realise he'd already made his own decision. "I doubt anyone's going to much care if I skip classes," he said. "So I suppose you might as well count me in."

Much later, as he lay in bed staring up at the arched ceiling, Durren finally thought to wonder just why he was going along with this dubious expedition of Tia's.

Certainly his motivation wasn't altogether to do with believing she was right. Tia was a rogue to the core, and her instincts always led her to solve problems the way a rogue would. Wouldn't it have made more sense for the four of them to simply take their concerns to Borgnin? Well, perhaps not, given Durren's current circumstances. Still, stalking an elderly storesmaster through the woods seemed about the least rational course of action he could imagine.

Yet the truth was that he didn't care. He'd follow Tia's lead anyway, simply because he'd rather that than be left out—and because, when the four of them had been questing together, relying only on themselves, he'd finally felt like the independent adult he'd told himself he was when first he crept away from home.

If Durren was really honest, there was more to it even than

that. He liked this new version of Tia, the one that actually spoke to him and even asked for his help. Something had changed in her, just as he himself had changed, and that transformation was a definite improvement. Perhaps he would never see her again after this, would never see any of them—but the prospect of one last quest together was more appealing than he'd ever have expected.

The intervening days, though, were among the most miserable of Durren's life.

He'd thought when Borgnin made the offer of letting him keep up his classes that it would be better to have even a little more time at the academy, anything to defer the moment when he'd have to put this life behind him. However, without the distraction of Tia's mission, Durren soon began to discover how wrong he'd been. His existence as a student was only a pretence now, one soon to end, and that fact was all he could think about through every lecture, every seminar, every training exercise. It was all futile—a lie he couldn't make himself believe.

On the second day after their meeting in the tower, during archery practise, Durren struck five bull's-eyes in a row. There seemed no point in pretending anymore. The two students who'd previously been the best in their group, Lyra and Tukver, looked at him with a mix of wonder and indignation. Tutor Tallowbyne, who surely knew that Durren's days at Black River were numbered, only pretended as though nothing unusual had happened.

Durren had thought that a little showing off might make him feel better, but doing so had entirely the opposite effect. All he'd accomplished was a glimpse into what his life might have been like, had he only made better choices over the course of these last months. Now, for all his recent efforts at friendliness, his fellow rangers would remember him solely as the boy who was expelled—the one who tricked his way into the academy and paid the price.

That night, Durren made a show of feeling ill at dinner and went to bed early. The next morning, he asked one of the other students to let that day's tutors know he still wasn't well. But that immediately backfired when the boy—it happened to be Arlo Mainbrow, the aficionado of Black River's architecture— proved so concerned that it was all Durren could do to get rid of him. Feeling as miserable as he ever had at the thought of all the potential friendships he'd soon be losing, Durren finally managed to persuade Mainbrow that all he needed was a few hours of bed rest and some peace and quiet.

With all of the other students absent, the room felt even emptier than it should have. Durren could hear faint sounds coming from around the building, murmurs of conversation and the tip-tap of feet, and from the main courtyard the muted clang of blades. However, those sounds didn't so much break the silence as deepen it. He wished he could have come up with a means of slipping away that didn't confine him here all morning.

Now, though, there was nothing to do but wait. As much as he tried to distract himself with the book on arrow-making, the period until second bell felt like an eternity. When eventually it came, the clang sent a shudder through Durren's whole body, as if his very blood were vibrating. Now he really had to go through with Tia's harebrained plot.

Once he was on his feet, however, Durren felt surer. By the time he left the dormitory, he'd already persuaded himself that there was no turning back. If he should be spotted wandering the corridors during lesson times, then he'd already be in grave trouble; perhaps admitting he was sneaking out to spend the day spying on one of the faculty couldn't even make matters worse.

When he arrived at the small courtyard, having nearly got lost half a dozen times on the way, Durren wasn't surprised to find that he was the last to arrive, as usual. The others were waiting in a huddle, looking impatient.

"I wasn't sure you were coming," Tia said.

"Of course I was," Durren replied irritably. Then he realised to his astonishment that Tia was smiling; she had only been teasing him. His scowl turned into a grin.

But already Tia's usual seriousness had reasserted itself. "Before we go any further," she said, "the three of you might want to check in those barrels." She pointed to a row of old casks against one wall, presumably left to be broken into firewood.

Puzzled, Durren went over to the nearest. "Not that one," Tia called from behind him, and so he moved on to the next. Trying the lid and finding it loose, he levered it free with his fingertips.

Even having been told to look inside, Durren had still half expected to find the barrel empty, and was surprised to see something bulky filling its base. The courtyard's high walls had shut out much of the day's light, and at first he couldn't make out what he was looking at—until he recognised the protrusions jutting from one side. They were the feathered tails of arrows.

"Oh! My pack," cried Arein from beside him, and from Durren's other shoulder he heard Hule huff with surprise.

Durren hauled his backpack out and slid his arms into the

straps, glad of the familiar weight. "How did you possibly get them?" he asked Tia.

"It wasn't difficult," she said off-handedly. "I just broke into the store late last night. Probably we'll have returned them before anyone notices they're gone. Now close up those barrels and let's get going; the last thing we want is for Cullglass to find us here."

Only as she led them to the small door in the wall did it occur to Durren that Tia's plan possessed at least one obvious flaw: their way out was certain to be locked. However, Tia was already kneeling before the portal, profound concentration etched on her face. He heard the scrape of metal on metal; then there came an abrupt click. Keeping one hand in place and steady, Tia reached with the other and drew the door open.

"Easy," she muttered, sliding her lock-picks back into a pocket.

Outside, the sun seemed brighter; its luminance made the spray rising from the river dazzling. Even Tia's black cloak looked cheerful. She was marching ahead with fast strides, and Durren had to hurry to catch her.

"That was really impressive," he said. "You know, you deserved to be the first of us to get promoted. Honestly, I'm surprised they didn't go all the way and let you graduate there and then."

Tia looked uncomfortable. "Actually," she said, "you and Hule aren't the only ones who haven't been telling the whole truth."

"Oh?" Durren tried to sound surprised, though it would never have crossed his mind that Tia wasn't keeping her share of secrets from the rest of them.

"The thing is," she said, "I didn't really get promoted to

level two. I just made that up to try and motivate you. Truthfully, I was told I'd never level up until my teamwork improved." Tia frowned with indignation. "They said that my charisma rating was one of the lowest they'd ever given."

Rather than laugh as he'd have liked to, Durren feigned coughing into his fist. "Ah," was all the response he could come up with. Having allowed himself a moment to make certain he wouldn't give himself away, he changed the subject; a question had occurred to him back in the courtyard and now he couldn't resist asking it. "Tia," he said, "I was wondering…you didn't do all this for me, did you? I mean, bringing us together, getting our packs, this whole thing? This isn't supposed to be one final quest before I get kicked out?"

Even by Tia's standards, the look she gave him was inscrutable. "No," she said, "of course not."

"Okay," Durren agreed. "I didn't think so. But, if you had—well, I'd have appreciated it." And with that, unable to bear the uncomfortableness any longer, he fell back and let her march on by herself.

It didn't take them long to reach the end of the riverside path. Durren struggled not to think about when they'd travelled this way in reverse, with Blackwing in tow. He hoped Arein had been wrong and that the unicorn was safe; as much as he hadn't much liked the beast at the time, the thought of anyone mutilating so magnificent a creature was hard to bear. At any rate, he had no doubt that Arein would be troubling herself with similar thoughts.

Tia picked out a spot near the corner of the wall, a little way down the river's steep bank, where a close patch of trees surrounded by low bushes offered the perfect cover from which to see anyone approaching. The day was warm and pleasant, the sun's heat mitigated by a fine mist coming off the water behind them. Insects buzzed and birds warbled, and every so often Durren would hear the splash and plop of a fish as it leaped after some prey. It almost seemed a shame that they couldn't just relax and enjoy themselves. This was the first time since he'd arrived, he realised, that he'd been outside the academy's walls for any reason other than an official expedition.

However, waiting in hiding wasn't a great deal of fun, especially when Tia insisted on shushing them whenever he, Hule and Arein tried to whisper among themselves. She seemed to be the only one taking this self-imposed mission seriously.

Fortunately, they didn't have long to wait. Just as Durren was beginning to feel sleepy—from the lapping of the river against the stones of the bank and the sunshine upon his neck—Tia whispered, "All right, here he comes."

Durren had long since shifted from the spot where he could see out over the path in favour of a more comfortable position, and so all he could do was rely on Tia's perspective. She held a hand upraised and stayed perfectly still, and he was reminded of a kestrel readying to stoop. After a while he thought he could hear what must be the patter of Cullglass's footsteps upon the packed dirt of the path.

The sound passed. Again, there was nothing to be heard but the birds, the insects, the fast-moving river.

Finally, Tia dropped her upraised hand. "Now," she murmured—and with that, she was gone.

15

Hule was next to break cover, with Durren and Arein close behind him. There was a patch of bare and rocky ground before the academy's front, which sloped down to the point where the highway entered the forest. Durren had a brief view of Cullglass in the distance, before a curve of the road stole him from view.

"I'm going to get closer," Tia said. "I'll take the lead, and all you have to do is keep me in sight. I don't think he can give me the slip between here and Olgen. Just in case though, Arein, did you manage to bring Pootle?"

Arein nodded, and reached into a baggy pocket. When she drew her hand out, the observer was nestled in her palm and blinking at the sudden daylight. Arein held the creature up to her face. "Now," she addressed it, "do you remember what we talked about?"

Pootle rocked its small body back and forth in a fair semblance of nodding.

"All right, then. Go on, and whatever you do, don't let him see you."

Abruptly, the observer shot straight up into the air and sped away, towards the forest edge. Tia watched for a couple of seconds, perhaps making certain that Pootle was following its instructions. Then she darted after, disappearing moments later amid the first trees. Durren hurried to close the distance between them, conscious that if he wasn't careful, he would lose sight of both her and Cullglass and that the entire endeavour might be over before it had even begun. Beneath the canopy, the dense upper branches shut out so much of the sun's brilliance that at first day seemed to have turned to evening.

Durren was already half convinced Tia had eluded him when he saw a flash of movement to his left, so brief that he nearly dismissed the flutter of darkness as a fleeing animal or a branch swaying in the wind. However, as he concentrated, he was sure that what he'd seen was the hem of Tia's cloak.

Hule and Arein were catching him up now, so Durren pointed wordlessly towards where he believed her to be. Together the three of them hurried in that direction, careful not to be visible from the road. As he dashed from tree to tree, Durren scanned the dense woodland. Keeping Tia in sight was far easier for her to say than for him to actually do. Of course, she was trying to keep hidden from Cullglass rather than them, which meant she shouldn't have been so hard to see from behind. Yet her ability to dissolve into every shadow, to merge her outline with even the narrowest trunks, was remarkable. It seemed to come instinctively to her, and certainly Durren struggled to imagine that every level one rogue was half so skilled.

Not losing Tia took all of his concentration. Even then, he might as well have been trying to watch a fish swimming at the bottom of a deep pool: he would see only the smallest flicker of motion, gone before his eyes had properly had time to register it. Durren quickly discovered that his only choice was to trust to his instincts and risk being wrong.

For all his efforts, though, he soon realised that it was Pootle who was their best hope and not he. Arein seemed to be doing an excellent job of communing with the little creature. She had taken off her glasses, and now wore an expression at once intent and glazed, as though she were both staring at a distant point and deep in meditation.

As useful as Arein's connection with the observer was, however, it had at least one drawback. Durren wasn't certain how much of the view before her own eyes she was actually seeing—but it certainly wasn't enough to keep her from walking into trees.

Hule was the first to notice, catching hold of Arein just as she was about to stumble into a sprawling spineroot bush.

A surprised, "Oh," was her only response.

After that, Hule apparently decided that his responsibility in the party would be to keep Arein from injuring herself. He stayed close to her and made a point of gently steering her aside from obstructions, leaving Durren the task of keeping Tia in sight.

All told, they had difficulty maintaining a remotely rapid pace. What made matters worse was that, to judge from the speed with which Tia flitted from trunk to trunk ahead, Cullglass himself was hardly dragging his heels. Their one slender advantage was that the road was winding, defined by the contours of the land. Though the route through the forest was more challenging, it was also more direct.

After a while, to Durren's great relief, Tia began to slow down enough for them to close the gap a little. They'd come to a point where the highway dipped well below the level of the surrounding woodland, and from the high bank Durren found that he could catch the occasional glimpse of Cullglass. In any case, there was only one place the storesmaster could be going, and that was the town now visible in the near distance, where wavering pillars of smoke and a few of the taller rooftops cut through the forest's emerald blanket.

That second leg of their pursuit was easier. So long as they were higher than Cullglass, keeping him in view was relatively straightforward, while for him to see them was all but impossible. And it seemed to Durren that the storesmaster *was* wary of pursuit; more than once he glanced sharply over his shoulder, or looked askance at the roadside. Perhaps he was only fearful of outlaws. Yet the area around Olgen was unusually safe, thanks to the presence of Black River itself and its many students constantly in need of excuses to test their mettle—a fact Cullglass surely knew.

The ground grew rougher about the town, as though twisted out of shape by Olgen's own presence. As they started down a rugged decline, Durren realised he'd lost sight of both Cullglass and Tia.

"Can Pootle still see him?" he asked.

Arein nodded, nearly lost her footing and clutched at Hule beside her—who looked gravely embarrassed, but was careful to hold her steady.

By the time they reached the slope's base, they'd strayed some distance from the road, and all they had to rely on was Arein and her connection with the observer. Durren let her lead the way, until they broke through a last dense band of trees and the edge of the town rose up before them.

Olgen was a small town by Durren's standards, or really by any standards at all. To his eyes, it barely qualified as a village. He suspected that the settlement existed first and foremost in service to the academy, though from what he'd heard, the locals would have denied the fact vehemently. After that, Olgen's function was as a hub for the surrounding area, offering trade and supplies. Nevertheless, it remained a primitive place in every way; the buildings were largely of wood, with only the very largest built from stone, and hardly any reached above two storeys.

Nor were there many people around. Durren was no expert in shadowing, but he suspected that wasn't in their favour. However, though he couldn't see Cullglass, Arein still seemed confident, and Durren concluded that his best approach was just to let her get on with things. In fact, for all Tia's skill, it occurred to him that Arein and her strange pet could probably have managed this self-imposed quest all by themselves.

With that thought still fresh in his mind, Durren started guiltily when Tia appeared at his elbow. Her arrival was like a magic trick; he hadn't even known she was near.

"Do you have him in sight?" she asked Arein.

"Pootle does." Even though Tia was right in front of her, Arein spoke as though she were talking to someone in a different room. "Yes, we can see him clearly."

"And how's Pootle doing? Does it mind helping us?"

"Not at all. I think it's enjoying itself."

"Good. Then we'll split into two groups," Tia decided. "Durren, you and I are going to get ahead of Cullglass. Arein, Hule, once he enters town you stay well back, at least a street away. If anything goes wrong, don't rush in; rely on Pootle. Cullglass might be on the lookout for someone following him, but I doubt he'll have thought to expect an observer. Can you do that?"

Arein nodded.

"Of course," Hule confirmed.

"Good," Tia said. "Don't worry about finding us, we'll find you."

"All right," Arein agreed—and narrowly avoided walking into an elderly couple, steered away at the last moment by Hule catching her arm.

"Are you sure it's a good idea to let those two…" Durren began—but Tia was already vanishing into a side street. Durren dashed after her.

This was his first proper visit to Olgen, having barely passed through on his way to Black River, and he was only growing less impressed. The place smelled of wood smoke and horse dung, and those odours seemed to have infected its colours too: everything, even the clothes of the people they passed, was either grey or muddy brown. The place made him a little homesick for Luntharbour, where the buildings were all of lustrous white stone and the streets were kept meticulously clean.

Well, he told himself, *you'll be back there soon enough.* And suddenly Olgen seemed more appealing, foul smells, drab colours and all.

Tia seemed to have a fair grasp of her way around town. Perhaps she didn't show quite the confidence with which she'd navigated Black River's passages; nevertheless, she barely hesitated as she took one turning after another, moving from alley to broad street to narrow passage between ramshackle houses. At any rate, it was apparent that she had a destination in mind—presumably one that would bring them out ahead of Cullglass, with minimal risk of their being seen in return.

Sure enough, the next junction deposited them in a sort of square, with buildings on every side that were at least marginally more impressive than those they'd been passing until now. At its centre was a cobbled area that Durren guessed would serve for weekly markets. There were more people around here, too—not exactly a crowd, but enough bodies milling back and forth that it would be easy to stay hidden among their number.

"There's something I need to do," Tia said. She pointed towards the opening of a side street. "If he's following the same route as last time, Cullglass will come out there. Hopefully I'll be back before he arrives, but if not then just stay on him. I'll catch you up in a minute."

"Wait, what are you—" But yet again Durren didn't have time to finish his sentence. Already Tia had disappeared into the open doorway of one of the nearby shops.

"Well, that's great," he grumbled. Hadn't this all been her idea? Wasn't she the expert in this kind of thing? And even a week ago it would have been impossible to imagine her delegating something she considered so important to the rest of them. Durren remembered what she'd said as they left the academy: *I was told I'd never level up until my teamwork improved.* That was all well and good, but couldn't she have picked a better time to begin putting her trust in others?

Still, Durren told himself, probably she was right and their race through the back streets had given them a good lead on Cullglass, enough that she'd be back long before he emerged.

The thought had barely crossed his mind when the storesmaster appeared.

Durren was wholly unprepared. Had Cullglass happened to be looking his way, he would surely have been seen. Fortunately, the storesmaster's gaze was directed straight ahead, all his attention focused on manoeuvring through the busy square. Durren ducked closer to the nearest wall, where at least he was within the building's shadow, and watched as Cullglass set out diagonally towards the opening of another street.

As before, he was maintaining a rapid pace, and Durren wondered whether Hule and Arein had managed to keep up. What if it was all down to him now? Should he be giving chase? Durren took a few indecisive paces, though Cullglass was already out of view. Then, on impulse, he glanced towards the rooftops. There, the slightest flicker of motion caught his eye. Yes, he felt certain that he'd seen Pootle, scooting from one observation spot to another.

When Durren looked down again, Arein and Hule were hurrying towards him, Hule still hovering close to prevent Arein from blundering into anyone.

Durren was about to tell them both how glad he was to see them, when Tia reappeared beside his elbow. To Arein she said, "You still have him?", taking charge as though she'd never been away.

"Absolutely," Arein said. "He's just turning the next corner, we can see him clearly." Then her face sank. "No, wait. I…I've lost him."

"But, you just said—"

Arein looked frantic. "I know what I said! One moment he was there, and then…I don't know. Pootle just can't find him anywhere." She rocked her head, as though expecting to see Cullglass standing before them—but it clearly wasn't her own eyes she was staring through. "I don't understand!"

"Look harder," Tia insisted. "Probably he's just stopped somewhere. Maybe he's getting suspicious."

"Wait," Arein said, "just wait. There's…there's someone else. Only, I think—" Her brow furrowed with concentration. "It just might be him. I mean, they're too short, and older, and the cloak is different, but the way he walks…and that bundle he's carrying, I'm sure it's the one Cullglass had. Yes, I think it might be him."

"Stick with them," Tia advised. "He might have turned his cloak, and it's not hard to make yourself look shorter or older than you are. If that really is Cullglass and he's disguised himself, then we know for certain something's going on."

Together the four of them hurried down the street that Cullglass had taken. Near its end, Arein pointed them towards a turn-off, and at the bottom of that road she led them to the right. The houses ahead, which were little more than shacks, gave way once more to forest. Even by Olgen's standards, this was a poor portion of town, some of the buildings already half tumbling down. Just as Tia had said, it was hard to see how anything in this direction could possibly interest the storesmaster; beyond the point where the track petered out, the woodland looked dense and uninviting.

Nevertheless, Arein was pointing towards a gap in the trees, so narrow that Durren would surely have missed it otherwise. "He's not far ahead," she said, in what she'd probably meant to be a whisper; her connection with Pootle even seemed to be affecting her hearing.

"I think we should stay together from now on," Tia proposed. "If we really are still following Cullglass, then probably he thinks he's safe for the time being."

Durren resisted the urge to point out that they should probably have stayed together from the beginning, and that she was the one who'd insisted on running off on her own. He could hardly bring himself to feel annoyed with her now that it was becoming apparent that everything she'd told them had been true. Assuming the man they were following really was

Cullglass, he was going to considerable trouble not to be discovered, while heading away from civilisation and deeper into the wilderness.

True to her word, this time Tia left the task of keeping the storesmaster in sight to Arein and Pootle. Anyway, there was only one possible route through the trees, and the difficulty was less of staying close to Cullglass, more of maintaining enough of a gap that they didn't accidentally blunder into him. Too, the path was badly overgrown, with cords of spineroot lying like tripwires and great mounds of stinging blackleaf to be avoided. The trail was so narrow and nearly erased, in fact, that it was hard to believe anyone but Cullglass—and perhaps the occasional passing deer or boar—had come this way in recent months.

Durren had lost track of how long they'd been walking for, or how often he'd been scratched and stung, when suddenly Arein gasped. "There's a building up ahead," she whispered. "Oh! It's huge. But it's all in ruins. And there are stairs, going down into the ground. He's following them. Should I send Pootle after him?"

"Can you lead us there?" Tia asked.

"Yes. It's just ahead."

"Then, no. Have Pootle wait and stay hidden. Unless there's another way out, Cullglass isn't going anywhere. We wanted to know where he went and now we do."

Less than a minute later, the forest abruptly opened out, the path dipped, and before them Durren saw the decaying building Arein had spoken of. He nearly jumped out of his skin when Pootle dropped from the treetops into their midst and hovered before them, blinking sleepily. Arein patted the observer's head and murmured, "Yes, you did very well, didn't you? Who's a clever Pootle?"

The ruins were evidently ancient. Of course, the surrounding forest had taken its toll, as branches thrust at crumbling walls and creepers dragged at the brickwork. Still, something about the cut of the stones and the sheer extent of the damage told Durren that what he was looking at belonged to centuries long past.

Where he came from, such an edifice would soon have been dismantled and its materials put to new purpose. Here, though, deep in the forest, it seemed there was no one around to bother. That the building had been left to rot was all the stranger for its prodigious size. Even ignoring the portions now roofless or too fragile to risk entering, a dozen families could surely have made their homes here without once worrying about having to share space.

And that was only taking into account the portion on the surface. Durren could see the stairs Arein had spoken of, descending steeply into the earth. Once upon a time they'd been covered, but the walls to either side had largely collapsed and the roof was altogether gone. The opening at their base must have been partly buried at one point, and someone—surely not Cullglass?—had gone to a great deal of effort to clear a passage.

Restoring that entrance would have been a considerable job. What could the point have been? If anyone had needed space for some purpose, then surely there were ample empty rooms on the surface that would have sufficed just as well. The more Durren thought, the stranger that underground aperture seemed—and the more the questions it raised sent shivers up and down his spine.

"How long do we wait?" he asked. The air was cool beneath the trees, and the sweat from their hurried pursuit through the forest was starting to chill his skin.

Tia shrugged. "As long as we need to," she said. There was a triumphant edge to her voice, as though she were a hunter who had trailed her prey back to its lair—which, Durren supposed, she was.

He settled down to wait. The knowledge that Cullglass, or whoever they'd followed here, might reappear at any moment—not to mention the fact that he might not be alone—was enough to keep them all silent. Still, that tension didn't make crouching in the bushes Tia had picked out any more interesting or comfortable. To occupy himself, Durren tried to guess at what the building might once have been.

But with so little evidence to go by, even that wasn't much of a diversion. The ruins reminded him somewhat of the monastery from which they'd stolen the Petrified Egg. The eccentricities of its design, as well as the smudges of weathered carving, made him wonder if this devastated structure hadn't once served a similar purpose. Perhaps priests had once prayed or meditated within those stubborn walls, maybe even to deities whose names were now long forgotten.

"Shush!" Arein whispered—though no one had said a word in what seemed an age. Her eyes had that glazed look again; Durren could tell she was seeing from Pootle's perspective. She had stationed the observer atop a ruined column, where it had a clear view down over the stairs, but was unlikely to be seen in return.

Durren tensed. Through the tangle of bushes before them, he could just make out the point where the steps entered the earth.

Finally, Cullglass reappeared. And this time, sure enough, it definitely was Cullglass. Tia had been right again, then;

somehow he'd disguised himself in Olgen, so rapidly that Pootle hadn't had time to register the change. Durren noticed, too, that the burden he'd been carrying had vanished. Whatever it had been, presumably it was now consigned to the mysterious underground realm he'd just left.

What could the storesmaster possibly be up to? A part of Durren wanted desperately to stand up and confront Cullglass right then and there. Perhaps he could offer some reasonable explanation; maybe he was here on legitimate academy business, even some vital, secret mission for Borgnin himself. Really, who knew what sorts of things went on at Black River that four level one students wouldn't be privy to? The more Durren thought, the more he doubted that following Cullglass had been such a good idea.

But by then Cullglass was gone, vanished around the first bend of the trail. Durren realised that he'd been holding his breath for longer than he could remember, and exhaled in a great sigh. At least one part of their mission was over; they'd found out where the storesmaster slunk off to twice a week, and had apparently managed to do so without him realising.

"So what happens now?" Hule muttered. His tone left no doubt that he hoped the answer would be, *We go home.*

Yet it was just as clear from Tia's face that leaving was the last thing on her mind. "What else?" she said. "We take a look inside."

16

A t their base, the stairs led onto a brief corridor carved of large rectangular blocks, which in turn gave way to a low archway, around which Durren could just make out faint traces of symbols cut into the stone. Beyond the arch he could see nothing but deep darkness.

"Are we sure about this?" he asked, before he could stop himself.

Tia's only answer was a scowl.

"I'm just saying, what if he wasn't alone? For all we know, he was bringing food to a gang of murderers that are hiding out here. Or maybe he comes to train his giant carnivorous moths and they're just waiting down there for their next meal."

"Then we'll deal with them," Hule declared, and smacked a fist against the flat of his hand to illustrate. Now that he was committed to exploring the building's depths, he seemed quite taken with the idea.

"Anyway, carnivorous moths live entirely on moonflies, and they'd be far more scared of us than we'd be of them," Arein pointed out.

"It was just an example," Durren said huffily. He didn't like being the one to admit that he was scared, but nothing he told himself made the feeling go away. There were just too many unanswered questions here. Still, he could see that the other three, for whatever their reasons, weren't willing to listen—and he certainly wasn't going to stay out here on his own. "All I'm saying is, we have to be careful. We don't know what we're getting ourselves into."

"Durren's right," Tia said. "We still have no idea why Cullglass came here, so everyone stay alert."

Durren couldn't tell if she was only saying it to make him feel better, but he was grateful anyway. Somehow he felt that so long as Tia was being cautious, the rest of them were likely to be a great deal safer.

"Also," Durren said, "at the risk of pointing out the obvious, you do realise it's dark down here?"

"Lucky I came prepared, then." Sitting at the base of the stairs, Tia began to rummage through her pack. She drew out a small oil lantern, which she set to lighting with a tinderbox. Once the lamp was burning, the light it gave off was limited but cheerful, staining the walls the precise colour of honey.

Now Durren could see that the passage before them ran on to a T-junction. The walls were plain, and offered few clues as to what this place might once have been. From what little he knew of such things, he felt that the craftsmanship was of good quality, and at the least it was fair to suppose that so much stone hadn't come cheaply. Whoever had built these tunnels long ago, they'd had money and sense enough to hire capable masons— or at least had the power to compel skilled slaves.

Without discussion, the four of them spread out into a column: first Tia with the lantern, then Hule close behind her, then Durren and finally Arein. Even had it not been obvious from the length of time Cullglass had spent down here, it was becoming apparent that at least as much of the ancient building lay below ground as above. Protected from the ravages of rain and wind, this lower level had fared better, but only a little. At the first intersection they passed, for example, two of the exits had been partially sealed when a section of ceiling had collapsed, decades or centuries ago. Great blocks were mixed with heaped dirt, and even the one way that remained clear required some clambering.

As he swiped loose earth from his trousers, Durren noticed another sound beneath the swish of palm on cloth. It was a low, steady scratching that set his nerves on edge. Worst was the comprehension that he'd been hearing it ever since they'd first come down here, without quite noticing until now.

The source of the sound lay ahead, he decided. It was coming from close to where Tia and Hule were—and seemed to be moving in step with them. Durren tensed. Was it rats? Insects, maybe? Or something worse? "Can anyone hear that?" he whispered, throat suddenly dry. "That...*skritch, skritch* sound?"

Ahead, Tia froze. "Now that you mention it."

The sound stopped.

"Um," Hule said.

Tia rounded on him. "What did you do?"

"Nothing!" Hule held up his hands—and Durren could see that one contained a sheet of paper, the other a wooden writing implement. On the paper, a crude series of interlocking lines and curves had been marked in an unsteady hand. "It's my item, all right? The label said 'map-making kit'. I thought it would be some magical device, but this is all I got." Hule brightened. "Still, at least I finally get to use it."

"Hule," Tia said softly, "look down." And she held the

lantern low to the ground to assist him.

Durren saw what she was indicating even as Hule did: in the thick dirt and dust were a succession of clear scuffmarks. Tia hadn't been wandering at random; she had been following Cullglass's footprints.

"Oh," Hule said. He looked a little defeated as he slid pencil and paper back into a pocket.

Tia only shook her head and began walking once more.

Around the next bend was a straight section of corridor. If there were any exits leading off, then the lamplight failed to pick them out. The passage was surprisingly long, its far end lost in shadow. Either these shafts ran further than the ruins above or those ruins extended deeper into the forest than Durren had suspected. Whatever the case, he didn't altogether like the look of this tunnel; but Tia had already started towards the far end and there was no choice but to follow.

They were perhaps halfway along when Durren noticed a curious sensation. It was a queasiness, as though his stomach was sloshing; it made him strangely dizzy. But at first he couldn't understand where the impression was coming from.

Then he realised: the ground was shaking.

Durren felt the tremors through the soles of his feet, even before he saw the way the paving slabs before them were shifting like the surface of a wind-ruffled sea. But stone wasn't supposed to move like that—and it certainly wasn't supposed to dip the way this was doing.

"Back!" he yelled, and was already moving himself. Arein, close behind him, hardly seemed to be reacting, so he caught her around the waist and hauled her with him, ignoring her yelp of protest. A moment later and Hule dashed to join them—but Durren couldn't tell where Tia was.

He could hear now what he'd seen and felt: the sound of stone grinding against stone. That awful cacophony was coming from all around him—and from *beneath*. Durren took another quick stride, not having to drag Arein this time. Though the passage was still shaking, he felt that the vibrations were subsiding now, and that the surface beneath his feet was sound. He turned back, not certain what to expect.

The floor was gone. Where it ended, just before him, the last blocks tilted steeply downward, held in place by who knew what. After that was only profound darkness, and no way to tell what it concealed. Possibly there was another passage down there, but Durren could as easily believe that he was staring into a fathomless gulf. He thought about throwing something down as a test, but wasn't certain he'd feel any better for knowing.

Only then did he realise—Tia had been in front of them. And now there was nothing where she'd been but that inky chasm.

Except that there was still light to see by. Surely light meant that Tia's lantern was intact? And even as the thought entered his mind, a voice called from beyond the abyss: "I'm alive. Are you three all right?"

Alive she might be, but Tia sounded shaken. Durren couldn't help but wonder how close a call she'd just had. Though, now that he considered, he couldn't have cut his own escape much more finely—and only then did he notice how his heart was thundering.

"We're fine," Arein called. "Can you get back to us?"

In the lamplight, Tia was only a shape cut from the blackness. Her silhouette took a moment to inspect the edges of the gap, then the walls to either side. "I don't think so. Even with my climbing spikes, the stone's crumbling in places; it's too risky."

Somehow, nothing could have made the situation more horrifying than Tia admitting defeat. Wasn't she always the one with an answer? Durren wracked his brains. What could they possibly do? There was Arein's magic, of course, but he suspected that transportation was a good few levels beyond her. *Think*, Durren told himself, *there must be something*.

There was. And it was obvious. "I have my rope," he said.

He'd fully expected the others to ignore him or to contradict him—but instead, Arein and Hule were looking at him expectantly.

Durren deliberated quickly. "There was a broken pillar back there. We could tie one end to that and throw the other over. Tia, can you look and see if there's anything that would make a good anchor point on your side?"

Tia didn't answer, but after a moment the lantern began to bob further down the passage—until it was all Durren could do to make out his own hand in front of his face. Seconds passed, and then the lamplight brightened once more, until he could again make out Tia's shape beyond the collapsed floor.

"It's no good," she called. "There's nothing on this side at all." She was trying hard to make a show of her usual confidence, but there was no disguising the disappointment in her voice.

"If we can't go backwards," Hule declared, "then we should go forwards. Probably there are other ways out. And we're supposed to be a party, aren't we? Where one of us is in danger, we all should be."

"That doesn't change the problem," Durren pointed out. "Tia's the lightest of us, so even once we throw the rope over, it still doesn't help. With nothing to brace against, she won't be able to hold it taut for the rest of us."

"Then we need someone else on her side."

"I *know*," Durren said, trying not to sound exasperated. "But we don't have any way to—"

"I can jump that," Hule declared. He was gazing meditatively at the gulf before them.

Arein looked at him in horror. "No! Have you seen how far it is? There must be a better way."

Hule shook his head. "If there's one thing I'm good at," he said, "it's jumping. I reckon I can clear that with enough of a run-up. Then, once I'm over, Tia and I can hold the rope for you two to climb over."

"Are you mad?" Durren wondered. "We don't even know how wide the gap is. You've no way to tell if you can make it."

"I can see," Arein cut in. "I mean, Pootle can see in the dark. It's—oh, about twice your height, I'd say, Hule."

"How much about?" Hule asked. He seemed a little less sure of himself now. "Would you say more or less than?"

Arein considered—or perhaps was only encouraging Pootle to move around for a better view. "A little more than," she concluded.

"I think I can make that." The fighter didn't sound anything like as certain as he had only moments before.

"We could bring more equipment from Black River," Arein suggested. "But oh, then Tia…"

There was no need for her to finish the sentence. By the time they returned to the academy and then came back here, Tia's little lamp would certainly have exhausted its fuel. And Durren doubted that any of them were willing to leave Tia here in total darkness with that gaping chasm close by. No, whatever they were going to do, it had to be done now.

"Wait," Arein said, "I think I have an idea. There's a spell— well, it can be used to lift heavy objects, even ones that are a long way away. I'm fairly sure I can cast it."

"You're fairly sure," Hule asked, "or you're sure?"

Arein drew a deep breath. "I'm sure."

"All right," Hule said, "I'm going to try."

Durren could tell that he'd made his mind up, and that there was no point in trying to talk him out of his recklessness. In any case, risky though it was, this was the best idea they had.

In silence, the three of them made their hurried preparations. Durren himself took the task of tying the rope, looping one end half a dozen times around the cracked pillar and then tying it with three of the sturdiest knots he knew. With that done, Hule retreated into the darkness to prepare for his run-up, while Durren and Arein pressed back against the wall, so that there was no risk of them getting in his way. Durren could hear Arein mumbling, though he couldn't make out the words.

"Ready?" Hule asked.

Rather than interrupt her monologue, Arein held out an upraised thumb.

"All right."

Then Hule was hurtling past them. Durren had never seen anyone run quite so fast; when Hule kicked off from the floor's broken edge, he was propelled like the stone from a catapult. He'd been telling the truth, he was an exceptional jumper, and he fairly flew towards the far side. His outstretched foot struck the distant brink.

But that was all. The rest of him hadn't made it—and now he was falling, dragged down by his own weight. Tia was reaching for him, but the distance between them was too great, the slabs too damaged for her to get close. And already the fractured block under Hule's foot was threatening to slip free.

The block stopped moving. So did Hule.

He was lying almost level now, supported by nothing, his arms and legs paddling at thin air. Then, by slow degrees, he began to drift, still at the same angle. Had the situation been only a little less dire, the sight of him travelling like that would have been the single funniest thing Durren had seen in his life.

Moments later and Hule's entire body was over solid ground. As Arein gave a small gasp of exertion, the fighter fell the brief distance to the floor. Tia reached down and helped him to his feet, and Hule set about swiping the dust from his trousers and jerkin with the flat of a hand. That done, he turned around to consider the crevasse that had so nearly claimed his life.

"See?" he called back. "I told you I could make it."

Getting the other end of the rope over proved considerably easier. Durren threw a coiled length, which Tia caught on the first attempt. Together, she and Hule drew the cord tight and leaned against it with all their weight.

As a means of transport, the rope still looked a long way from safe. "I'll go first," Durren decided. If he or Arein were to plunge into the depths, he didn't much like the thought of it being Arein.

However, before he could move, Arein said, "Please…can I?"

The look on her face told Durren all he needed to know: she wanted to get this over with, while her courage still held.

"If you're sure," he agreed.

Arein nodded, slid her staff into the sheath on her pack and grasped the rope. With an effort, she swung her legs up and hooked them over. Durren could see Tia and Hule straining on the other side, but it seemed that they had her. Tentatively, Arein began to shuffle along. Within moments she was above the gulf of nothingness where once the floor had been.

Then, abruptly, she came to a dead halt—and Durren's heart once more began to hammer. Had she already exhausted her strength? How would they possibly rescue her?

But Arein had only paused to rest, for already she was moving again. Twice more she stopped, and though each time Durren felt afraid on her behalf, she began again as soon as she'd recovered her strength. And eventually she was over, lowering herself onto unbroken paving slabs.

"That wasn't so bad," she said, though the quaver in her voice suggested otherwise.

Now there was just Durren. Even having watched Arein cross, he hadn't quite realised until then how daunting the prospect was. Yet Arein had made it, and moreover she'd now joined Hule and Tia in holding the rope, meaning he even had an advantage she'd lacked.

Durren gripped the rope, looped one leg over and then the other. It felt less taut than he'd expected. As he began to shuffle along, shifting hands and feet in turn, he was all too conscious of the fact that by now there would nothing beneath him except fathomless drop. Still, he was making good progress. Another minute and—

Durren stopped. There was a sound coming from beside his ear, a sort of slithering. He could feel, too, the barest tremble of movement against his back. For an instant his mind went to all the worst possibilities—snakes, centipedes, maybe bats— until he heard a faint clatter from far below and realised what was happening.

He'd forgotten about his quiver. And with the angle he was now hanging at, the arrows it contained were sliding free.

On the one hand, that was better than snakes or bats. On the other, he might well need those arrows, for who knew what lay ahead? On impulse, Durren gripped the rope tight with his left hand, tried with his right to cram the slipping shafts back into place. However, that only made matters worse. A rattle from beneath announced that surely he'd just lost at least half of his remaining ammunition. Durren clutched frantically behind his head, caught a few—but by then he'd set himself swinging.

It was all he could do to tell up from down. The price he'd paid for saving a handful of arrows was that he'd altogether lost his equilibrium. Cold panic squeezed his heart. Rationally, he knew that all he had to do was let the shafts fall and clasp the rope once more. But his fingers felt greasy and his muscles burned.

Durren clenched his knees together. The way the ceiling was rocking was making him nauseous, so he closed his eyes. He couldn't persuade his hand to move. It was as though his entire right arm had gone numb—and the numbness was spreading. He couldn't shake the absurd conviction that if he only stayed perfectly still, somehow everything would be all right.

"Durren!" Arein cried.

"I'm fine," he managed. His voice sounded tiny.

"Durren, listen to me," Tia called, "Just let them go."

There was such authority in her voice that he could hardly imagine disobeying. Durren jabbed the shafts as firmly as he could back into their quiver and released them. A couple immediately tumbled away.

Very slowly, desperate to keep his body from swaying, Durren returned his free hand to the rope. He should have felt better for having it there, but he didn't. Regardless, he tried to edge his knees forward. When nothing terrible happened, he moved his hands. Still he didn't fall. He tried again: legs and then arms. More arrows fell, bouncing or shattering below. He did his best to ignore them. Legs, arms, legs, arms, that was all he dared focus on.

"It's all right, Durren," Arein said, from close by. "You've made it. You can let go."

Durren opened his eyes, to find that the three of them were just ahead of him, still gripping the rope. Embarrassed, he swung to the ground. His legs felt jelly-like and at first he wasn't sure they'd hold him, but they did. Slipping off his pack, he counted his remaining arrows: three had survived. He cursed beneath his breath.

"At least you're alive, idiot," Tia pointed out.

"I just thought I might need them," he mumbled.

"Not if you're dead."

Before Durren had a chance to reply, she'd already set off down the remainder of the passage. He noticed, though, that she was taking considerably more care now, treading softly and sweeping the lantern ahead of her with each step.

Hurrying to follow, Durren diverted himself by wondering whether Cullglass had known about the damaged stretch of floor. Had they simply been unlucky, having it collapse like that? Perhaps Cullglass's weight alone had never been sufficient, and it had taken the four of them together to wreak such catastrophic damage. Then again, there was an equal possibility that someone had worked to undermine that section from a lower level, in the knowledge that more than one person would be required to bring it tumbling down.

Just who or what were they dealing with here? Durren could just about accept that the storesmaster might be involved in something suspicious, but he couldn't imagine Cullglass as the type to casually murder strangers.

The next corridor they turned into was nearly as long as the last, and ran at a right angle. Halfway along, another passage cut across, and the footprints they were following turned left. Durren had altogether lost his bearings in relation to the stairs they'd descended by, let alone what he'd seen of the layout of the building above. For all he knew, they were somewhere deep beneath the forest by now.

They were halfway down the passage when Tia came to a halt, so sharply that Durren nearly collided with her. "Everyone, stop," she said—and her voice sounded strangled.

"What is it?" Arein whispered.

With immense slowness, not moving her legs at all, Tia bent to bring the lantern closer to the floor. At first, Durren couldn't make out what she was drawing their attention to. Then, as if his eyes had refocused, he saw the hair-fine thread that ran between the two walls—and how it had been stretched to breaking point by Tia's left ankle.

A tripwire. There was a tripwire across the passage. And Tia had tripped it.

"Where does it lead?" Durren asked softly.

Tia unstooped, moving with the same impossible patience, and held the lantern out at arm's length. First she played its light across the nearest wall—Durren could see where the thread ran through a loop of metal hammered into the stone—and then she raised the lamp over her head.

Above her, high up, Durren could just discern where the

wire ended. It was connected to a wooden peg, and the peg held in place a small and fragile-looking orb of glass. Within, he could distinguish a tangle of dark vegetable matter splotched with ugly red pustules.

"Rotwart bulbs," Durren breathed. He was certain: they'd been shown an illustration in a lecture just the week before. The tutor who'd given that talk had looked nervous just to be holding up the picture.

Despite their unpleasant name and odour, rotwart plants were basically harmless. Their bulbs, however, were another matter. They had a unique defence mechanism that ensured most animals had learned from experience to leave them alone—one that had backfired once humans discovered how extraordinarily dangerous they could be. Since then they'd become a favoured tool of assassins, and had even been used in open warfare once or twice, to devastating effect and much controversy.

Durren turned his attention back to the simple mechanism the glass orb was suspended by. If Tia moved her foot even a fraction further, the peg would pull all the way free. But if she tried to withdraw, it was entirely possible that the wire's retightening would have the same effect. Probably the peg was already growing looser by minute degrees, and even to do nothing wouldn't save her.

At any rate, sooner or later the orb would fall and shatter. Roused by the impact, the bulbs would unleash the toxin they held, and Tia would be left standing amid a cloud of the most singularly poisonous substance known to humankind.

In that moment, Durren made his decision. Before he'd even had time to consider, he had his bow unslung and an arrow nocked.

"Hule and Arein," he said, "get well back. Tia, in a few seconds I'm going to shout 'move', and then you come towards us, all right? As fast as you can—and hold your breath. Whatever you do, you have to hold your breath."

He knew Tia would expect him to explain, but there was no time. Instead, Durren dashed back up the passageway, into the shadows. The orb was so close to the ceiling; that made the angle he needed almost impossible.

Almost, he told himself, wasn't the same thing as entirely. Anyway, if he hesitated long enough to think this through then he'd never be able to do what had to be done—for he knew without doubt that the slightest miscalculation would cost Tia her life.

He drew a deep breath. Nothing mattered but the shot, and it had to be now. He made one last, minute adjustment. "Move!" Durren yelled, and loosed.

The arrow's flight was too fast to see. He knew it had struck home only by the tinkling of broken glass. Tia was moving towards him, half running and half flinging herself. But if he'd misjudged even slightly then all he'd have accomplished was to pin the bulbs to the ceiling—and she would still be well within the foul cloud they spat out. Durren could see the air darkening above her, as though it were water and ink had been poured in.

Yet Tia was already clear of that sinister miasma and, even as Durren watched, the fog began to dissipate.

"You're safe," he cried.

He hurried back to her. Tia looked badly shaken, though she was trying her best to hide it. He realised then that if he'd recognised the rotwart bulbs, she certainly would have. And if she'd recognised them, she would have known, too, what lay in store for her if she inhaled even the tiniest particle of their vapour.

"Come on," Durren said, striving to sound light-hearted, "I want to see where they ended up."

Tia hesitated, and then moved to follow.

"Are you sure that's a good idea?" Arein called nervously.

"Don't worry," Durren told her, "the gas disperses almost immediately. If it was going to kill us, we'd be dead by now."

They found the bulbs at the end of the passage, fixed to the wall by Durren's arrow. With their poison expended, they didn't look at all impressive; the red blotches had faded to a nondescript grey. Durren yanked out his arrow, pleased to note that the head was blunted but intact, and the bulbs slopped to the ground.

"Maybe the floor was just bad luck," he said, "but those didn't get up there by themselves. Someone must have set that trap, someone with no qualms about killing. And if Cullglass didn't trip the wire, that means he at least knew it was there."

"It means more than that," Tia said. "You don't just find rotwart bulbs lying around. Even an academy storesmaster would have a hard time laying hands on them."

Arein and Hule had caught up by then. "So Cullglass is dangerous?" Arein asked.

"Death by rotwart toxin is so horrible that there are professional assassins who refuse to use the stuff," Tia told her. "If he was behind this, then he's something worse than dangerous. And if he wasn't, then he still has plenty of questions to answer."

Yet if Tia was worried, she hid the fact well. For once again she set off without discussion, her eyes locked upon the footprint trail that still snaked into the gloom. Durren followed, alert now for whatever pitfall might lie ahead—though there was every possibility that none of them would see it until far too late.

They took a couple more turns in quick succession, and passed a number of openings in the walls. This portion of the underground labyrinth seemed different to the other, somehow more like the inside of a regular building. What little Durren had glimpsed through the doorways suggested that they led off to rooms, which implied in turn that people had once used this region for a purpose, maybe had even lived down here. Durren tried to imagine that, and what those ancient dwellers might have been like. *Assuming*, he thought with a shudder, *that they ever actually left.*

"I can feel something ahead," Tia said.

She didn't need to say, *Something bad.* That information was clear in her voice—and in any case, by then Durren had sensed the same himself. Yes, there was something terrible around the next corner. He knew so with certainty. He wanted to turn and run, but Tia had the lantern and she wasn't stopping. Durren would have liked to cry out to her, but the prospect of making a sound, of drawing the attention of whatever lay in wait, was somehow even worse.

The light seemed strange now, as though it were thicker than before. Ahead, he heard Tia gasp, a small noise of suppressed horror. Durren was almost at the corner. Another step would carry him past. Yet he knew that whatever threat Tia had encountered, it lay not only ahead of them. The danger was behind him too, close behind. And, try as he might, he couldn't resist the urge to turn and face his fear.

There before Durren, veiled in shadow, stood his father.

Urden Flintrand said nothing. He only glowered, his eyes made black as pitch by the scant light. Durren understood all too well his unspoken meaning: that he was a failure of a son, a disgrace, and his punishment would be to be dragged home and forced into a life of—

No. This wasn't right. As much as his senses tried to persuade him, as much as the fear strived against his doubt, Durren couldn't shake off a sense of wrongness. Then he remembered—and couldn't believe he'd forgotten, even for an instant. This had happened before. It hadn't been real then and couldn't possibly be real now. Anyway, this nightmare was already coming true; any day now he would be carted back to Luntharbour and his father's home. Nothing he thought made the feeling of dread go away, but abruptly Durren found that he could see beyond it. He knew what was going on here.

"It's the Petrified Egg," Tia declared, from ahead. Her voice was tense, but Durren could tell that she too had mastered her imposed fear. "Arein, please will you come here and deal with it?"

Arein hurried past. As before, she seemed entirely impervious to the Egg's power. An instant later and so was Durren himself, the feeling of artificial terror abruptly vanished.

Hule trotted past. "Damned spiders," he muttered, just loud enough for Durren to catch. Then, at his normal volume, "I suppose we know now why somebody wanted us to steal the thing."

Durren didn't enjoy hearing what they'd done phrased so bluntly, but Hule was right: they'd stolen the Petrified Egg from those poor priests, who he felt sure now had been innocent of the slightest wrongdoing.

"Another trap," Tia agreed, "to protect or guard whatever's down here. One that was bound to work, too—against anyone but us."

It nearly worked on me all over again, Durren thought. The fear had certainly been convincing enough.

"Obviously Cullglass, or whoever's pulling his strings, knew a great deal about the Egg," Tia added. Durren saw that she was examining something in the centre of the passageway: a waist-high column, down the edges of which ran a series of carved runes. It closely resembled the pedestal that had housed the Petrified Egg back in the monastery tower—though how such a replica came to be here was yet another mystery.

"I think we must be getting close," Arein said. "Otherwise no one would just leave something so valuable lying around."

As they set off again, it soon became apparent that she was right. Since Cullglass's footprints had suggested he'd ignored the rooms they'd passed earlier, so had they. This time, however, halfway down the next passage, the imprints turned off into a doorway—currently a vacant arch, for nothing remained of the door itself but three blackened hinges. An unpleasant smell came from beyond the entrance, one that made Durren think unmistakeably of overflowing latrines.

He didn't much like the idea of going in, but there could be no turning back now—and in any case Tia had already slipped through. Noticing that she had her knife in her hand, Durren drew his, and tried to take some reassurance from its heft.

The space beyond the doorway was shallow but long, so much so that Durren could barely make out the farthest wall. However, for the first time in what seemed an age, there was natural light to be seen: narrow, sloping channels had been cut into the ceiling, and through them fell slivers of dusty, green-tinged sunlight.

At first, Durren couldn't say what the room's purpose had been—not until he noticed the glint of metal. Then he understood: half of the chamber, divided lengthways, was cut off by vertical bars, and those bars in turn were subdivided into a series of cages.

"There's someone here," Arein murmured. Obviously her vision in the darkness was considerably better than Durren's own—or else she was still relying partly on Pootle's perspective.

The four of them drew closer together. And now Durren could see what Arein had seen, there in the most distant of the half-dozen cells: a shape that seemed to him more or less human.

They crept nearer. The shape wasn't moving. Durren could tell, though, that it was a person, crouched with their back to one wall.

"Wait, isn't that..." Hule began.

He didn't need to finish. They'd all seen by then. For the shape had glanced up, and the face it had turned their way was undeniably familiar.

There could be no question. The man they were looking at, the man imprisoned here deep beneath the earth, was Lyruke Cullglass.

17

At first, the second Cullglass barely seemed aware of their presence. It was obvious that the lamplight troubled him, and he shielded his eyes with one bony hand. Other than that, however, all he did was sit there, swaying slightly, as the four of them gazed through the bars at him.

The Cullglass before them differed in a few crucial ways from the one they'd come to know over the last few weeks. For a start, he was a great deal thinner: his cheeks were sunken, his eye sockets were dark pits, and Durren found it unpleasantly easy to perceive the contours of his skull beneath the skin. His hair and beard were long and straggling, reaching well past his shoulders. He looked older as well, though perhaps that was only another result of the obvious mistreatment he'd endured. Durren didn't doubt for one moment that he'd been in that cage for a very long time indeed.

Tia set down her lantern before the cage and studied the lock with an expert's eye. "I can get that open," she decided. "But are we certain I should?"

"What do you mean?" Arein asked. "We can't just leave him in there."

"I'm just saying—" Tia dropped her voice to a whisper.

"*We don't know for sure what it is we're looking at.*"

"He's…" Clearly Arein had been about to say, *Cullglass*, before she'd realised Tia's meaning. Her brow scrunched in thought.

Then, when the man in the cage spoke, she nearly jumped out of her skin. "Are you…real?" he croaked. "Or are you…like *him*?"

"Sir," Arein said, "we're students from Black River Academy. My name is Areinelimus Thundertree—but you can call me Arein if you like. These are Hule, Durren and Tia."

The second Cullglass scrutinised them. "Is this another trick?"

"It's not a trick," Tia assured him. "But why would you believe it was?"

"I think I know," Arein murmured. To the caged Cullglass she said, "Just a moment, sir. We'll be right back, and please don't worry about anything." She caught hold of Tia's arm and drew her into the shadows, nodding for Durren and Hule to follow.

Some distance away from the occupied cage, Arein crouched, motioning for the others to join her. "Listen," she said, "I think that our Cullglass is a shapeshifter. Do you remember I told you about them, Durren? They're magical creatures, but ones that started out as men—at least so far as anyone knows. They used to be a big problem a long time ago, always stirring up trouble, and in the old days people would kill them whenever they were found out." She shuddered. "I thought the last one had been executed centuries ago. Still, it's the only possible explanation."

Durren was ready to argue, for the explanation seemed too outlandish to be real. Was he really expected to accept that the

Lyruke Cullglass they'd spoken with so many times had in fact been some magical imposter? Only, a memory came to him then, and he knew suddenly that she was right. "That's how he gave you the slip the first time you followed him, Tia," Durren said. "And how he nearly lost us before. That wasn't a disguise—at least not in the way we thought."

"Is there any way to be sure?" Tia asked.

Arein considered. "There must be a test. Like I said, there was a time when everyone thought they'd wiped shapeshifters out for good, so they have to have had a way of finding them. Whatever it was, though, I don't know it."

"But," said Durren, "it's not exactly likely that the real Cullglass would have locked up a shapeshifter duplicate of himself." Only as the words left his mouth did he realise what Tia was getting at. Yes, that was unlikely—but it was perfectly plausible that the storesmaster was keeping imprisoned a shapeshifter that had, at the last moment, taken on his appearance to confuse them. "I think we've no choice but to trust this Cullglass," he decided. "After all, our Cullglass has been behaving suspiciously. Isn't that enough?"

"No," Tia said, "it isn't. We know now why he wanted the Petrified Egg. Maybe he had an equally good reason for needing a unicorn. And he could hardly just say to us, 'Here's a list of things to steal for me, so that no one can come along and rescue the shapeshifter I have locked up out in the forest.'"

"You know, I can hear every word you're saying," came a weak voice from behind them. "So perhaps you'd like to include me in your discussion?"

Tia sighed, clearly annoyed by the stupid mistake they'd all just made. She turned back to the cell. "If you've been listening, then you heard what we want to know," she said. "How can we be sure we can trust you? If you're claiming to be the real Cullglass—"

"I *am* Lyruke Cullglass," the caged man said. Annoyance gave his tone a strength it had lacked before. "I was drugged and kidnapped by that filthy creature and brought to this foul place, where I've been kept for…" His words choked off, and Durren realised he must have no idea how long he'd been incarcerated down here in the darkness. "For a long time indeed," the old man concluded. "Now I would very much like to get out."

"If you're the real Cullglass," Hule put in, "then why was the fake Cullglass visiting you? Why did he even bother keeping you alive?"

"I think I know the answer to that," Arein said. "Shapeshifters don't just turn into people. It takes a constant effort, and relies on their memories of the person they're imitating. If the fake Cullglass had just let the real one die, then he could only have kept the impersonation up for a few days."

"Exactly," agreed the man in the cage. "That creature kept me here because he needed me. Twice a week he would bring me food and question me so as to perfect his imposture, while reminding himself of precisely what I looked and sounded like. Until your arrival, that has been the entirety of the company I've received—and I can tell you honestly that I didn't much enjoy listening to that vile thing."

Arein glanced from face to face. "I really think this is the real Cullglass," she whispered.

Durren was inclined to agree with her, while Hule's expression suggested that he had no real opinion either way. Only Tia seemed still to have doubts.

She took a few steps closer to the bars and knelt before the second Cullglass. "Who's head of the rogue class?" she asked him. "No, wait, that's far too easy. Who was the academy's third head tutor?"

For all his malnourishment and dishevelled appearance, the caged Cullglass still managed to scowl at her convincingly. "There were no head tutors in those days," he grumbled. "However, the third arch-dean of what was then the Conto Martial Academy was Lord Rufus Conto, fifth son of the founder Lord Rafael Conto. He was something of a wastrel by all accounts, which was why the academy was sold off and renamed."

"I didn't know any of that," Arein said, sounding impressed. "Did the academy really used to have a different name?"

"Yes," Tia confirmed, "it's all true. And unless the shapeshifter did a great deal of preparation, I can't believe it would have known that much."

Without waiting to ask their opinions, she began at once to work at the lock with her picks. The task took her considerably longer than opening the door from the courtyard had done, and every so often Durren would hear her tut or curse beneath her breath. Finally, the mechanism gave a definite click, and Tia drew the barred hatch open. Then she backed away, so as to give Cullglass space.

His first step, the one that carried him across the perimeter of the cell he'd dwelled in for so long, was hesitant—as though he was having second thoughts about leaving or, perhaps more likely, as though he couldn't quite persuade himself that this chance of freedom was real. He was bent half double, and the way he moved belonged as much to animal as man.

Then, perhaps conscious of their eyes on him, he drew

himself to his full height. Even with his beard and hair matted and filthy, even dressed in stinking rags, Cullglass had a certain authority.

"Well," the storesmaster said, "I'm grateful to you for my rescue. But now, if none of you have any further objections, I'd be very glad to get out of here."

Getting out of there was not so easily said as done.

Only as they turned into the long passageway did Durren remember that they were trapped. Hadn't the plan been to hunt for another way out? However, now that he really thought, they had no guarantee that there was another exit, and it would be all too easy to become lost—especially if Tia's lantern, which already seemed less bright, should exhaust the last of its fuel. Anyway, Cullglass was clearly in no state to be wandering for hours in these subterranean depths.

Therefore, their only remaining option was to find a way back over the chasm. Eventually, after much discussion, they arrived at a solution: they tied the free end of the rope to the curved hilt of Hule's dagger and anchored the blade deep in a crack in the floor, propping a broken chunk of paving stone on top to keep it in place. Even then, Durren had his doubts that the arrangement would hold, but Tia volunteered to go first, arguing that she was the lightest, and she shimmied over without incident, moving as easily as though she'd spent half her life crossing horizontal ropes over gaping holes.

After that, they began to discuss what to do with Cullglass—who cut them off with a curt, "I can manage perfectly well by myself, thank you."

Durren wanted to argue. Even had the storesmaster been at full strength, it was hard to imagine him capable of such an athletic feat. But Durren hadn't the nerve to contradict him, no one else tried either, and so the only option was to let him make his attempt. Durren spent the entire time with his teeth gritted and his fists clenched. Yet a couple of minutes later and Cullglass was safely on the far side with Tia, chuckling to himself with obvious self-satisfaction.

Arein went next, and had the most difficulty. However, with the same stubborn patience she'd shown on her first crossing, she made it over in one piece. Hule had considerably less trouble, and even managed to carry their flagging lantern in one hand—though his overconfidence was nearly as nail-biting as Arein's nervousness had been. Then there was only Durren left.

Everyone else had had the failsafe of another party member to catch the rope if it should slip. Only Durren had to rely solely on the anchor of Hule's knife—and the memory of his passage in the other direction was still fresh in his mind.

As it turned out, however, the going was considerably easier this time. Durren was careful to secure his remaining arrows in his pack, and without that distraction to throw him off, it wasn't long before Hule and Arein were helping him to his feet on the other side. He gave the rope a last grateful glance—it hadn't proved such a bad choice after all—and the three of them, with Cullglass beside them, followed Tia as she led the way.

Finally, they ascended the flight of stairs back to the surface. Durren felt as though hours had passed, and certainly the way the shadows had lengthened told him they'd been underground for a considerable while.

In the daylight, Cullglass made for a pitiful sight. He reminded Durren of those poor souls who lived on the streets of Luntharbour, the sailors too devoted to drink to take ship and the petty craftsmen whose debts had consumed their fragile livelihoods. However, as he watched, the storesmaster seemed to pull himself up, as though simply by being free of his prison he was beginning to recover some of his vigour.

"We need to hurry," Cullglass said. Even his voice sounded firmer. "It's possible and even likely that my imposter set wards on my cell to alert him if I should ever manage to escape. If he's to be brought to justice, the sooner his presence is made known, the better."

Durren nearly pointed out that they could make far better time without the storesmaster in tow. But it would have been cruel indeed to leave Cullglass alone after everything he'd been through, and nor could Durren imagine any of them wanting to stay behind to escort him.

He shared a glance with Tia, and knew she was thinking the same. Yet all she said was, "You're right, sir. We'll have you back at Black River as soon as we possibly can."

Just as Durren had suspected, the return journey with Cullglass accompanying them took considerably longer than trailing his imposter in the other direction had done. The storesmaster did his best to keep up, aided by the restorative of some bread and cheese that Tia had brought along in case of emergencies. But he had been confined for weeks or months, and his muscles were wasted from disuse.

Eventually, the forest pathway deposited them back on the edge of Olgen. Durren nearly suggested that they attempt to hire a horse and cart, but he didn't know if anyone had any money, and given the time they'd take to find a seller and haggle and explain why they were accompanied by a half-starved man in rags, he suspected it would be quicker simply to walk.

At any rate, the last stretch through the forest proved even slower. Cullglass was hobbling by then, but—aside from the loan of Arein's staff, which he took gratefully—rejected all offers of help with a stubborn scowl. As the walls came finally into sight, evening was drawing in, bathing Black River in lurid rose and amber light.

Immediately, Durren noticed a problem he hadn't considered: the two night guards on the gate. "Should we go around to the side?" he asked.

"Of course not!" snapped Cullglass. "Since when does Black River's storesmaster have to sneak into his own academy?"

Since he was replaced by a shapechanging duplicate, Durren resisted pointing out. Instead, he tried to indicate with his eyes alone why the appearance of an inexplicably emaciated, shabby, bearded version of the storesmaster might raise difficult questions.

In the end, Cullglass registered how Durren—and by then, Hule and Tia as well—were looking at him. He glanced down at himself, acknowledged the filthy robe that hung from his wasted frame. "Ah. I take your point. Still, we are in a hurry."

"I think I can manage this," Tia said. "Only, what I'm going to do—perhaps you could not tell anyone about it afterwards?"

Cullglass seemed surprised by the request, but all he said was, "You may rely upon my discretion."

As they approached the two guards, who were by then watching them with unveiled interest, Tia reached within the folds of her cloak. She drew out a square of parchment, which she unfolded and held up before her.

"Tia Locke," she said, "from the rogue class. These are my

companions. We've been on a special rescue mission, but our observer is malfunctioning. We've had to walk back."

One of the guards studied the document she was holding in front of his nose. "Fine," he grumbled, and nodded to the other, who opened the small side entrance beside the main gate. Tia marched through, and the rest of them hurried along behind her.

Fortunately, the yard beyond was empty at this late hour, so there was no one else around to be curious about their strange party. As soon as the door had closed behind them and he was confident the guards were out of earshot, Durren asked, "All right—what was that?"

"A special dispensation to travel outside the walls, signed by Borgnin and Head Rogue Lune Torr," Tia said. It was the first time Durren had heard her sound even slightly smug.

"But how did you convince them to—" Arein began. Then her face lit with comprehension. "Oh. You didn't."

By then, Cullglass had caught them up. "I'm as good as my word," he said. "However, I must ask you to promise that in future you will not cozen academy staff with forged documentation."

Tia sighed. "I promise."

"Thank you," the storesmaster said. "Now, I have a request to make of the four of you. I'm going to talk to the Head Tutor and explain the grave danger in our midst. But Adocine Borgnin is a thorough man, and I don't expect him to accept what I tell him lightly, nor to act without due preparation.

"Assuming that my doppelganger hasn't already departed, will you keep him occupied until I can join you with sufficient strength to subdue him? I realise I ask a great deal, but you should be in no real danger. The creature hasn't any reason to suspect you, and certainly won't wish to give himself away."

Durren was startled by the request—but only a little. They had already explained on the way from Olgen that the false Cullglass had been acting as their mentor. As such, though he might not like the real Cullglass's logic, he couldn't altogether fault it.

The four of them exchanged glances. Arein, at least, looked every bit as nervous at the prospect as Durren felt. But none of their faces suggested that they were willing to turn down the storesmaster's request—and, Durren realised, neither was he. Because Cullglass was right: delaying the imposter for a few minutes might prove crucial, and no one was better suited to doing so than they.

However, as was often the case, it was left to Tia to speak for all of them. "We'll do our best," she said.

All the way up to Cullglass's stores, Durren could tell that something was going on in Hule's mind. Finally, as they turned into the last passage, the fighter announced, "This talk of being a distraction is nonsense. I say we deal with him ourselves."

"No!" Arein looked appalled. "Hule, you don't understand what a shapeshifter is. The most powerful wizards in history spent centuries trying to eradicate these creatures—and now we know that even they didn't succeed."

"We do have one advantage, though," Tia said thoughtfully. "Assuming he didn't see us following him—and I'm certain he didn't—then, like the real Cullglass said, the imposter has no idea we suspect him. You're right, Arein, he's dangerous, and he may already be wary. If a dozen tutors burst into his storerooms and start making accusations, that could end very badly. Whereas the four of us just might be able to capture him before he ever realises what's going on. Can it be done?"

Arein looked as though she would much rather not be made their expert on the subject of apprehending shapeshifters. "I suppose so," she said. "I mean, there must be limits to how much they can change themselves. If we could tie his arms and legs, or just pin him down, then in theory..." She let the sentence trail off, perhaps unwilling to sound too certain.

"I bet they'd make us at least level two if we captured a shapeshifter that had been hiding right under their noses," Hule said. Then, realising how they were looking at him, he added, "What? You were all thinking the same thing."

Durren would have liked to contradict him. Yet, while it hadn't occurred to him until just then, there was no denying that this might be his only opportunity to win his way back into Black River and Borgnin's good graces.

Still, that didn't make the prospect any less intimidating. "We have to take a vote," Durren said. "This is too big a risk, unless we all absolutely agree."

"I don't like it," Arein said—and Durren couldn't resist a slight surge of relief, until she added, "But I think Tia has a point. I don't want other people to get hurt just because I was scared."

"You know what I think," Hule said. "I don't see what's so dangerous about a shapeshifter, anyway. If it's got a face, then I can hit it."

"My opinion hasn't changed in the last minute," Tia said. "It's the right thing to do." Her gaze fell on Durren. "So I suppose the decision is up to you."

Durren's chest tightened. He didn't want this to be his responsibility. The fact was, they had no real idea what the shapeshifter might be capable of; all of their knowledge came from Arein's vague recollections. Yet Tia's argument was persuasive. The four of them were better placed than anyone to catch the imposter Cullglass unawares.

"I think that if we have the opportunity, we should take it," Durren said. "But no unnecessary risks, all right? I'm looking at you, Hule. And if it seems as though he suspects anything, we make our excuses and get out of there—even if that means letting him escape. Is everyone agreed?"

The other three all nodded.

"Fine," Durren said. "Then let's talk about a plan."

Tia had knocked four times, and her fist was hovering for a fifth. Durren had just persuaded himself that the door wasn't going to open, that Cullglass—or the thing pretending to be Cullglass, he tried to remind himself—was long gone, when the portal swung inward.

But only a sliver. From that gap, Cullglass peeked out. "My young friends," he said. "This is surprising. Could it be that I summoned you here and then forgot? I confess, my memory isn't always the most reliable. Whatever the case, I'm afraid this isn't the best of times."

For all his attempts to disguise the fact, Cullglass seemed genuinely flustered by their appearance. That hardly unexpected, but it didn't bode well for their prospects of catching him unawares. A lot would depend on whether Arein could be convincing—and given how nervous she looked, Durren had his doubts on that score.

She said, "It's just that we wanted to discuss something with you. I mean, we need to. Something important."

Cullglass considered her steadily. "Is that so?"

"Yes. To be honest, we nearly went straight to the Head Tutor, but we thought it would be rude not to talk to you first. But if you're too busy—"

"Not at all." Cullglass's smile was probably meant to be reassuring. "After all, I am your mentor. All I ask is that you be quick; I really do have matters of the utmost urgency to attend to. Nevertheless, do come inside."

With that, the storesmaster opened the door further—but only enough for the four of them to squeeze through one by one. Durren realised that, rather than leading them to the central portion that served as his office, his intention was to speak to them here by the entrance.

"Now," asked Cullglass, "what are these concerns you're so eager to unburden yourselves of?"

"Well," Arein began, "I hope you won't be angry with me for bringing this up again, but we haven't heard anything about the issues we raised. I know you said you'd speak to us when we next had a quest—only it's been preying on my mind all this time. I mean, on all of our minds, really. We can't stop thinking about those priests worrying over their lost stone, and about poor Blackwing. Um…"

Arein's eyes flickered towards Durren, and he could see the desperate question there: *Aren't you supposed to be moving?* This had all seemed so simple when they'd prepared it out in the passage. Arein would provide the diversion, the rest of them would edge closer, and once they were near enough it would only be a matter of leaping upon the storesmaster.

Only, now that they were here, things weren't so straightforward. You didn't simply creep towards people, not without them noticing. It seemed that every time Durren so much as thought about doing so, Cullglass's gaze drifted in his direction. And Hule and Tia were having no more luck. That made Durren feel better in a way, for if Tia couldn't sneak up on someone there was certainly no hope he could. But it meant that their fragile scheme was falling apart moment by moment—and poor Arein was left trying to hold it together.

"I know we're just level one students," she continued, before Cullglass had had a chance to respond, "and I know no one owes us any answers. But the thing is—I also know that we have to be willing to own up for the things we do. Even if someone tells us to do them, that doesn't make the consequences not our fault. So, if anything bad should have happened to Blackwing, if those priests were really trying to help people and now they can't, that's as much our responsibility as anybody else's. And—I'm just afraid that maybe we've been a part of something we shouldn't have been."

Durren's heart was trying to hammer a path through his chest. This wasn't the speech they'd prepared—and it was dangerously close to what he suspected Arein had really been feeling. The idea had been to keep Cullglass talking, not to provoke him with the truth.

However, the storesmaster looked merely concerned. "Areinelimus, all of you…you have my sincerest apologies. I see now that I was wrong to wait in addressing your doubts. Please believe me when I say that I've given them a great deal of thought over these last days. And I promise you that you'll have your answers soon—even tomorrow. But, I'm afraid, not now. I'm truly sorry, but the business I have to attend to is exceptionally vital."

Durren had managed to sidle a half step closer as Cullglass had been speaking. For the first time he had a clear view past him, to the centre of the room. The storesmaster's office was considerably more disordered than usual, the tables buried beneath an assortment of random-seeming clutter. The impression was that Cullglass had decided to inventory every last object in his storerooms, all at once.

Prominent upon the nearest table was a long bundle of dark fabric. The package was bulky, misshapen, its outline suggesting that items of all shapes and sizes had been carelessly crammed together. Yet what caught and held Durren's attention was that, protruding from one end where the cloth had torn, there was a spike of some pale substance. At first he took it for a weapon. Then he noticed its curious pattern, the deep groove coiling towards the tip. Nor did the spike resemble metal. Though it had a certain lustre, it looked more than anything like bone.

Durren felt himself rooted to the spot, all thoughts of getting closer to Cullglass vanished from his mind. He understood now that he hadn't altogether believed before, not really. Somehow he'd been hoping that everything would prove to have a reasonable explanation in the end, and even the fact that there were two Cullglasses hadn't quite overcome his stubborn resistance.

But this did. Because there could be no question: that was Blackwing's horn, and it was most certainly not attached to Blackwing.

Cullglass cleared his throat, and finally Durren managed to tear his eyes away from the bundle and its all-too-revealing protrusion. When he looked round, he could see that the storesmaster had followed his gaze—as had Hule, Tia and Arein, their faces registering various degrees of shock and horror.

"Ah," Cullglass said. "My going-away presents to myself." His own expression showed conflicting emotions. There was annoyance there, frustration too, but was it Durren's imagination, or did he see an inkling of pity? "I had hoped," the storesmaster said, "that you wouldn't see that."

Then, with a ripple like wind-stirred water, the thing that had been calling itself Cullglass began to change.

18

"Children," the creature that a moment before had been Cullglass said, "this is most unfortunate."

Its voice, now, couldn't possibly have been mistaken for anything that would issue from a human throat. The syllables had sounded like the rattle of iron nails in a lead pipe, with beneath that a faint serpentine hiss.

Yet if its voice was strange, its appearance was much stranger. The thing was still roughly the same height that Cullglass had been. It had two arms, two legs and a head, and it wore his clothes—though they looked odd and ill-fitting now. However, its face was all but vanished, reduced to a thin slash of a mouth, two pinprick nostrils and wide eyes of solid white.

Its skin was even worse. It rippled; it refused to stay the same colour. It made Durren think of the sea on a stormy day, patterns of light and dark flickering, spots rising beneath as though something alive was about to burst upon the surface. But, even more so, the shapeshifter's ever-changing skin reminded Durren of the Petrified Egg—and he remembered what Arein had said about where that object might have come from and whose hands might have crafted it.

"This need not end badly." The creature smiled a lipless

smile. "Though it might. I'm going now, with my possessions, and you'll not try to stop me. But first I ask you, who knows that I'm here? Has my former twin somehow freed himself? Tell me everything you know and tell it quickly, and you might yet leave this room alive."

"You should give yourself up," Arein said. Her tone was surprisingly firm and tremor-free. "You're right, no one has to be hurt."

The shapeshifter eyed her with its head aslant. "So others are coming? Having used you children for a distraction?"

"No one used us," she said. "We made a choice, to do the right thing. And if that means we have to stop you leaving, we will." Her jaw clenched, the very picture of stubbornness. "You shouldn't have hurt Blackwing," she said. "Maybe if you hadn't done that, things would be different. But you did."

"Very well then." It was almost impossible to read meaning into that alien, dissonant voice, but for a moment Durren thought that he'd heard something faintly like regret. Nevertheless, the creature raised its hand towards Arein, palm flat and fingers slightly clasping. "If you stand in my path, you leave me no choice."

At that same moment, Hule barrelled into the shapeshifter.

The fighter had been working his way around while the Cullglass-thing had been distracted, and now he struck from behind. The one advantage Hule undoubtedly had on his side was muscle, and the shapeshifter didn't look strong at all; the way its skin shifted like water suggested that it might blow away in a strong breeze. Sure enough, taken by surprise, the creature staggered.

But only for an instant.

Then it had regained its balance, and Hule was the one

looking surprised. For he was clearly pushing with all his considerable strength and the shapeshifter was moving not even slightly, but only gazing down at him with its lightless eyes.

Before Hule had time to fully realise his predicament, the creature had clamped grey fingers around his throat and was plucking him from the ground.

Like that, the shapeshifter held Hule up, inspecting him as one might a bug in a jar. "Do you even understand what you're doing?" it asked—though it was obvious from the fighter's contorted face that he could barely breathe, let alone answer. "I was old before your great-grandparents were conceived. I've learned the lessons of a dozen lifetimes. Do you imagine I don't know how to *fight*?"

Durren found himself retreating. His feet seemed to be moving of their own accord. He had already placed a couple of tables between himself and the shapeshifter, yet he felt no safer for the fact. He was beginning to understand, now, just what they'd set themselves against. For all Arein's talk, he'd somehow imagined that they'd be fighting Cullglass himself; but this thing had nothing in common with the frail storesmaster whose image it had borrowed. It was a monster from nightmares, and the very sight of it made Durren's flesh want to crawl from his body.

Now he held his bow, with an arrow nocked to the string. He didn't remember how either had got there; his hands, too, had taken on a life of their own. Under other circumstances, he might have worried about hitting Hule, or the fact that the shapeshifter was a moving target, or any of a dozen other things—but there was no time. He didn't doubt that the Cullglass-thing had the strength to snap Hule's neck in two, and surely would at any moment.

Durren couldn't quite bring himself to aim for its head. Monster it might be, but it still looked awfully like a person. However, he felt certain that an arrow through the arm holding Hule would be enough to persuade it to let go.

Durren picked his shot. He loosed. His aim was perfect; the shaft flew true.

The arrow shattered.

It had struck precisely where Durren had intended, just below the Cullglass-thing's elbow—and only now did he understand the risk he'd taken, how small a mistake would have led to him inadvertently skewering Hule. Still, Durren had hit his target, and the force of the impact should have buried the arrow deep in the shapeshifter's forearm.

Instead, there were only spinning fragments, splinters pirouetting through the air. Durren thought he saw the metal head spiral past, was certain he heard the chink as it struck a wall. Had he fired at solid stone, he might have expected a similar result. But the shapeshifter was still only flesh—wasn't it?

Perhaps. But that flesh had just become hard as iron.

Durren's distraction had been enough, at least, to make the creature release its grip on Hule. Already the fighter was lurching away, crashing through tables, sending bric-a-brac and scrolls and glass receptacles tumbling to the floor.

The creature watched with evident distaste, as though Hule were a naughty child thoughtlessly spoiling its carefully ordered space. "Ah well," it uttered, apparently to no one in particular. "I won't deny it's a relief to shed that ugly meat. Rarely have I been anything quite so tedious and trivial as Lyruke Cullglass." The shapeshifter's inchoate features darkened into something like a frown. "You know, there are such treasures here—objects wasted on a hoarder like Cullglass, or on this schoolhouse for the spoiled and desperate."

Since the shapeshifter seemed momentarily preoccupied, Durren took the opportunity to glance around for the others. Hule was easiest to find, for he'd only scrambled far enough away to take cover behind a stack of shelves. Arein took more effort; she'd wedged herself beneath a particularly laden table near the entrance.

That left only Tia—but Tia was nowhere to be seen. Durren knew he had no right to be surprised, for of course a rogue's first instinct in any fight was to vanish. Still, he felt a pang of disappointment. The fact that she'd also hidden from her allies seemed all too like the behaviour of the old Tia, the one who'd insisted on always working alone.

Then Durren heard something. The sound was faint, muffled by distance and layers of stone, but familiar nevertheless. It was the anguished whinny of a horse—or of something like a horse.

Following the noise, Durren finally found Tia. There was a door in the farthest corner of the room, and he felt certain the dark shape scurrying towards it must be her. He couldn't guess what she was up to, but even as he watched, she drew the door open—and then disappeared through.

So he'd been right. Tia was still only following her own agenda. Durren was surprised by how much the realisation felt like a fist around his heart. Just as he'd begun to really trust her, here she was letting them down—and at a time when her actions risked all of their lives.

Durren's gaze swung back to the shapeshifter—and he was horrified to discover that it was watching him back. Of all of them, he was the only one who'd made no attempt to hide, settling for putting distance between himself and their adversary. Only now did it occur to him that distance might not be the impediment he'd imagined. For if the creature could make a shield from its very skin, Durren hardly dared imagine what else it might be capable of.

"You know," the shapeshifter said, "it's ill-mannered to shoot arrows at people." It held up its sleeve to show the ragged hole Durren's shot had torn. "I assure you, all I desire is my freedom and the prizes I've won; no harm need come to you or anyone else. Which is more than can be said if you insist on prolonging this fool's quest. Surely you've seen by now how outclassed you are? So I offer you one last chance, boy. Take your friends. Walk away. Allow me to do the same."

Durren was startled to realise just how tempting he found the offer. Because the creature was right: they couldn't harm it, and it was more than capable of hurting them in return. The best they could hope for was to buy enough time for the real Cullglass to arrive with reinforcements—but what would be the cost? Would it be Hule's life? Or Arein's? Or his own?

Yet, as much as he willed it not to, Durren's mind kept drifting to that misshapen bag on the table, and the contorted ivory point teasing through the ripped cloth. The thought that this monster should be allowed to make its escape, having mutilated Blackwing and picked the stores clean of their greatest treasures, twisted in his gut.

"Leave the things you've stolen," Durren said. "Do that and you can go."

The shapeshifter's dead-eyed gaze was unreadable. "Don't be ridiculous."

How could Durren possibly make this decision? When all of their lives were at stake? Yet he knew what the others would say. He dared a glance at Arein, where she was still crouched beneath her table—and, sure enough, though even at a distance he could see the fear in her eyes, she nodded.

That was all he'd needed. Suddenly all of Durren's doubts were gone. "Then," he said, "I'm sorry, but you're not going anywhere."

"So be it." Yet this time Durren was certain it wasn't his imagination: the shapeshifter actually sounded disappointed. "I suppose that, as your mentor, I ought to be proud. Truthfully, though, I take no pleasure in watching children throw their lives away. Since time is of the essence, I promise at least to make this quick."

With a jolt, the Cullglass-thing raised one arm. It splayed its fingers and clutched at empty air. Durren flinched back, came up against a table. Still the creature's hand grasped at nothing. Was this some magic, the beginning of a conjuration?

It was—but not at all of the sort Durren had been expecting. For abruptly, with a scrape of metal on stone, one of the weapons displayed on the wall slid free of its mount and flung itself into the shapeshifter's outstretched hand. The scimitar was beautiful, an antique diligently cared for; despite its obvious age, its blade glistened in the torchlight.

For an instant, the shapeshifter considered the weapon. Then it leaped.

That one bound covered a third of the distance between them. No human could have done such a thing. The creature landed deftly on a table, managing even to avoid the clutter there. It twirled the sword speculatively, and the light glinted from its perfect edge.

In a flash, Durren had an arrow nocked and loosed.

Had he not been acting on pure instinct, he'd never have

made the attempt, assuming the result was sure to be the same as last time. On the other hand, had he spent even a second in aiming, the fight might have been over right then. As it was, the arrow grazed the shapeshifter's cheek, leaving an angry crimson stripe in its wake.

Durren was astonished that he'd managed to draw blood, almost as much so that the creature's vital fluid was the same colour as his own. He had no time, though, to be pleased at his small victory. The shapeshifter tipped back its head and let out a sound such as a furious cat might make: a sort of baleful hiss. Then, once again, it bounded towards him.

Durren had a moment in which to realise that the shapeshifter wasn't stopping before it had leaped again. Then it was right before him, sword descending, and there was no time to so much as think about drawing his own short blade. Yet he still held his bow—and even as he tried to tumble over the table behind him, Durren flung the weapon up in both hands.

An instant later, he was holding two severed halves of what had been his oldest possession, and the shapeshifter's sword was wedged deep in the table between Durren's spread legs. A hair's breadth closer and he didn't dare to think about what would have happened. Durren dropped his destroyed bow and struggled frantically backward, sending crystalline flasks, glassy-eyed stuffed birds and other assorted curios hurtling to the floor.

He'd half hoped that the Cullglass-thing might have lost its weapon, but it yanked the blade free without the slightest hint of effort. By then, Durren had rolled off the table's far side and was struggling to drag his own sword free of its scabbard. As he did so, he continued to retreat—until his free hand pressed cold stone and he knew there was nowhere left to go.

Was his only choice to fight? He was at best an adequate swordsman, and even if the shapeshifter had been bragging about its centuries of experience, its raw strength was phenomenal. As though to illustrate the point, the creature grasped the corner of the table, and—despite its obvious weight—flung it effortlessly aside. The table crashed into a set of shelves, in a shower of broken glass and loose parchment, and abruptly there was nothing between Durren and the shapeshifter—or between him and the shapeshifter's sword.

At least Durren had his own weapon in hand by then, for all the good that was likely to do. When the shapeshifter swung for him, he just barely managed to deflect the blow. The next, though, was quicker, more deliberate. This time, Durren tried to dodge instead—but the creature had foreseen that. It had flicked its blade from one hand to the other, and was scything a slash towards Durren's off hand. He got his sword in the way, though the resultant clang numbed his forearm to the elbow.

Surely the Cullglass-thing could have had him then, but its follow-up was slower, almost clumsy, and even with his right arm almost useless, Durren still somehow managed to turn the strike aside. He staggered again, looking for an opening, a way out—but the shapeshifter moved with him, as casually as though it had read his mind. Wherever he tried to go, its scimitar was waiting.

The thing was toying with him—or else had some last qualms about dealing the fatal blow. Whatever the case, the moment it decided this fight was over, Durren's life would be too.

"Hey! Monster."

The cry came from behind them. Even had he not recognised the voice, Durren would have known to expect

Hule—because anyone else would have had the sense to stab the shapeshifter without first drawing its attention.

In less than an eyeblink, the Cullglass-thing had spun about and had brushed away Hule's blow. Then it was counterattacking, with greater ferocity than it had shown against Durren; clearly, it sensed Hule was a worthier opponent. Durren took the opportunity to hack at the shapeshifter's back, and was startled when it twisted to face him, swatting his blade aside. Hule seized upon that moment's distraction to dance around the creature—he was surprisingly light on his feet—and sliced hard for its shoulder. But the shapeshifter had anticipated the attack and was already sliding away, already preparing its response.

Had Durren been more than a passable fighter, they might have had it then. Two against one was good odds, especially when their opponent had so little room to manoeuvre. However, Durren knew he was little help, and though Hule was a solid swordsman, he wasn't a tenth the creature's match. Its scimitar was a whirlwind now, batting away their blows and following up almost more quickly that Durren could keep track of.

For the first time, it occurred to him that they really hadn't a hope. His arm ached terribly, each parry he was forced to make sending pain throbbing from wrist to elbow. Soon he wouldn't have the strength even to try. Hule, too, for all his size and stamina, was clearly beginning to flag. Yet the shapeshifter moved with the same easy grace it had shown since the beginning, as though their conflict required no exertion at all. Durren had no doubt that either he or Hule would drop their guard long before it did, and then the fight would be one-on-one again—for the thing wouldn't miss its chance to strike.

"Hule, Durren—get out of there!"

Even the effort of making sense of Arein's words nearly proved fatal. In that momentary loss of concentration, the shapeshifter's blade came dangerously to close to opening Durren's throat. He stumbled back, his breathing laboured, looking at once for somewhere he might briefly be in the clear and to see what Arein was up to.

When he did, the sight sucked the last air from his lungs. Arein stood a little distance away. In one hand she held her staff, as always. In the other, upraised, was the Petrified Egg— and the Egg was glowing. So was the hand that held it and much of Arein's arm. Even her eyes possessed a certain fierce light that hadn't been there before.

"Dwarf girl..." the Cullglass-thing growled. "That isn't for you."

Arein paid no heed. "Get down!" she bellowed.

Durren did as he was told. But not quite quickly enough— so that he still saw the beginnings of her spell. From her fingers sprang a thousand sizzling glimmers in a thousand different shades, and all of them streamed towards the shapeshifter. Even a glimpse made Durren dizzy to his core, and he could only imagine what it must be like to have that cascade of light and colour and sparking energy surge towards your face.

"Now! Grab him," Arein cried—and then she added, "Oh."

When Durren opened his eyes, he understood that last, plaintive syllable. Though even now the air around its head was crackling and humming, the shapeshifter was completely unaffected. Instead, it had used the distraction to close the distance between itself and Arein.

"Child," it spat, "you'd throw magic at me? I *am* magic,

down to my blood and my bones. Now give me back what's mine."

The shapeshifter raised its palm and Arein cowered. With the creature's back to him, all Durren could see was that smoke was curling in oily threads from its outstretched fingers. Suddenly the smoke was fire, a smouldering globe of orange edged in purple. Arein was scrambling away, but a stack of laden shelves blocked her path.

Durren tried to drag himself towards the shapeshifter. He could see Hule moving too, but it was as though the two of them were swimming through tar. He knew they couldn't reach the creature in time. A flick of its wrist and that ball of condensed flame would fly meteor-like towards Arein, and nothing they could do would save her.

Then the fireball was gone, potent magic dissipating to nothing. The shapeshifter stood with its head cocked—a weirdly inhuman pose. It was listening, and now that Durren wasn't focused on the prospect of Arein's imminent death, he could hear what it heard too.

The sound was coming from the far side of the room— where Durren had last seen Tia, he realised—and had already grown noticeably louder. The noise made him think of the great, clanking cranes that moved cargo upon the Luntharbour docks, of the steady drumbeats that accompanied marching soldiers. But most of all, it sounded like—

Hooves. He was hearing hooves.

Durren knew then what was coming, and just why Tia had skulked away. He understood that the door she'd crept through must lead down to a second, private storeroom, the room into which they'd once watched the imposter Cullglass lead Blackwing.

Still, the sight was astonishing. If the unicorn had been imposing out in the wild, it was somehow even more impressive charging at full tilt through the cluttered space, avoiding furnishings where it could and charging through them where it couldn't. Even as Durren watched, a table spun out of the beast's path, shelves exploded into firewood, and still the unicorn was gaining speed.

The shapeshifter's blank eyes weren't made for showing emotion. Nevertheless, Durren was certain he read fear there. The creature flailed a clumsy blow towards Hule, which the fighter fended off easily. Realising its error, the Cullglass-thing crouched, readying to spring away—so Durren lashed at its shoulder, forcing it to block and stumble. Again it tensed, desperate to leap free.

But by then there was no more time.

Had the unicorn still possessed its horn, what happened next would surely have been the end of the being that had passed itself off as Lyruke Cullglass. Perhaps the shapeshifter could stop an arrow, but that horn was an object of raw magic, and Durren had no doubt that it would have sliced through the creature's strange flesh like a spoon through stew.

Maybe that was even what the beast had intended. Maybe, in its fury, the unicorn had forgotten its mutilation. In any case, the actual result was merely a head-butt rather than a skewering. But a head-butt from a huge horse travelling at full tilt still counted for a lot.

The unicorn struck the Cullglass-thing with a sound like a thunderclap—and kept going. The shapeshifter was lifted bodily from the ground and carried the remaining distance to the wall, which it crashed into with another cacophonous impact. Then, for good measure, the unicorn tossed its ivorymaned head, flinging the battered creature up and watching as it plummeted to the stone floor.

"Now!" Arein yelled.

She was the first of them to hurl herself onto the shapeshifter, but Hule was close behind, dropping his entire considerable weight upon its thrashing legs. Durren followed, grasping for an arm and pinning the limb with all his might. The shapeshifter was strong, incredibly so; but flat on the ground with its extremities beneath their bodies, it could gain no leverage. Despite all its efforts, it couldn't shake them off.

Still, perhaps the Cullglass-thing would have freed itself eventually, had Tia not appeared just then with a length of rope, presumably recovered from the half-demolished stores. She bound its legs, and Durren, Hule and Arein worked together to tie its arms and wrists. All the while, the creature snarled and spat, its wordless rage only encouraging them. By the time they'd finished, the shapeshifter looked more cocooned than bound.

Just as they were finishing, Durren heard the creak of the great door. When he looked up, there in the opening stood none other than Adocine Borgnin himself, surrounded by a coterie of the academy's highest-ranking staff; Durren recognised Eldra Atrepis close behind the Head Tutor.

Beside Durren, Arein gasped. When he glanced back to see what had startled her, his own reaction was the same—for, in the instant they'd been diverted, the shapeshifter had resumed its charade. Their captive was now, to all appearances, Lyruke Cullglass.

For a moment, Durren's heart sank. Could it really be that, after everything they'd been through, the monster would trick its way free? But then, behind the Head Tutor's shoulder, he saw the real Cullglass, scruffy and emaciated. He was watching his imposter with an expression of the most pronounced loathing—and Durren knew that, finally, their battle was over.

19

F our of the burliest tutors carried the shapeshifter away. It didn't try to resist. Durren had no idea where they'd take it or what they intended to do, and found that he didn't much care. Whatever happened now was no longer his problem, and he was glad of that fact—for he was suddenly aware of just what he'd put his body and mind through in the last minutes. The one thing he wanted, very badly, was to sit down.

He looked around at the others. Hule had perched himself on the edge of a table and was massaging one arm. Arein and Tia were fussing over the unicorn; the beast was obviously uneasy at the presence of so many people, but stayed calm so long as they kept near.

At first none of the tutors paid them much notice. The safe removal of the thing that until recently they'd all believed to be Cullglass absorbed everyone's attention. Everyone's, that was, except for the real Cullglass; to Durren's surprise he seemed eager to ignore his imposter. Instead he wandered about the stores, alternately chuckling like a child reunited with his favourite toys and frowning at every patch of damage and disorder.

Once the shapeshifter had been safely bundled out, the tutors turned their focus upon Blackwing—and at first it looked as though the unicorn would pose the more difficult problem. However, once Arein had explained that the animal didn't get on well with men, one of the female tutors stepped in, a young woman in wizard's robes whom Durren didn't recognise. After a minute of soft whisperings and coaxing, the unicorn decided it trusted her sufficiently to allow itself to be led away, presumably in the direction of the stables.

Only with those two immediate dangers safely dealt with did Borgnin acknowledge the four students waiting nervously to discover their fates. The Head Tutor looked severe as he strode over to them—but then, Durren reminded himself, he always looked severe.

"Storesmaster Cullglass told me he'd sent you here to keep his doppelganger talking," Borgnin said. His eyes roved across the destruction that had claimed whole portions of the stores. "It seems to me you did rather more than talk."

"We had no choice," Tia said. "It was that or let him escape."

Borgnin sighed. "Then you should have let him escape. You had no right or mandate to brawl in academy premises. What you did put your own lives and the lives of everyone in this establishment in grave jeopardy."

The Head Tutor's stern gaze examined each of their faces, and Durren fought the urge to avert his eyes.

"However," Borgnin continued, "you've also shown remarkable courage. Especially since Storesmaster Cullglass assures me that you braved great perils to rescue him. And there's no question but that you helped root out a formidable threat to Black River's security. Therefore, I thank you."

Borgnin cleared his throat. "Now, I'll have to ask that you each take a few minutes to speak with your class tutors and give them your accounts of what occurred here."

As Borgnin turned to beckon the group of academy staff milling around the entrance, Durren took the opportunity to sidle closer to Tia. He felt that there should be a lot he wanted to say, but nothing in particular came to mind. "I suppose this is it then," he said softly.

Tia smiled. "You're such an idiot."

"What's that supposed to mean?" Durren snapped, too stunned to be properly angry. Then he saw Eldra Atrepis, summoning him with the brisk wave of a hand. He almost said, *I'll see you around*, realised that in all likelihood he wouldn't. "Well…goodbye."

And before Tia could answer, Durren had hurried over to Atrepis and was letting her lead him away.

For two days Durren had been confined to his dormitory.

This time he had no desire to be anywhere else. He didn't want to go to classes or lectures. He would have liked to see Arein, Hule and Tia, but even then he didn't altogether mind that he couldn't. After all, what was there to say? Only more goodbyes—and those were better left unspoken.

He would be leaving soon. And perhaps that was all right; perhaps he could finally accept the fact. He'd had three months at Black River and, now that he looked back, they'd been three good months—without doubt the happiest time of his life. He'd made friends, and he'd been part of a quest that would go down in the academy's annals, all the more so because it was one they'd set themselves. He'd helped save a man's life, and to vanquish a real and genuine monster.

Maybe his father could keep him locked indoors for the rest of his years, could force him to study nothing but how to use money to make yet more money. But he couldn't take what Durren had accomplished in these last weeks away—and that was worth more to him than any mountain of gold.

Still, by the end of the second day, the isolation was starting to wear upon Durren's nerves. It was impossible not to notice how the other ranger students had grown wary of him, how they glanced his way and whispered among themselves. Now not only was he the student who'd tricked his way into Black River and been expelled for his efforts, he was confined to dorms amid rumours that he and his party had inexplicably decided to demolish half the stores. He was already a legend—though for all the wrong reasons.

On the morning of the third day after their clash with the shapeshifter, Eldra Atrepis came for him. *This is it*, Durren thought, as he saw her there in the doorway—and he couldn't tell if what he was feeling was sorrow or relief.

"Durren Flintrand," Atrepis said, "will you come with me, please?"

Her face gave away nothing of her thoughts. Still, it was easy enough to guess where they were headed and what awaited him. Perhaps Borgnin wouldn't feel quite so good about ejecting Durren from the premises now, but rules were rules, and Durren hardly blamed the Head Tutor for having to enforce them. After all, he'd begun to realise over the last couple of days just how wrong he'd been to fake his way into Black River—and, ironically, it was their run-in with Cullglass's imposter that had made him understand. No good could come, Durren saw now, from pretending to be something other than what you were.

He was surprised to see that Hule, Arein and Tia sat waiting on the bench in the passage outside Borgnin's door. He nodded to them, and Arein smiled back. Then Atrepis was knocking on the door, opening it and ushering him through.

Borgnin sat behind his desk, which was clear but for a single, furled scroll. "Young Master Flintrand," the Head Tutor said. "I trust you're recovered from the recent excitement?"

In truth, Durren had bruises he suspected might take weeks to heal, and even lying perfectly still was enough to make them ache—but there was no need for Borgnin to know that. "I'm fine, sir," he said.

"Excellent." Borgnin hemmed into his fist, with uncharacteristic awkwardness. "Well, as you know, before this recent incident I wrote to your father to notify him of your presence here. His return letter arrived this morning. And Durren, your father's response is...I suppose the word I'm looking for is 'disappointing'."

Durren hadn't the faintest idea what to make of that word, or of the fact that Borgnin's manner seemed almost apologetic. They were already off to a stranger start than he'd expected, and the only reply he could manage was, "I'm sorry to hear that, sir."

"Yes," Borgnin agreed, as though Durren had said something genuinely perceptive. The Head Tutor considered, chin resting upon steepled fingers. "Perhaps," he decided, "it would be easiest if you were to read the communication yourself." And he indicated with a tilt of his eyes the document resting before him on the desk.

Durren took up the scroll. He felt a strange, fluttering sensation in his chest, as though something were trying to escape from inside him. He realised with sudden alarm that this was the first contact he'd had with his father since that day all those months ago when Durren had vanished without trace or explanation. He couldn't altogether persuade himself that he wanted to read what lay within; but Borgnin was watching expectantly, and Durren realised he had no choice.

The seal was already broken, so he unfurled the scroll. He recognised immediately the cramped handwriting as his father's. There was not a needless stroke anywhere, the sign of a man who resented even the tiniest waste of his time and considered most things as falling within that category.

The letter read:

> *Head Tutor Borgnin,*
> *Regarding your recent communication and the matter of my ungrateful offspring: since he is already in your care and you advise me that your grossly inflated fees have been settled until the termination of his schooling, I can only conclude that he is now your problem and not mine. I have no wish to see him back here, where he would no doubt only cause further embarrassment. My sole requirement is that, amid the nonsense you fill his mind with, you try and inculcate a greater esteem for other people's money than it would appear he currently possesses. Other than that, I ask only that you never again waste my time with trivialities such as this. I assure you that, short of dying or admitting the copious error of his ways, there is nothing my son can do while at your so-called academy that will interest me in even the smallest way.*
> *Signed in all sincerity,*
> *Urden Flintrand*

Durren read over the single paragraph again, and then rerolled the scroll and placed it back where he'd found it. The handwriting had undoubtedly been his father's, and there was no question but that the signature was his. For that matter, the tone was so precisely the one his father liked to employ that Durren could almost hear the bitter words falling from his lips.

Yet something about the letter just didn't feel right. Perhaps it was simply that Durren couldn't imagine Urden Flintrand, however angry or indignant he might be, tolerating his son's presence in a place like Black River.

Still, there was no point in saying such a thing to Borgnin— who, Durren realised, was once more waiting for his response. "I'm sorry, sir," Durren tried. "My father...he doesn't have a great deal of respect for..." He wanted to say, *Anything that isn't himself and his greedy merchant friends, and even them he only tolerates because they're useful.* Instead he said, "Well, he doesn't have a very high opinion of education."

"It would appear not," Borgnin concurred.

The Head Tutor was giving nothing away. With no idea what was expected from him, Durren decided he might as well ask the one question he urgently wanted an answer to. "Sir, what happens now?"

"You read your father's letter," Borgnin said. He still seemed uncomfortable—and only in that moment did it occur to Durren that perhaps the Head Tutor might simply be feeling some sympathy for his plight. "As he notes, your tuition fees have been paid in full. Since he also confirms quite explicitly that he's willing for you to study under our care, I can see no further objections to your presence. That is, Master Flintrand, assuming that you still desire to be trained at Black River?"

"I do," Durren said. There was more he'd have liked to say,

much more, but he wasn't certain he could trust himself to make the words come out properly.

"Excellent." To Durren's surprise, Borgnin actually did sound pleased. "Then perhaps you'd be so good as to call in your companions?"

As he crossed to the door, Durren couldn't bring himself to feel pleased, nor hurt by his father's callousness. He had a distant sense that both emotions would come in time, but just then they were drowned out by numbness; this was entirely too much to absorb. He opened the door, glanced out. Atrepis had left, but Arein, Tia and Hule were still sitting on the bench, and all looked up at the noise.

"Head Tutor Borgnin would like to talk to us together," Durren said.

As the three of them trooped in, Hule and Arein both glanced at Durren curiously. But the look Tia gave him was altogether different. Was there something knowing in the slight smile that flickered across her face as she passed?

They lined up together before Borgnin's desk. Durren suspected that none of them quite knew what to expect. On the one hand, they'd certainly done the academy a service; on the other, they'd broken any number of rules in doing so, and Adocine Borgnin was notorious for taking rules seriously.

The Head Tutor's expression offered no insights. "This academy," he said, "has been here, in one form or another, for a great many years now, and its affairs are well documented. Often my duty as Head Tutor is merely to consult the records and to rely on the wisdom of my predecessors. Rare indeed is the occasion when I encounter circumstances with no precedent."

Unexpectedly, Borgnin stood, walked to the corner of the

room and inspected a small painting that hung there. The image was of a man in antiquated-looking clothing, and the style and faded colours made Durren suspect that the portrait itself might be decades or even centuries old.

Borgnin's attention remained upon the painting rather than the four of them as he continued, "It's of the utmost importance that the imposter Cullglass's infiltration of this academy should remain a secret, at least until we've had time to conclude our investigations. As yet, we have only the barest understanding of the creature's motives. We know that its intention was to abscond with a number of magical objects— at least one of them, the item you know as the Petrified Egg, in itself most likely of shapeshifter origin.

"We suspect, however, that its plans ran much deeper. And of course, there remains the possibility that the creature had allies. For these reasons and others, I cannot publicly acknowledge the part you four played in defending Black River. Though you've done this establishment a great service, I have no choice but to conclude that rewarding you publicly would be an unacceptable risk. This disappoints me, as it must disappoint you."

Durren had never once considered that they might be rewarded for anything they'd done, let alone that Borgnin would have given the question so much thought. Glancing at the others' faces, he could see they were every bit as surprised as he was.

In the end, it was left to Tia to say, "We understand, sir."

Finally, Borgnin turned away from the painting that had been consuming his attention.

"Still," he said, "there are yet further difficulties. It won't surprise you to know that the thing posing as Storesmaster

Cullglass has not been keeping adequate records. Not only that, but these events have clearly had a detrimental influence on your academic progress, and on our ability to measure that progress. To be blunt, aside from the details you yourselves have given, we have no idea of what you accomplished on your quests—and therefore no grounds by which to advance you."

A week ago, this would have been terrible news—worst, perhaps, for Tia, who'd always been so preoccupied with advancement. Yet now Durren found it hard to be concerned, and though Tia was frowning, that was her only reaction. So what if they'd need to undertake a few more quests before they reached the elusive level two? After surviving a booby-trapped dungeon and battling a monster out of ancient history, it was hard to imagine any challenge proving beyond them.

"As I say," continued Borgnin, "an unprecedented situation. In such cases, it falls to me as Head Tutor to rely upon my own initiative, good judgement and conscience. And those faculties tell me that four young people who have accomplished what no level one students should be capable of cannot rightly go on being considered level one students.

"Therefore it's my pleasure to announce that, as of now, you have all ascended to the second levels of your respective classes. Congratulations, and I trust that this is only the beginning of what I expect to be four fine academic careers here at Black River."

"Thank you, sir," the four of them chorused—and they each sounded as stunned as Durren felt.

"Well," Borgnin said, "I'm certain you'll have much to be getting on with; I won't keep you further. Except to say that my door is always open to students who need me." Borgnin smiled—a wholly unexpected expression on those severe features of his. "Perhaps the next time you suspect misdeeds at my academy, you'll consider discussing the matter with me first?"

Durren had imagined that the other three would go their own separate ways once they left Borgnin's office. But they didn't, and though a part of him badly wanted to be alone to try and untangle the confusion of his thoughts, neither did he. With Tia in the lead, the four of them trooped through the passageways in stunned silence. The only one who spoke, after a minute had passed, was Arein—and then only to murmur, awestruck, "Level two!"

When finally Tia came to a halt, Durren realised she'd led them to the small garden where they'd interrogated Hule, what seemed half a lifetime ago. Even then, nobody said anything at first. Instead, the four of them stood awkwardly, barely looking at each other.

Again, it was Arein who finally spoke up. "So I suppose this means you're not expelled anymore?" she asked Durren.

"That's right," Durren agreed. And he explained to them about the letter that had arrived from his father, describing its contents and Borgnin's unexpected reaction.

Yet as he did so, he found his attention more and more drifting to Tia's face, seeking for he knew not what. Only as he was finishing did it come to him: she didn't look surprised in the way the other two did. Not that he'd have entirely expected her to; Tia was never one to let her reactions show. Still, even then her response didn't feel quite right—just as, Durren thought, his father's letter hadn't felt quite right.

"Tia," Durren said, "can I speak to you in private?"

She looked momentarily startled, but all she said was, "I

suppose so."

Durren led her to the far end of the small garden. Satisfied that they were out of earshot, he said, "You know, when Borgnin let me read that letter, I couldn't help thinking there was something off about it. But at the time I couldn't put my finger on why. The handwriting definitely looked like my father's, and so did the signature; I should know, I spent long enough learning to forge them. And the style couldn't have sounded more like him. Only—I've thought hard, and that was exactly what bothered me. Somehow, it was just too much like how he'd write."

"That doesn't make much sense," Tia pointed out.

"I know. That's why it took me so long to realise. What I mean is, my father might have written two or three of the things in that letter, but even he wouldn't be so obnoxious quite so consistently."

"Ah, I see what you're saying," Tia mused. "It was overdone." She shrugged carelessly. "Well, I didn't have long; I did the best I could. And since it fooled Borgnin, I think I did a good enough job."

So Durren's theory had been right. Yet, even with Tia having confessed, he still felt none the wiser. "But that's not possible," he said. "I mean—so you faked the letter, you must have, but *how?*"

Tia's expression became suddenly solemn, as though she were a tutor about to lecture her class. "The handwriting and signature were easy enough; just a case of borrowing your entrance forms. Of course, I was forging from a forgery, and for all Borgnin knew the handwriting on the paperwork was nothing like your father's, but I suppose that must not have crossed his mind."

"All right," Durren said, "I can see that—though I won't ask how you 'borrowed' a form that was locked in Borgnin's office. But that letter read exactly like something my father would have written. Surely you're not telling me you've met him and just never felt the need to mention the fact?"

"Do you spend much time in the library, Durren?"

The question was the last he'd have expected. "No more than anyone, I'd say," he lied. If he were honest, he'd avoided the main library as much as he possibly could.

"There are all sorts of strange things in there," Tia said, "if you know where to look. Copies of public announcements, official documents, even private letters that the tutors don't have space to keep in their own offices. Well, it turns out that, ten years ago, one Urden Flintrand discussed some minor business dealings with the then head tutor of Black River; the academy is always investing shares of its profits into one venture or another.

"Anyway, the head tutor had some ethical concerns, which your father didn't take kindly to. He wrote back at length, and the letters eventually found their way into the library. It was just luck, really; otherwise I'd have had to improvise." She grimaced. "I wanted to fool Borgnin, of course, but ideally I'd have fooled you too."

Durren realised that he'd never heard her say half so many words in one go before, or sound quite so enthusiastic about anything. "But what about the real letter?" he asked. "I mean, what if another one turns up from my father saying the opposite? Borgnin's bound to figure out the truth."

"It won't," Tia said, "because Borgnin's own letter was never sent. I made sure that it vanished before ever leaving Olgen."

"And when we were in Olgen," Durren realised aloud, "you were taking the fake reply into the courier's office."

Tia nodded. "I told them to wait a couple of days and then send it on to the academy."

"I suppose I should thank you," Durren said.

"Yes, you should."

He laughed. "I'm sorry. I mean, of course I should. You saved me. That's the kindest thing anyone's ever done for me."

At that, Tia looked bashful. "It wasn't that big a deal." Then, her usual self again, she added, "It didn't exactly look good for me, did it, having one of my party expelled? And what were the rest of us supposed to do? We'd have had to start over again, breaking in some other idiot. Anyway, you were just beginning to look as though you might conceivably be of some use."

This time, Durren managed not to laugh; she would only get more defensive. "Whatever your reasons," he said, "I appreciate what you did."

When they rejoined Hule and Arein, the pair were deep in one-sided conversation, with Arein doing all of the talking. She glanced round at the sound of their approach, and Durren couldn't help but notice how glum she looked.

"I was just telling Hule," she said, "about something I overheard yesterday. A couple of students who'd just gone up to level two were talking. They said they'd been allowed to disband their parties and join up with whoever they chose." Arein sniffed, shuffled her feet. "So I suppose this means we're not stuck with each other anymore."

Durren took a moment to process that. Thanks to Tia, he didn't have to worry about his father finding him, or about being thrown out. There was no more reason to hide his skill with the bow, and he felt certain he could develop his other abilities to match, given time. He was a level two ranger, now; his foot was on a ladder that led towards the sort of future he'd always dreamed of. If he should reach level six or even seven, then he could end up leading expeditions into the wildlands, or perhaps captaining a border fort, protecting people and doing real good. Now that he had no reason to pretend to be mediocre, the possibilities seemed limitless.

He was free to look for a wizard who wasn't afraid of using magic. He could find a fighter who didn't pretend to be a moron, a rogue who wasn't always disappearing off on their own. He could join a party that actually worked together, and which didn't end up inadvertently kidnapping unicorns or robbing innocent priests or battling deadly shapeshifters.

Only, that wizard wouldn't be Arein, with her endearing awkwardness, her courage in the face of absolutely everything. That fighter wouldn't be Hule, stuck in a ridiculous role he'd accidentally invented and yet somehow managing to make the best of it. And that rogue certainly wouldn't be anything at all like Tia.

"Of course," Arein added, "that isn't to say we *have to* form new parties. Just that we can. If we want to. But if we don't want to…"

"Who can be bothered with such nonsense?" Hule asked, sounding more like his old self than perhaps he'd intended. "As far as I'm concerned, one party is as good as any other."

Durren realised he'd already made his own mind up. "I'm with Hule," he said. "Replacing you three? That sounds like a lot of work."

Together, the three of them looked to Tia. But she was glancing away from them, frowning, and Durren's heart sank.

Of course she wasn't about to stay with three losers like them; of course she'd want party members who were every bit as skilled as she was.

Then Tia met his gaze—and to Durren's surprise, she was smiling. "Who knows," she said, "maybe there's some hope for you three yet. Let's just see how things go, shall we?"

THE END

ACKNOWLEDGMENTS

Given the level of assistance David and I had putting together this first book of The Black River Chronicles, these acknowledgments could be the longest *chapter*. But I'll try to keep it brief—just know that there was a lot of help, a lot of input, and we owe everyone a lot of thanks.

In no particular order, we'd like to thank our very first beta readers, Luke Forney and Stephen Helleiner. They managed to stumble through very early drafts and come through the other side with heaps of excellent ideas and helpful comments. Level One is a better book because of Stephen and Luke.

Then there's our editor, Anne Zanoni. Her professionalism and skill took the book to the next level—right along with Durren, Tia, Arein, and Hule. And to our oh-so-carefull proofreader, Mike Reeves-McMillan. Thank you both.

With additional help from a handful of so called *final draft* readers, the book shape-shifted just a little more. A sincere thank you to Evan, Noel, Marc, Craig, and my big broth Rob for their time, comments, and encouragement. Also, my daughters Ivy and Charlotte, whom I only let read a little less than half—so the end would be a surprise!

For the cover art we turned to Emmanuel Xerx Javier. I have worked with Emmanuel before, I like his style, and he's a pleasure to deal with. The cover is a lot of fun, but I know there's a lot more visual art ready to spring forth from the Academy. We can't wait to see it. Thank you, sir.

And for the final reads, our professional fantastic fellows, Ed Greenwood and Adrian Tchaikovsky. Fantasy giants from each side of a rather large pond. Thank you guys!

Thank you for reading our *Digital Fantasy Fiction* novel, **The Black River Chronicles,** and for supporting speculative fiction in the written form. Please consider leaving a reader review so that other people can make an informed reading decision.

Find more great stories, novels, collections,
and anthologies on our website.
Visit us at <u>DigitalFictionPub.com</u>

Join the Digital Fiction Pub newsletter for **infrequent**
updates, new release discounts, and more:
Subscribe at - <u>Digital Fiction Pub</u>

See just some of our exciting fantasy, horror,
crime, and science fiction books on
the <u>next page</u>.

MORE FROM DIGITAL FICTION

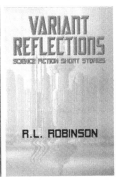

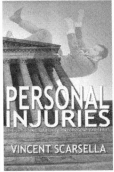

COPYRIGHT

The Black River Chronicles: Level One
Written by David Tallerman and Michael Wills
Foreword by Ed Greenwood
Edited by Anne Zanoni
Cover illustration by Emmanuel Xerx Javier

This story is a work of fiction. All of the characters, organizations, and events portrayed in the story are either the product of the authors' imagination, fictitious, or used fictitiously. Any resemblance to actual persons or unicorns, living or dead, would be coincidental and quite remarkable.

ABOUT THE AUTHORS

David Tallerman

David Tallerman is the author of the Tor.com novella Patchwerk and the comic fantasy novels Giant Thief, Crown Thief, and Prince Thief, as well as the graphic novel Endangered Weapon B: Mechanimal Science.

David's short science fiction, fantasy and horror has appeared in over seventy markets, including Clarkesworld, Lightspeed, Nightmare and Beneath Ceaseless Skies, and fourteen of his stories were recently brought together in the collection The Sign in the Moonlight and Other Stories.

He can be found online at **DavidTallerman.co.uk**

Michael Wills

Michael Wills is the co-author of The Black River Chronicles: Level One. He is a husband, father, part-time geek, and full-time lawyer. He owns and operates Digital Fiction Publishing Corp. in his spare time. The Black River Chronicles, as conceived by Michael, is his first full length novel; which was realised only through the effort of his co-conspirator, David Tallerman.

He can be found online at **DigitalFictionPub.com**

60900855R00177

Made in the USA
Lexington, KY
22 February 2017